children and two dogs. Her writing career came as a lovely surprise when she decided to write a book to teach her children a valuable life lesson and show them that they are capable of achieving their dreams. Christie's dream was to become a writer and the book she wrote to prove a point went on to become a #1 bestseller in the UK, USA, Canada and Australia.

When Christie isn't writing she enjoys playing the piano, is a keen gardener and loves to paint and upcycle furniture. Christie is an ambassador for the @ZuriProject alongside Patron of the charity Emmerdale's Bhasker Patel. They raise money and awareness for communities in Uganda. Christie loves to hear from her readers and you can get in touch via Twitter, Facebook and Instagram.

christiebarlow.com

facebook.com/ChristieJBarlow
twitter.com/ChristieJBarlow
bookbub.com/authors/christie-barlow
instagram.com/christie_barlow

Also by Christie Barlow

The Love Heart Lane Series

Love Heart Lane

Foxglove Farm

Clover Cottage

Starcross Manor

Standalones

The Cosy Canal Boat Dream

A Home at Honeysuckle Farm

THE LAKE HOUSE

CHRISTIE BARLOW

One More Chapter
a division of HarperCollins*Publishers* Ltd
1 London Bridge Street
London SE1 9GF
www.harpercollins.co.uk
HarperCollins*Publishers*
1st Floor, Watermarque Building, Ringsend Road
Dublin 4, Ireland

This paperback edition 2021

1

First published in Great Britain in ebook format
by HarperCollins*Publishers* 2020
Copyright © Christie Barlow 2020
Christie Barlow asserts the moral right to
be identified as the author of this work
A catalogue record of this book is available from the British Library

ISBN: 978-0-00-841307-1

Printed and bound in Great Britain by
CPI Group (UK) Ltd, Croydon CR0 4YY

For Gary Barlow,

I'm now single so please call me… in fact hold that call… in my mind every guy I've met has been an arsehole so if you are an arsehole I never want to know. *Sighs*

So I think it will be best just to stay friends.

Prologue

Ella Johnson's life was in turmoil. She just couldn't understand how this could even be happening to her. She'd barely slept in the last forty-eight hours and was consumed with worry and confusion, as her whole world was shattering around her.

Her fiancé, Dr Alex James, had gone to work as normal on Monday morning but had never come home. There was no trace of him; his mobile phone no longer connected, their brand-new Range Rover had vanished and there had been no withdrawals from their bank account. None of it made any sense, and Ella checked her mobile phone and local news reports for the umpteenth time that day.

Hours earlier, with the constant pain of not knowing what might have happened to Alex twisting in her heart,

Ella had been sitting at the kitchen table in front of two policemen, giving a statement.

'And nothing out of the ordinary happened between you? An argument, perhaps… anything?' The police constable was poised with his pen.

With tears rolling down her cheeks Ella shook her head. 'Far from it. We cuddled in bed and Alex brought me a cup of tea, like he has done every morning since he moved in.'

'And how long have you lived together?'

'Ten months,' replied Ella, remembering the day they'd met like it was yesterday. 'But we've been together for just over a year… we're getting married next year!' Ella was distraught and none of this made any sense. They'd already picked the venue, organised the invitations and, knowing how difficult it was getting time off work, Alex had booked his leave already.

'And Alex's friends, have you spoken to them? Has he been in contact with any of them?'

Ella was silent for a moment. 'I've never met any of his friends.' She knew as soon as the words left her mouth that it sounded lame, but although Alex spent a lot of time mentioning friends and colleagues, after he'd finished his shift at the hospital, he always wanted to spend time with her alone, which of course she never objected to.

'Never? How about work colleagues?'

Ella noticed a look pass between the two officers. 'No, but Alex talks about them all the time and he plays football with them every Thursday night… five a side.'

'At which sports club?' The policeman was poised with his pen again, waiting for Ella's answer.

'Christ, I don't know.' She stood up and raked her hands through her hair. 'All these questions.' Ella was beginning to feel a little agitated. They shouldn't be here talking about football – they should be out looking for Alex. 'I've never asked! He goes and plays football, then comes home.'

'Try and keep calm, Miss Johnson, take a seat. These are just standard questions, so that we can try to build a picture of Alex's routine,' the officer soothed.

'You need to get out there and find him. He can't just disappear off the face of the earth with no trace. Something has happened to him, I know it. He wouldn't do this to me, he messages me all the time.' Ella's voice wavered as she sat back down at the table.

'And his phone? Have you rung his phone since Alex has disappeared?'

Ella nodded. 'Yes, of course I've rung his phone. I've lost count of the times I've rung his phone, but all it says is my call can't be connected. Alex never has his phone switched off. Please, please just find him!' she pleaded.

'We'll do our very best. It's our job to investigate, and our first stop is the City Hospital.'

'Good, because they wouldn't tell me anything.' Ella was taking in huge gulps of air as she tried to catch her breath. 'They said they can't give out any information about any member of staff, due to data protection.'

'Leave that to us. Have you got anyone who can come and sit with you?'

Through her tears all Ella could manage was a nod. 'My friend Callie is on her way. She's travelling from Scotland, but her train gets in...' Ella glanced up at the clock on the wall, 'any time now.'

Both policemen stood up. 'That's good. We'll be back in touch after we've visited the hospital.'

'Will that be today?' Ella just wanted answers.

'Yes, hopefully today.'

Hearing a knock on the door, Ella's eyes widened. She scraped back her chair and rushed to the door. 'Alex... Alex!' she shouted and flung the front door open... to find her friend Callie standing on the doorstep.

Feeling like her legs were going to buckle underneath her, Ella held on to the door tightly. 'He's got a key, Alex wouldn't be knocking, he's got a key.'

Callie opened her arms wide and grabbed on to her friend. Ella could feel her whole body physically shaking. 'Thank God you are here. I can't believe this is happening.' Once again, a tsunami of tears ran down her cheeks.

'I'm going nowhere,' replied Callie, noticing the two

policemen standing behind Ella. 'Is there news, have you found him?'

Ella shook her head and let go of Callie as the police constables walked outside.

'We're going to the hospital now and we'll be in touch as soon as we have some more information.'

'Thank you,' replied Ella, watching them head out towards the police car that was parked outside.

As soon as Ella closed the door behind them, she turned towards Callie. 'I just don't understand this, Callie. The ache in my heart is killing me. Where is he, Cal? What the hell has happened to him?'

'I don't know, I just don't know.' Callie hugged her friend again, then passed her a tissue from the box in the hallway. 'I'll make you a drink. Have you eaten?' she asked, following Ella into the living room.

Ella dabbed her swollen eyes. 'I can't think about eating, showering or anything. I haven't even slept, in case I miss a call from him. Where is he?'

'I wish I knew, Ella, I really do. You can shower now I'm here, and I'll make you something to eat. You have to keep your strength up.'

But Ella wasn't listening. She'd sat down on the sofa and pulled her knees up to her chest, hugging them tightly. She began to rock gently. 'He just needs to come home.'

'The police will do their best to find him.'

'I've got this horrible sinking feeling. Someone can't just disappear with no trace.' Ella swallowed down the lump in her throat.

'We'll have news soon, I'm sure,' soothed Callie.

'All I keep thinking about is the worst-case scenario. They're going to find him dead, aren't they?'

Callie slipped her arm around Ella's shoulder and pulled her in close. 'Try not to think like that, stay positive.'

For a moment, they sat in silence. The last forty-eight hours had taken their toll and an exhausted Ella finally fell asleep. Gently, Callie removed her arm, then laid Ella down on the sofa and covered her up with a soft grey throw. Tip-toeing out of the living room, Callie headed towards the kitchen and switched on the kettle to make a cup of tea.

She would let Ella sleep whilst she could, but hopefully there would be some news soon.

———

Three hours later, Ella woke up startled. Hearing a loud knock on the door, she was up on her feet to find the same two policemen standing back on the doorstep. There was something about the look on their faces that she didn't like. This wasn't good news.

'What is it? Have you found him?'

'Are we okay to sit down?' asked Constable John Price.

'Yes, please do.' Ella gestured towards the chairs, whist Callie perched next to Ella on the sofa and took her hand.

'There's no easy way to say this. We've been to the City Hospital…'

Ella's heart was thumping so fast, she thought it was going to burst through her ribcage at any second. Callie gripped her hand tighter.

'What is it?' Ella's voice faltered, her whole body trembling. 'Have they found him? Is he dead?' she blurted.

'I'm afraid there is no Dr Alex James working at the City Hospital. We've checked and double checked.'

Ella's mouth opened and closed. The words hung in the air whilst she tried to process what she'd just heard. 'But… but…' Ella looked towards Callie, confused. 'He's worked at the City Hospital for the last three years. I drop him off and pick him up from the car park there. He has his doctor's coats hanging in the wardrobe, his spare lanyard is in the drawer. There must be some sort of mistake.' Ella felt a tightening in her chest as her mind raced.

'Could we possibly have a look at his lanyard?' asked the Constable.

Ella was already up on her feet, pulling open the

drawer. 'Here it is.' She handed the lanyard over to the policemen, who passed it between themselves.

'See, there has to be some mistake.' Ella's voice was hopeful.

'Ella, this isn't a lanyard from the hospital. It's a fake.'

Feeling baffled, Ella looked towards Callie, then back towards the policemen. 'I don't understand what you're telling me.'

'I'm afraid that the man you knew as Dr Alex James isn't a real doctor. We aren't sure that's even his real name.'

Ella felt the burn of bile in the back of her throat, and an uncontrollable shudder swept through her entire body. Her breaths were now coming in short sharp bursts. The initial shock of what she was hearing just didn't make sense.

'It's going to be okay,' Callie reassured.

'It's not, though, is it?' Ella knew she was being sharp, but she couldn't help it.

'Ella, please can you start from the beginning. How did you meet Alex?'

'Take a deep breath,' encouraged Callie, handing her a glass of water from the coffee table.

After taking a sip, Ella exhaled. 'I'm the owner of the gift shop on the corner of Barton Square next to the City Hospital.' She noticed that Constable Price was tapping away on an iPad whilst the other officer was writing in his notepad.

Barton Square was home to small boutiques, coffee shops and a deli which was popular with the medical staff from the hospital, and that was where Ella had first spotted Dr Alex James, sitting outside at a wrought-iron table, reading a newspaper and drinking coffee. The second Ella clapped eyes on him she knew there was something about him – the way he carried himself, his Mediterranean olive skin and deep hazel eyes. He was drop-dead gorgeous and even though he was a stranger to her, Ella had a feeling that this man was going to be in her life. And she was right.

'My parents had passed away…' Ella let out a long shuddering breath and the tears slipped down her cheeks.

Callie quickly passed her a tissue. 'Take your time,' she soothed gently.

'Their deaths made the local news but that escalated to the national news.' Her voice quivered.

'What happened?' asked the policeman.

'Carbon monoxide poisoning,' replied Ella, 'given off by the old gas fire in the Edwardian property they were living in. There was an article in the newspaper and I was sitting in my shop reading it, when Alex walked in. I was mortified, all blotchy-faced from my tears, with greasy hair,' Ella reminisced. 'But he introduced himself, asked if I was okay, and as soon as I explained about my parents' death, he insisted on making me a cup of tea. He comforted me for an hour, the whole of his lunch break. I felt dreadful – he went back to work not having anything to eat.'

'And he said at that very first meeting that he worked at the City Hospital?' asked the police officer.

Ella nodded.

'And when was the first time you picked him up from work?' asked Constable Price.

'Literally a week after. His flat was on the outskirts of the city and he used to ride the bus into work. He didn't like crawling through the slow city traffic, so it was easier for me to pick him up, as I live closer to the hospital, and for him to come back to mine. It was a couple of months before we moved in together.'

'And what's the address of his flat?'

All eyes were on Ella.

Ella's voice faltered. 'I... I don't know.' As soon as the words left her mouth, she noticed both policemen raise their eyebrows. 'I know saying that out loud, it doesn't sound very good, does it?'

'Did you think it was strange that you never went to his home?'

Ella looked towards Callie who gave her hand a little squeeze.

'No, I didn't think about it. It was just easier for him to come to mine when he finished work.'

'When he moved in, did he bring his belongings?' the policeman probed.

Now Ella felt like she was under investigation. Why were they questioning her like this? She hadn't done anything wrong. Her only crime was to fall in love. She shared a look with Callie, raising an eyebrow. 'Do you think it's weird I never went to his flat?'

Callie hesitated. 'If you thought it felt right and he was being genuine…'

'Alex *is* genuine! What are you saying? He could lying at the bottom of the river… murdered… anything! And you're asking me ridiculous questions about his clothes, what he moved in with.' Ella was bordering on hysterical now. She didn't want the police sitting there asking her stupid questions. She wanted Alex to be found and brought home.

'Ella, I'm on your side,' reassured Callie, 'but I can hear what the officers are saying. Alex James is not who he says he is and doesn't work at the hospital.' Callie's voice was calm.

Ella was quiet for a second, and she felt a quiver in her stomach. She wanted to turn back the clock to Monday morning before Alex had left for work, when everything in her life had been normal. At this moment in time she wanted to be anywhere but here, listening to this. She'd spent twelve months with this guy. She knew who he was!

'Your friend is right,' added the policeman. 'That's exactly what we're saying. So, did Alex move in with any possessions?'

Ella tucked her feet up on the settee and cast her mind back. 'It was a weekend; I remember because I was working in the shop and he borrowed my car to move stuff. He brought one suitcase full of clothes and shoes…'

'Was that it?' continued the policeman. 'No furniture from the flat? TVs, electrical devices?'

'No, he didn't need to bring any furniture, as I had all my stuff and most of it belonged to his landlord. All he had was his clothes and white coats for work, a few shirts.'

'Any photographs of family?'

Ella shook her head. 'Nothing.'

'Can we go back to the death of your parents?' questioned the police officer. 'Did your parents leave you any inheritance?'

Ella looked puzzled. 'What's that got to do with anything?' She was starting to feel a little agitated. 'Why is this relevant?'

The policeman was staring at her, waiting for her to answer the question.

'Yes, I received two hundred and fifty thousand pounds. But I'd rather have my parents than the money.'

'And did Alex know that you were going to receive a large sum of money? Have you lent him any money?'

The room fell silent, and Ella felt a tightness in her chest. The colour drained from her face as everyone watched and waited for her answer. 'Yes... but... he's going to pay me back.'

The policeman raised an eyebrow. 'How much money did you give him?'

Wearily Ella walked over to the dresser and pulled out her savings account book and slid it over the table.

'You gave him the whole two hundred and fifty thousand pounds?'

Ella nodded her head sadly.

'Why?'

'He had cash-flow problems and needed the money to help his brother out of a business predicament. But he said he'd have all the money back in my account by the end of the month. He promised.'

'Have you met his brother?'

Ella felt her chest tighten again. 'No.' Every time she answered their questions her mind whirled.

'What about credit cards? Bank accounts?' questioned the officer.

'I barely use my credit cards. If I don't have the money, I don't spend it. I have no debt whatsoever.' Ella headed for the kitchen and returned with a pile of unopened statements. She tore the top one open and stared at the statement in her hand. She frantically began tearing each one open.

She had difficulty focussing on the numbers in front of her, feeling disbelief as she pushed the statements across the table towards the officers.

'I-I didn't spend all this money!' Ella stammered. 'This wasn't me. How am I ever going pay this back in a lifetime?'

The police officers cast a glance of the statements. 'There's over ten thousand pounds' worth of debt on this card, and you had no idea?'

Ella was in a state of shock, and she shook her head. 'The card is in my purse. It can't be possible; I just don't understand.' She muttered as she reached for her purse. She desperately searched all compartments for the card, but it wasn't there.

'It's gone,' admitted Ella, suddenly feeling exposed and judged. 'What am I going to do? He's maxed out my card.'

'Our guess is the man you know as Dr Alex James is a professional fraudster. He targeted you when you were at your most vulnerable after your parents' death and pursued your inheritance,' shared the police officer gently.

Ella buried her head in her hands. With her heart thumping fast and the tears falling down her cheeks, she felt sick to her stomach. She had nothing left; Alex had stolen everything from her, including her heart. With all the evidence laid out in front of her, Ella had to face facts. The man she'd let into her life was an imposter and she didn't know anything about him at all. Everything had been a lie. Whoever Alex was, he'd played the long game and swindled Ella out of everything. And he was never coming back.

She fell into Callie's arms as she sobbed and clung on to her for dear life. Ella couldn't believe he'd planned the whole thing, she couldn't believe anyone could be so cruel. She thought they'd been in love. He'd kissed her like she'd never been kissed before, he'd made her laugh and feel beautiful in her own skin. They were going to be together forever. He'd said so and she'd believed him.

'What the hell am I going to do? I've lost everything!'

Ella's Johnson's whole life had just fallen apart... again.

Chapter One

SIX MONTHS LATER

With her stomach rumbling, Ella emptied the contents of her purse and stared at the ten-pound note and a handful of coppers as they rolled on to the kitchen table. She was absolutely broke and this was all the money she had to her name. Next to the shrapnel lay the pile of credit card statements that had accumulated over the last six months. Alex had certainly gone to town spending without her knowledge, and she was liable for all the debt. The last six months had taken their toll on Ella. She'd sold every scrap of furniture in her home and her business to try and make ends meet, but she was still struggling to keep on top of her finances.

And now, with all of her belongings packed inside a suitcase, her emotions were all over the place. One second she was angry, then embarrassed, the next, heartbroken. And unless the police managed to track Alex down, it was unlikely she was ever going to get her money back. She'd lost everything and the police had no new leads at all.

Another wave of emotion hit her, and she blinked back the tears and looked at the clock. Callie had arrived a couple of days ago. She'd been a tower of strength for the last six months and had helped Ella to sell as much as she could from the house.

'I'm not going to ask you how you slept.' Callie walked into the kitchen. 'You look shattered.'

'I am shattered.' Ella pushed the loose change towards Callie across the table. 'This is it – all I have to my name.'

Callie sat down opposite Ella. 'I know it's easier said than done, but try not to worry about that right now. These things have a way of working themselves out, and you need to start thinking about you. I've booked the train tickets. We're on the 12.15pm train to Inverness.'

Ella went to open her mouth but was shut down by Callie. 'No arguing, and don't worry about the cost. What you need is good, decent people around you, and Heartcross is the place for that. Trust me.'

Ella was extremely grateful to Callie. She was a true friend and had stepped in to help Ella get her life back on track. It was hard giving up her life here, this was her home, but Ella had no other option.

'This place was a happy home once, but for the past six months it's just felt like an empty shell and tainted in some way.'

Everywhere she looked reminded her of Alex, and she couldn't wait to hand the keys back and move on with her life.

'I'm ready when you are.' Ella looked towards Callie. 'Can we just get out of here?'

Within ten minutes Ella was standing on the pavement outside number 17 Ellerbeck Close, next to her battered old brown suitcase. With the door firmly lock behind her, she exhaled. 'A new chapter,' she said, her eyes teeming with tears.

'You've got this,' replied Callie, linking her arm through Ella's.

'Thank you, for everything, and especially for coming to my rescue. It's just what I need.'

'That's what best friends are for,' replied Callie, glancing at her watch. 'Come on, we have a train to catch.'

'Heartcross, we are coming to get you.' Ella attempted a smile as she wheeled the suitcase behind her, and began the short walk towards the train station and the next chapter of her life.

Ella had never visited Heartcross before, but she'd

seen it on the news eighteen months ago, after all the villagers had been stranded when the only bridge in and out of the village had collapsed due to a storm. For the next six months, thanks to Callie, Ella was going to be working as a waitress at The Lakehouse, a restaurant owned by millionaire property tycoon, Flynn Carter, and would be sharing a flat above the village shop with Callie. Ella couldn't be any more grateful to Callie; this was exactly what she needed to try and forget the past and get her life back on track.

Full of emotion, Ella bit down on her trembling lip and didn't look back. Dr Alex James – or whatever his real name was – was not going to break her. She was going to come through this with the help of Callie.

As the train pulled on to platform ten, Ella and Callie climbed on board. With Ella's suitcase safely stored in the luggage compartment, they sat down and within minutes the train slowly pulled away from the station. This was it, her new life started right now. Ella knew living in a tiny tourist village was going to be a huge change compared to the hustle and bustle of city life. And working at The Lakehouse restaurant was going to be different from owning her own business, but she was excited about the challenge.

Once the train picked up speed, the towns and the countryside whizzed by. Ella knew it would be perfect hanging out with Callie. It would help to heal her hurt and put the past behind her. She was looking forward to their girly time; being Callie's lodger was going to be fun. Ella had visions of late-night films, glasses of wine and proper belly laughing, just like the old days at university. She had every intention of getting her life back on track and getting herself out of this financial mess, but she just hadn't worked out all the details yet.

Despite the distance between Chester and Inverness, the journey flew by. Ella and Callie reminisced about their university days, they dozed a little, and finally the train reached its destination. This was it. Ella had arrived in Scotland. With mixed emotions she stepped off the train behind Callie.

'How are you feeling?' asked Callie, throwing away their rubbish in a nearby bin.

'Excited, scared… sad,' admitted Ella.

'That's understandable, but I promise you, you're going to love it here. When Dan and I broke up, I came to stay with Julia at her B&B and instantly fell in love with the place. I've no intention of ever living anywhere else. There's something about Heartcross…'

Compared to Chester, this had to be the world's tiniest station, comprised of a coffee shop, and not much else. Ella admired the wonderful blooms hanging from their baskets as she followed Callie over to the taxi service outside the wrought-iron railings.

'Where to?' asked the taxi driver after he placed Ella's suitcase in the boot of the cab.

'Heartcross, please,' Callie told the taxi driver and climbed in the back of the taxi next to Ella. He nodded and began to drive.

Heartcross was a tiny village separated from the local town of Glensheil by a temporary bridge, the original having been brought down in a storm. Cut off from civilisation, the village had become famous in the national news, and since the TV coverage of the disaster, tourism had been growing at a rapid pace. In the last twelve months alone, property tycoon Flynn Carter had added a new five-star hotel, a boat house and a fancy restaurant to the quaint village.

The driver wound down his window. 'Sorry, the air-con is broke,' he mumbled his apology. They were both thankful for the fresh air and inhaled the country aroma of cow dung as they spotted the culprits loping across the lush fields. Ella noticed alpacas grazing, vintage caravans dotted in the distance, and a magnificent castle standing on the craggy hill. The cab whizzed past numerous cosy dwellings, white-washed terraces and cottages entwined with pink clematis and roses tumbling around the oak-framed porches. This place was like somewhere out of a novel. In the distance stood the beautiful mountain of Heartcross covered in purple heather with numerous ramblers dotted around, hiking the paths, enjoying the weather.

'Look at this place,' she murmured, still watching the views through the window.

The taxi continued to bump over the steep mountainous track, approximately half a mile long, and pulled up outside the village shop opposite the pub. After the driver was paid, they stepped on to the pavement. Ella slung her bag over her shoulder and held on to the handle of the suitcase. 'So this is Heartcross,' she muttered, casting a glance around. People were going about their business; kids ambling up the road, clutching their fishing nets; dog walkers sitting outside the pub enjoying a pint. It was a beautiful warm evening.

'Welcome to Heartcross, your new home!' exclaimed Callie, nodding towards the flat above the old village shop in front of them.

'I feel like I'm on holiday,' shared Ella.

'That's exactly how I felt when I turned up here too. Honestly Ella, you are going to love it here. I promise.'

Ella took in the sight. The lovely little shop in front of her was quaintly old fashioned, with postcards stacked outside in the spinning carousel. A metal ice-cream sign swung in the light breeze and fishing nets were lined up behind the fresh fruit laid out in wooden crates on a table.

'What an adorable shop,' she said, turning the carousel and taking a look at the postcards.

'Welcome! Welcome!'

Ella spun round to see the shopkeeper standing in the doorway, holding a bottle of wine. 'You must be Ella.'

Ella's first impression was, *What a lovely man.* At a guess, he was in his mid-sixties. He had rosy cheeks and such a welcoming smile.

'I am, I am,' replied Ella, taking the bottle of wine that was being thrust towards her.

The man stretched out his hand. 'Hamish, shopkeeper and your new landlord. Welcome to Heartcross!'

'Thanks very much,' replied Ella, shaking his hand.

'I've been looking out for you both. How was the journey?'

'Long,' replied Callie with a smile, touching Hamish's arm.

'Very, very long,' replied Ella, also with a smile. In fact, even though she'd been sitting on a train doing nothing for hours, she actually felt completely exhausted.

'But you are here now. Wait there!'

Before they could object, Hamish disappeared back into the shop and reappeared with a serving dish covered over with tin foil. 'Courtesy of Meredith.' He nodded towards the Grouse and Haggis pub standing opposite. 'She thought you may appreciate a home-cooked meal after such a long journey.'

'Both you and Meredith are superstars. This is just what we needed, thank you.' Callie took the dish from Hamish's hands. 'This is perfect!' She beamed.

Ella was taken back; she'd only arrived literally a few moments ago, and everyone was so welcoming. The familiarity of being with Callie and the welcoming warmth of everyone brought tears to her eyes. She flapped a hand in front of her face. 'Look at me, I've come over all emotional. These are happy tears. Everyone is so kind.'

'That is what Heartcross is all about.' Callie gave her a warm smile. 'Let's get you settled in. Just wait until you taste Meredith's home-cooked food, it's out of this world.'

Hamish hurried back into the shop to serve a couple of children patiently waiting for ice-cream, and Ella turned back towards Callie. 'Is everyone this lovely in Heartcross?' she asked.

'You better believe it.' Callie smiled as she took a peep under the tin foil. 'Lasagne, and it's still warm. I'm famished.'

They climbed the short, steep steps to the upstairs flat, and Ella followed Callie into the tiny hallway which led into the living room. 'Woah! I wasn't expecting that.'

The magnificent view through the French doors was simply breath-taking. Ella abandoned her suitcase and placed her bag down on the settee before standing in awe. Heartcross Mountain was towering in the background, the River Heart tumbling over the rocks, and the town of Glensheil standing tall in the distance. 'I feel like I'm in a different country.'

'You are,' laughed Callie, opening up the French doors which led out on to a tiny balcony. There were two bistro chairs, a handful of potted plants and pastel floral triangular bunting draped above the doors. 'This place was a great find. The rent is reasonable, there's two bedrooms, one bathroom and a small kitchen. It's tiny, and for the time being all mine... and yours.'

'How long have you been here?' asked Ella, pulling out a chair and folding her arms on the railing. 'I could wake up to that view every morning. It beats looking out on a street full of cars and overflowing bins.'

'It is pretty spectacular, isn't it? I've been here around eight months now. At first I was staying with Julia at the B&B, but I needed my own space, and to cut down on her amazing full Scottish breakfasts every morning, which weren't doing my waistline any good.' Callie patted her stomach with a chuckle.

'I wish I had that problem.' Ella pulled at the waist on her trousers. Her clothes were hanging off her thin frame. 'I've lost so much weight in the past six months.'

'That'll be stress. Hopefully things will begin to change now, and working at The Lakehouse will keep you distracted... There's also discounted meals, and if there's any food left over after the late shift, we're able to bring it home... The desserts are to die for.'

'That sounds just what I need.' Ella picked up the bottle of wine that Hamish had given her and looked over the label. 'Shall we get this open?'

'Absolutely,' replied Callie. 'I'll get the glasses and plates,' she said, peeling back the tin foil on the dish of lasagne.

Just at that second Ella's stomach rumbled, sounding like a growl of thunder rolling out across a valley.

Callie laughed. 'Let's eat.'

Two minutes later they were tucking into the best lasagne Ella had ever tasted. She took what felt like seconds to clear her plate before diving in for more.

'You seem to have got your appetite back. And we are going to get you back on track, if we keep busy and enjoy life. I know the job isn't what you're used to... after running your own business and not having to answer to anyone.'

'I'm looking forward to not being in charge,' admitted Ella.

'And Flynn is just the best boss. It's going to be just fine.'

'Everyone needs a Callie in their life. Thank you.' Ella took a sip of her wine. 'But I do still wonder where the hell he is?' Even though months had passed, Alex was still very much on her mind.

'Probably seeking out his next victim.' Callie was straight to the point. 'We are not giving that man any more head space. Fresh start… starting now. Deal?'

Ella nodded but put down her knife and fork. 'Deal, but Callie – I'm not going to be able to pay you much rent.'

'I'm not expecting you to pay me any rent. You are here to get yourself back on track, and I'm not adding to your worries.'

'But—' Ella went to object, but Callie was having none of it.

'No buts, you'd do the same for me.'

'Thank you.' Ella swung a look towards the mountains. 'This does beat the city.'

'It does, and wait until you see The Lakehouse. There's no point me even trying to describe it to you, as it wouldn't do it justice. It's stunning.'

'I can't wait, even though I have to admit, I'm not sure I'll make the best waitress. I'm the clumsiest person ever and am always dropping stuff or tripping up. Remember when we were at university, and I got sacked from the pub on campus after the plate of spaghetti I was holding slipped into the lap of the woman wearing the white dress?' Ella rolled her eyes. The manager had sacked her immediately and at the time Ella thought she'd never work again.

'Oh my God, don't remind me of that now!' Callie

burst out laughing. 'You can't go throwing spaghetti over the diners at The Lakehouse.'

'I'll do my best.' This was what Ella had missed, old friendships full of banter. Even though her debts were weighing heavily on her mind, she knew being here with Callie would do her the world of good.

'Hindsight is a wonderful thing.'

'And love has a lot to answer for, Callie. What's that noise?'

Their conversation was interrupted by the sudden sound of singing coming from the balcony below them. Ella raised her eyebrows.

Callie was chuckling. 'That's Dolores! She's amazing. I absolutely love her and you're going to absolutely love her too. Come and meet her – you're in for a treat.'

Ella took another sip of wine before following Callie down the stairwell to another duck-egg blue door. There was no answer after Callie rapped on the knocker, so she pushed down the handle and walked straight inside.

'Dolores, it's me, Callie,' she shouted over the noise of the music.

Wide-eyed, Ella thought she'd walked into some sort of hall of fame. The walls were lined with faded photos and magazine cuttings of Dolly Parton, and there was an old-fashioned olive-green telephone on a small round table with a brown velvet stool tucked underneath it.

'Dolores, it's me,' Callie called again, competing with

the warblings that were belting out from the balcony. 'She's a huge fan of Dolly – I mean fangirl!'

'No shit, Sherlock,' whispered Ella, still staring at the walls in the small hallway and wondering what she was going to find on the other side of the door.

'Is that you, Callie dear?' Suddenly the music was turned down.

'It is. I've brought a friend to meet you.' Callie pushed open the door and walked into the living room.

In her head Ella had pictured a minimalist space with a wooden floor, neutral colours on the walls and a little old lady wearing a grey cardigan with her hair in a bun, singing along to the radio, but instead Ella was mesmerised. Standing in front of her was a tiny, slim woman wearing cherry-red lipstick and a matching bright-red beret on the top of a mass of blonde curly hair, a vivid peacock-blue blouse over a large chest that was draped in orange beads, a black skirt and green tights. The outfit was completed by a black feather boa draped around her neck and fluffy animal-print kitten-heel slippers.

The living room was cosy with two armchairs, a sofa and a coffee table facing a pretty tiled fireplace. To the left a bookcase was stacked with romantic comedies, and to the right an old record player sat with hundreds of vinyls piled next to it. There was a TV like no other Ella had ever seen, the carpet was a vision of brown paisley swirls, and the walls, decorated in red and gold stripes, were covered in frame after frame of photographs.

'Wow, what an amazing room,' exclaimed Ella, feeling like she'd stepped inside some sort of museum.

Dolores smiled at Ella and stared from underneath her heavily mascaraed lashes. 'Who do we have here?' she asked, taking a seat. 'You look like you are in need a good meal.' Dolores clearly wasn't afraid to say what she thought.

Callie tipped a wink at an astonished Ella who was captivated by Dolores' appearance. She knew she was staring but she couldn't take her eyes off her.

'Dolores, this is my friend Ella. She's staying with me for a while.'

'A while? Are you in trouble or mending a broken heart?' Dolores was watching Ella carefully. 'In my experience, it's usually one of the two.'

Ella snagged a fleeting glance towards Callie, who was grinning. 'She doesn't miss a trick,' whispered Callie.

'And there's no need for whispering. I may be old but I'm not deaf – not yet, anyway.'

'No, I'm not in trouble,' replied Ella with a smile.

'Mmmm… boy trouble, then? It will tell me in your leaves.'

'Leaves?'

'Dolores can see your future in your tea leaves.' Callie

gave her a knowing look.

'They aren't worth it, you know... boys. Everyone needs a McCartney and Fred instead.'

Ella looked bewildered. 'A McCartney? A Fred?'

Dolores pointed to the bird cage on the balcony. 'Fred, my canary.'

'Named after Fred Astaire, as he dances around the cage,' chipped in Callie.

Ella glanced at the blue-and-yellow canary that was happily pecking away at the bird food before bobbing his head. He looked comical.

'And McCartney,' Dolores pointed her stick to the tiny Yorkshire Terrier asleep on the bed in the corner of the room.

Ella was surprised he hadn't moved a muscle since they arrived.

'Please tell me he's not stuffed,' whispered Ella, looking for the rise and fall in his chest.

'He's deaf,' mouthed Callie. 'But very much alive.'

'Obviously named after the great Paul McCartney. Well, sit yourselves down, there's tea in the pot. And take a biscuit, but only if it's one of those rich tea ones – they're so boring, and they stick to the root of my mouth.' Dolores nudged the plate towards them. 'Go on, take one. I have to get rid of them somehow. Hamish brings them. He thinks I've not noticed they are past their sell-by date.'

'Thank you,' replied Ella, eyeing up the chocolate biscuits but only daring to take a rich tea.

'More importantly, do you like Dolly?' asked Dolores, eyeing Ella with interest.

'I absolutely love Dolly!' Ella replied enthusiastically.

Dolores stood up slowly and, with the help of her stick, walked over to the old-fashioned record player. She placed the needle back on the stand and the record stopped spinning. Then she slowly walked back to her seat.

'Where was Dolly born?' asked Dolores, watching Ella carefully.

'Tennessee,' answered Callie, thankfully coming to Ella's rescue.

'Which Bee-Gees song did Dolly and Kenny Rogers score a hit with?' continued Dolores, leaning back and stretching her arms out along the arms of the chair.

'I know this one…' Ella clapped her hands together. Callie looked at her with amusement. '"Islands in the Stream".'

Dolores nodded, clearly impressed. 'Who is Dolly Parton's god-daughter?'

'I know this one too… Miley Cyrus.' Ella beamed, getting into the swing of things and thankful for the pub quizzes at university.

'Last one…' Dolores was thinking. 'Who wrote Dolly's hit, "9 to 5"?'

Ella looked towards Callie for help, who mouthed 'Dolly'. 'That'll be Dolly, herself,' answered Ella triumphantly.

Dolores' mouth hitched into a smile. 'You, Ella, are a friend of mine. Take a seat and you can have a chocolate biscuit – but only one, mind.'

Ella was chuffed she'd passed the test and sat on the floral sofa covered in a patchwork crochet blanket of many colours. Callie sat next to her.

'I might even open up the fruitcake.'

'Save the cake for another day – we've just finished dinner and are stuffed. We just heard your beautiful voice and thought we'd say hello. We'll pop back tomorrow for cake,' replied Callie warmly, finishing her biscuit and catching the crumbs with her hand.

Dolores looked please, then nodded towards Ella. 'Let me read your leaves.'

'Of course, I'd like that,' replied Ella, giving her a wide smile followed by a yawn. 'Please forgive me! We've been travelling all day.' She would have liked nothing more than to pull on her PJs whilst finishing the wine.

'I feel very much the same,' admitted Callie.

'You get yourselves off, but come and see me tomorrow,' instructed Dolores, waving her stick in the air.

After they said their goodbyes and before the door

was even shut behind them, the record player crackled, and Dolores began singing again.

'Oh my God, are you sure that dog is alive?' exclaimed Ella, stepping into the stairwell. She was convinced he wasn't breathing.

'He's definitely alive,' confirmed Callie, much to Ella's relief.

'I hope I'm just as wacky as that one day – living with my canary, my deaf dog and obsessed with Dolly.' She giggled, thinking the whole visit was surreal.

Callie let herself back into her flat and they sat back out on the balcony and poured the wine. 'Dolores is Hamish's ninety-something-year-old mother.'

'Ninety-something?' Ella let out a low whistle. 'Wow… just, wow!'

'She's as bright as a button, doesn't miss a trick and on the whole is still able to take care of herself, but since I've been here, I do check in on her every day. She brightens up my days to no end.'

'Amazing.' Ella was in complete awe. Ninety-something years old! She couldn't believe it. 'She seems wonderful, absolutely wonderful,' confirmed Ella, thinking if their first meeting was anything to go by, Dolores must have a very interesting and colourful past.

Having only arrived in Heartcross an hour ago, Ella was already feeling relaxed and very much at home. They sat in a comfortable silence, staring out over the mountainous terrain. 'I hope I'm as switched on as Dolores when I get to her age,' Ella thought out loud.

'I'm just hoping I'm still alive,' replied Callie with a chuckle.

'Can you believe we are both sitting here… single?' Ella looked at Callie. 'I really can't thank you enough for inviting me to stay.'

'You don't have to thank me – you'd do the same for me. It's a funny old world, isn't it?'

'It certainly is. You know what, Callie? We need to be more like Dolores.'

'What – idolising Dolly Parton, owning a canary and a deaf dog?' Callie gave her a funny look.

Ella threw back her head and laughed. 'No! Living life to the max… that's my new motto… be like Dolores.'

'You'll be getting a T-shirt made next,' teased Callie.

They were still chuckling as they finished their wine. With her feet propped up on the balcony, Ella tilted her face up towards the sky and shut her eyes. It was late September, and the weather was still glorious. Ella inhaled and they exchanged contented smiles. In her heart she knew that Heartcross was a good place to get her life back on track after leaving her old life behind. 'Today is the start of the rest of my life,' she announced.

'I'll drink to that.' Callie reached forward and clinked her glass with Ella's.

'So Dolores reads tea leaves – that's what she said, isn't it?' asked Ella, who had only ever had her fortune told once before, by Gypsy Petrulengro on Blackpool's seafront after getting totally inebriated on a hen weekend.

Callie let out an involuntary laugh. 'I can see where this is going.'

'Have you had yours read?' Ella was intrigued. She didn't disbelieve the whole theory about seeing into the future, but of course was a little sceptical. 'This could be fun.'

'Whoa!' Callie held up her hand. 'Don't bring me into this! I'm not sure I believe in all that looking-into-the-future malarkey. I'm a firm believer in letting fate take over. But as your friend, I'm willing to participate, if I have to.'

This perked Ella right up and a flicker of a smile spread across her face. 'You know what I love, even after all this time? We just fall back into being the best of friends. It's just so easy being in your company. Thanks for all this, and sorting out a job for me too.' Ella was genuinely grateful.

'It's exactly the same for me, after splitting with Dan after all that time. If it wasn't for Flynn and Julia giving me a job and a home when I first arrived... There's something about Heartcross, and you being here will do me the world of good. It's great to have some company, especially when it's yours. We used to have the best times.'

Ella was unexpectedly moved. Callie was a loyal friend with a good heart, always kind and a well-meaning person. She'd stepped up to the mark, and that was what true friendship was all about. 'Let's have a toast to us.' Ella held up her glass and tapped it against Callie's. 'Here's to life, happiness and my new job. Let's hope it's all happy sailing.'

'I hope so too, as the only way to work is by water taxi.' Callie gave a little chuckle.

Ella's mind glimpsed back to her younger self – slender, gorgeous and maybe a little gobby at times. Now in her mid-thirties, she'd never thought it would be written in the stars that she was going to be a waitress, bunking up with her old uni friend, miles from home. But now she was here, she was going to grasp the opportunity with both hands. Of course, she was going to throw herself into life in Heartcross, and hopefully soon she'd have more of a clue about what she was actually going to do with her life.

'You never know what's around the corner,' added Callie, holding up her glass. 'To us! And our future, which starts right here, right now.'

'To us,' mirrored Ella. 'And the start of a brand-new chapter.'

Chapter Two

The next morning Ella woke just after 9am, pushed back the duvet and swung her legs to the floor. Already she knew it was going to be another magnificent day ahead. The sun was beaming through the gap in the curtains, leaving horizontal patterns across the carpet. Sliding back the curtains, she stared at the splendid view. What could be more glorious than waking up to the view of Heartcross Mountain? She pushed open the window and breathed in the air before pulling on an oversized jumper and wandering into the living room.

Callie was already sitting out on the balcony reading a newspaper. 'Good morning!' She gave Ella a huge smile. 'Did you sleep well?'

Ella sat down opposite and smothered a yawn. 'Ha, look at me, still yawning – but yes I slept well.'

'I've slept well every night since arriving in Heartcross – it must be the mountain air.' Callie nodded to the breakfast laid out on the table. 'Help yourself. There's cereal, croissants, fruit, and tea in the pot.'

Breakfast was a small feast and Ella reached across the table and grabbed a croissant from the basket, along with the pot of strawberry jam. 'Is that Dolores, singing already?' Ella swung a look over the balcony and saw Dolores sitting below at the table and chairs on her veranda. Fred was chirping away in the cage on the table whilst McCartney was curled up on her lap. Dolores was belting out a song like she didn't have a care in the world.

'Every morning, without fail.'

'She has got a pretty amazing voice,' remarked Ella, tilting her ear towards the balcony.

'The dog thinks so,' joked Callie.

Ella laughed, pouring herself a glass of orange juice from the carton. 'So, what's the plan for today?' Ella was curious to get out and explore Heartcross, maybe meet some of the locals too.

'It's up to you. We could wander around Heartcross so you can get your bearings. There's The Boathouse, which is perfect on a day like today. I've got the day off work, and we do need to go over to The Lakehouse to pick up your uniform ready for Monday at some point, but you choose. We can do whatever you want to do.'

Callie folded the newspaper and pushed it to one side. 'And the postman has pushed this through the wrong door by mistake – it's a letter for Dolores. I've got a little bit of paperwork to do, but apart from that I'm all yours.'

'I'll have a shower and drop the letter into Dolores',' offered Ella. 'And once you've finished your paperwork we can go and do some exploring.'

Ella couldn't wait to go out and about. She'd woken in a good mood and as far as she was concerned, today was going to be a good day. Ella had every intention of grabbing it with both hands, and hopefully she could begin to put the past behind her.

Thirty minutes later, after a quick shower, Ella found herself standing outside Dolores' front door clutching the letter. It was hand-written with spider-like writing in an old-fashioned ink pen. Ella knocked but there was no answer. Dolores was probably still sitting outside, so she turned the handle and gave a little shout.

'Dolores, it's Ella!' She stepped into the living room.

Dolores was sitting in her chair with her eyes closed and McCartney was curled up on her lap.

'Dolores,' Ella spoke softly. The last thing she wanted to do was frighten her. Maybe she should just leave the letter beside her for when she woke up. Padding lightly over the carpet, Ella was just about to place the letter on the arm of the chair when Dolores opened her eyes and screamed. McCartney didn't move a muscle.

'I'm so sorry, I didn't mean to make you jump!' exclaimed Ella, sitting down on the couch. 'It's just me.' Ella touched Dolores' arm, then brought her hand up to her own chest to calm her beating heart.

'We didn't hear you, did we, McCartney? Must have dozed off for a second.' Dolores patted McCartney's head, who eventually opened his eyes and jumped down from the chair and straight on to Ella's lap.

'He's adorable.'

'Don't be fooled, he's a grumpy old man. I often joke about which one of us will go first. I'm hoping it's him, even though it will break my heart. I just couldn't leave him in this world alone.' Dolores was staring at McCartney with such love that Ella immediately felt emotional and swallowed down a lump in her throat. 'And what have you there?' asked Dolores, noticing the letter in Ella's hand.

'It's for you, a letter. The postman pushed it through the wrong letterbox.' Ella handed over the letter.

The rapid beam that spread across Dolores' face didn't go unnoticed. She clutched the letter to her chest. 'Thank you.'

Ella was intrigued. 'Something important?' she asked, noticing that Dolores' eyes had brightened.

'It certainly is.' Dolores wasn't giving any more away.

Ella noticed that she slipped the letter into her bag at the side of the chair before turning back to her.

'Are you in a rush?' asked Dolores.

'Callie is just catching on up on some paperwork, so I have a little time before she shows me the sights.'

Dolores reached for her walking stick and rose carefully to her feet. Ella's eyes were fixed on her as she walked over towards the dresser and reached for a bone-china cup. 'This is what we need. Shall we see what your future holds?' asked Dolores, resting her stick against the chair and sitting back down.

'Absolutely,' replied Ella, leaving Dolores looking pleased as she placed the cup on the table and began to swirl the teapot. After a few seconds Dolores poured the tea into the cup and looked up at Ella.

'Can you really read tea leaves?' asked Ella, intrigued by what she was about to find out.

'Of course, it's an ancient tradition dating back thousands of years – nearly as old as me. My Granny taught me. The tea is brewed but this time we don't use a strainer, we need the leaves to do the reading all by themselves.' Dolores was clearly taking this very seriously. 'What I need you to do is prepare yourself mentally, think about your life, any unanswered questions you may have, while the tea is brewing and you're holding the cup.' Dolores passed Ella the cup, who wrapped her hands around it and shuffled back on the settee and sat up straight.

Ella had many unanswered questions, more than Dolores could ever imagine: why she'd allowed Alex into her life and why he'd caused her so much pain.

'Now drink your tea carefully. You need to leave the tea leaves in the cup, and a little liquid too.'

Ella nodded her understanding and began to drink the tea. 'I think I've finished,' she said, looking down into her cup before passing it back to Dolores.

With much concentration on her face, Dolores swirled the cup around slowly, then carefully she poured the rest of the liquid away. Dolores remained silent whilst Ella moved to the edge of her seat, waiting for her reading to start. Dolores scrutinised the leaves and made a few noises. 'What I'm looking for is the most prominent pattern,' she murmured. 'Tea-leaf reading is a way to give us answers. These shapes can tell us of our successes, downfalls, relationships and life in general.'

Dolores gazed at the cup for a moment longer. 'Are you ready?' She glanced up at Ella.

'I think so.' Ella could feel her heart racing and had no clue what to expect.

'Okay, we have numerous shapes and symbols, which all mean different things. I can see a cloud. You, my dear, have had a difficult time.'

Ella blew out a breath – that was an understatement!

'You've had significant difficulties and grief. Grief that will live with you every day of your life.'

Immediately, thinking of her parents, the tears welled up in Ella's eyes. She nodded and swallowed. Dolores was spot on.

'You may not feel it now, but whatever happened to you will make you stronger. See this straight line here?' Dolores tilted the cup towards Ella. 'This means your journey is going to become peaceful and full of happiness. So don't give up on yourself just yet.' Dolores offered her a warm, reassuring smile. 'And you have an anchor. Not only does that mean good fortune in your work, but your love life too. Your happy ever after is not too far away.'

'I'm not looking for anyone,' shared Ella, thinking the last thing she needed in her life was another relationship.

'And that's when it happens – when you are least expecting it.'

'But I do start my new job on Monday.'

'There you go – this job is going to be good for you. It will make a difference to your life and it's going to bring you opportunities. Thankfully, I can't see an hourglass.'

'And what would that mean?'

'An hourglass indicates upcoming danger, but I can see a goat, which means you may encounter an enemy from the past – so have your wits about you! But on the whole, your move to Heartcross is going to be a good one. Embrace it!' Dolores' voice lifted.

Ella liked the idea of the move being a good one, but she certainly wasn't interested in coming face to face with anyone from her past, and there was only one person who sprang to mind.

'How long are you staying for?' asked Dolores.

'Six months, initially. And I really am not looking for love at the minute.'

'Very wise,' agreed Dolores. 'Make time for you, but sometimes love smacks you in the face, right out of the blue.'

Dolores put the cup down and reached over and took both of Ella's hands. She squeezed them tightly. 'You've been through the mill.'

'I have,' agreed Ella, and briefly she shared with Dolores what had happened between her and Alex.

'Time is a good healer, and you are in the right place.' Dolores smiled at Ella with such warmth. 'And McCartney and I will look after you.' Dolores looked towards McCartney with adoration.

'Thank you, Dolores. Once I'm distracted with work and I work out a way to pay off all the debts…'

'And you will, dear. You're a bright girl who has had a difficult time. This cup shows comfort and peace in your future. You will find happiness. I think you are going to be just fine, Ella.'

'That's just what I needed to hear. But in the meantime, I think I'll put my heart on hold.'

'Look after you, and the rest will come in time… And there's one more thing. See that shape there?'

Ella leant forward to take a look.

'That means your next journey is to Bonnie's teashop to pick me up a slice of Victoria sponge. McCartney will keep you company,' Dolores gave a little chuckle.

'Of course, I will. Just point me in the direction of Bonnie's teashop.'

Dolores reached for her purse, but Ella put up her hand. 'My treat – payment for reading my leaves. Where is McCartney's lead?'

Dolores pushed herself up on her stick and gave Ella directions to Bonnie's teashop, just at the top of Love Heart Lane.

Ambling down the High Street, Ella and McCartney made slow progress. They were stopped by everyone who crossed their path who immediately went all gooey-eyed over the dog. Everyone was friendly, passing the time of day, and Ella couldn't believe the difference between village and city life. Usually, she found it difficult to cross a road due to the amount of traffic whizzing by, but in the last five minutes she hadn't seen one car. Everywhere there seemed to be a slower pace of life, and people were actually standing around having conversations, catching up with each other's lives, instead of rushing about speaking into telephones and clutching their laptops like their lives depended on it.

Ella carried on walking for another five minutes before she discovered the whitewashed terraced houses of Love Heart Lane. Bonnie's teashop was at the top of the lane. Ella breathed in the mountain air. 'Wow,' she muttered to herself, gazing up at the magnificent mountain standing in front of her. 'What a view.'

McCartney had discovered the bowl of water outside the entrance to the teashop, whilst again everyone commented on how delightful he was. Ella stepped inside and the old-fashioned bell tinkled above her head, alerting the woman behind the counter to her arrival. She turned around with a welcoming smile.

'McCartney and…' She wiped her hands on her tea towel then stretched a hand out towards Ella.

'Ella, a friend of Callie's. Her cousin Julia owns the B&B.'

'Ella! Welcome, welcome to Heartcross. I'm Rona. We heard you were arriving. Felicity… F-E-L-I-C-I-T-Y!' Rona bellowed towards the door at the back of the teashop. 'Come and meet Ella.'

Felicity appeared from the kitchen, balancing a freshly baked Victoria sponge on a blue china plate. 'Hello.' She beamed. 'Welcome! Callie told us you were coming.'

Ella couldn't believe the welcome she was receiving from everyone in the village. They were all so lovely.

'Pleased to meet you both, and that's exactly what I've come in for.' Ella pointed at the plate Felicity was holding. 'A slice of Victoria sponge for Dolores – good timing!' Ella marvelled, looking around. 'This place is foodie heaven.' Her eyes widened as she took in all the delicious-looking pastries, cakes and sandwiches displayed in the front counter.

'Have you settled in?' asked Felicity, grabbing a knife and beginning to cut up the cake into over-large slices.

'I only arrived last night but I've already made a new friend in Dolores, and I've a day of exploring ahead of me before I start work on Monday at The Lakehouse.'

'Did you pass the initiation test?' Rona raised an eyebrow.

'I can confirm that I got all my Dolly questions correct, with a little help from Callie.'

They all chuckled as Felicity handed over a white box wrapped up with a pink ribbon. 'Dolores' cake.'

'And The Lakehouse – has business picked up?' questioned Rona, with a look of concern on her face. 'The last I heard was that Flynn was finding it difficult to fill the tables.'

'Really? I don't know anything about that.' Ella's first thought was, if business wasn't booming, how long would her job last?

Rona must have noticed the look on Ella's face. 'I'm sure there's nothing to worry about. Flynn is a businessman, and if anyone can make that place work, it will be him. Sometimes these things take time to get off the ground,' added Rona, bending down and giving McCartney a dog biscuit from the jar at the far end of the counter. 'And we hope you settle in quickly. Once you arrive in Heartcross…'

'… You are here for good,' Ella chuckled, finishing off Rona's sentence. 'I already feel like I'm at home. Everyone is so welcoming, and that view! It must be amazing, working here, staring at that mountain every day.'

'It's pretty special,' admitted Rona. 'The whole village is pretty special, but we're biased.'

'I think I'm going to feel the same.' Ella handed over the money for the cake. 'Thank you,' she said, holding the box. 'Have a lovely day.'

'You too,' answered Rona and Felicity in unison.

Ella ventured back outside. *What a lovely little teashop,* she thought, strolling back down Love Heart Lane towards the village. Hearing her phone ring, she pulled it from her pocket and swiped the screen. Callie was checking up on her.

'Have you got lost, going down the stairwell?' Callie asked.

Ella grinned. 'No, I haven't got lost. I'm just running a quick errand for Dolores. I'll be home in five.'

As Ella stuffed the phone back into her pocket, she stepped off the kerb.

'Woah! Look out.'

Startled, Ella looked up to see a man on a bike wobbling towards her. She'd stepped straight out in front of him without looking where she was going. Time slowed as the front tyre hit the kerb and catapulted his shopping bag up in the air. He was flung forward but managed to hold on, before he bounced back on to his seat and placed his feet firmly on the ground.

Feeling a fool, Ella opened her mouth to apologise. 'I'm so sorry, it's all my fault!'

But the man wasn't looking at her, he was staring down at the ground. 'Sausages, MY SAUSAGES!'

McCartney might be deaf but there was nothing wrong with his sense of smell, and with his nose buried deep inside the man's bag, he was currently enjoying the rich pickings he'd found. Ella tugged on his lead and gave the man an apologetic smile. 'I'm so sorry! Really, I am.'

'Foxglove Farm's finest pork sausage with caramelised onions. That dog has taste!'

'He might have taste but you've no dinner,' exclaimed a mortified Ella, taking her first proper look at the man. She knew she was staring, but she couldn't help it – he was drop-dead gorgeous. His thick blond hair was wild on top, and at a guess he was mid to late thirties – her sort of age. She noticed a tiny scar at the side of his eyebrows, which were blond too. His eyelashes and deep-blue eyes were to die for. His face was tanned, and he had that unshaven thing going on, and a beaming smile that showed a perfect set of white teeth.

He gave her a wolfish grin and they stared at each other for a moment, then burst out laughing.

'It's okay, at least one of us will be fed today. Hi, I'm Roman.'

She scanned his outfit and approved: a very casual look, white T-shirt, cargo shorts, white trainers and a woven leather band around his wrist.

'I'm Ella,' she said, shaking his hand. 'And this is McCartney, aka Sausage Thief.'

'McCartney, one of the Fab Four. Very cool name.'

'And also not my dog, I'm just walking him.' Ella handed the cake box to Roman while she fumbled inside her purse. 'Let me pay for your sausages, it's the least I can do.'

'I wouldn't hear of it,' he said, handing the box back, which forced Ella to shut her purse.

'Are you sure? It's all my fault, I really wasn't looking where I was going.'

'Very sure,' he replied, holding her gaze, causing her stomach to give a little flip. 'With that accent, my guess is you aren't local... Tourist?'

'I think I'm classed as a temporary resident. I only arrived last night.'

'Welcome!' He smiled as he leant his bike against a wall and picked up the bag of half-eaten sausages, then climbed back on to his bike. 'No doubt I'll see you around, Ella...?' He raised his eyebrow hopefully.

She cleared her throat. 'Ella Johnson,' she replied, liking the idea that he was going to see her around. Suddenly feeling a little shy, she felt a crimson blush on her cheeks and could have kicked herself. 'And you are Roman...?'

'Roman Docherty,' he shared. For a moment they stared at each other in a contemplative silence before he put his foot on the pedal. As he rode away, Roman looked back over his shoulder and gave her a warm smile. Ella watched him all the way to the end of Love Heart Lane before he disappeared in the direction of the bridge, heading for Glensheil. There was something mesmerising about Roman Docherty, but Ella gave herself a little shake. The last time she'd found someone intriguing, he'd ripped her off, and she wasn't here to find a man... far from it. But, surprisingly, Roman had put a spring in her step as she walked down the lane.

Over on the far side of the pavement, Ella's eyes skimmed over the metal sign flapping in the breeze, the entrance to an impressive farmhouse called Foxglove

Farm. In the fields were a herd of alpacas being walked around by children – a sight Ella had never seen in the city. This place was just a different way of life. 'Less than twenty-four hours I've been here, McCartney, and already I'm feeling relaxed. This place is going to be good for me.' But McCartney didn't answer; he was too busy ferreting around underneath the hedgerow without a care in the world.

Chapter Three

With McCartney and the slice of Victoria sponge safely delivered to Dolores, Ella bounded up the stairs to discover Callie was sitting out on the balcony reading a book.

'I'm home! I've met Rona and Felicity. How lovely are they?!'

Callie was smiling at Ella's enthusiasm.

'Oh, and I nearly killed some guy on a bike.'

Callie cocked an eyebrow. 'What do you mean, you nearly killed some guy on a bike?'

'He's okay, he's still breathing… no ambulance was needed,' replied Ella, pulling out a seat, 'even though, at a push, I would have been willing to give mouth to mouth. However, his sausages were not okay, and McCartney has had an almighty breakfast.' Callie looked mildly amused as Ella explained how she'd stepped out in front of Roman's bike. 'I wasn't looking where I was going.'

'Blooming heck, you have had a busy morning,' replied Callie, noticing a slight sparkle beneath the dark shadows of Ella's eyes. Callie waggled her finger round in a circle in front of Ella. 'See, baby steps – and look, you're already smiling.'

'Oh, and in other news, Dolores read my tea leaves. She confirmed that Heartcross is going to be good for me.' Ella gave Callie a knowing look.

'And I'll be predicting you'll be seeing Roman again – very soon.'

'What do you know that I don't?' queried Ella.

'I'm saying nothing, except watch this space.'

'It doesn't matter anyway. I'm not being taken for a fool again.'

Callie reached over and took her hand. 'You aren't a fool. Alex was a professional scammer, but we're no longer talking about him or giving him head space. One day you'll meet someone genuine, who treats you like you are the only girl in the world. Everything will fall into place.'

Ella poured herself a juice and sat down at the table. 'There has been something worrying me since my visit to the teashop. Rona seems to think The Lakehouse is in trouble. Should I already be looking for another job?'

Callie gestured to all the papers strewn over the table. 'I've just been looking at the bookings and it's not doing as well as Flynn would have liked, but that doesn't mean to say we are laying off staff just yet.'

'But there's a possibility?'

'Flynn is working on marketing strategies. He's turned many businesses around and I'm sure there isn't anything to worry about. Sometimes it just takes a little time for word to get around. Most restaurants are based on reputation.'

'Okay, but if I need to start looking for another job, please let me know in good time. I'm not sure I can take many more surprises this year.'

'You'll be the first to know,' reassured Callie. 'And while you've been out I've rustled us up a packed lunch. The Boathouse is open, and I thought we could mosey on down, have a mess about on the river before the weather changes. Then we could catch the boat over to The Lakehouse to pick up your uniform, and you can have a look around. You're going to love it there. Hopefully Flynn will be there, so you can say hello.'

'Sounds like a perfect plan to me,' replied Ella. Even though she felt a little nervous, Ella couldn't wait to meet Flynn in person.

'We can pick up your rota too. It's going to be good working together,' insisted Callie.

'Will I be working every day?' asked Ella, thinking about the money.

'Luckily for you, I'm in charge of the rota.'

'Do I need to call you Boss?'

'Absolutely you do.' Callie grinned. 'Nah, only joking!'

'I'll just change my shoes. I feel like a comfy trainer day.' Ella was just about to make a move when her phone pinged.

'My latest credit card statement is ready to view online... the joy.' Ella didn't dare to even look. Since discovering that Alex had maxed out the cards, she'd paid off six minimum payments, leaving her completely stony-broke each month. It made Ella anxious just thinking about it, but trying to focus on what was good in her life was helping. She had Callie and a job and was staying in a beautiful place which was good for her mind and soul.

'What you need to do is win the lottery and life will become simple.' Callie pointed her finger at Ella. 'You have to be in it to win it!'

'I can't even afford a ticket.' Ella rolled her eyes and Callie chuckled.

'I was in the same boat when I turned up here – not with the same amount of debt, but I was lucky Julia owned the B&B and didn't charge me anything until I'd sorted out my finances. We all help each other whenever we can.'

'And now we're both in the same boat,' added Ella with a smile, 'the one that takes us over the river to The Lakehouse each day.'

'And you might know the captain of that boat.' Callie tipped her a wink.

'Huh? What do you mean?' asked Ella.

But Callie deflected the conversation and pointed to the balcony. 'Listen!'

The sound of Dolores' voice filtered up from the balcony below. She was pitch perfect and Ella couldn't help but think that she had an amazing recording voice. Dolores was belting out the song like she didn't have a care in the world. 'I wish I could sing like that – I'm tone deaf,' shared Ella.

'I know! I remember when you attempted karaoke in the uni bar, everyone thought you were joking around until we realised you couldn't actually sing,' teased Callie.

Ella placed her hands on her heart, pretending to be hurt, then giggled. 'However, Dolores really can sing. She's a very colourful character.' Ella admired how a woman in her nineties still oozed star appeal, glitz and glamour. She hoped she lived life to the max in her later years, just like Dolores.

Ella took another swift look over the balcony. Dolores had now sat down at the bistro table, and in front of her was the slice of Victoria sponge looking scrumptious on a china plate. McCartney was stretched out by her feet, most probably still with a full belly after stumbling across the bag of sausages. Dolores was tilting her head from side to side and talking to Fred like she was expecting him to answer. Fred hopped on to the swing and suddenly began chirping.

'She's like a bird whisperer,' claimed Ella.

They admired how Dolores was dressed to impress. Her top was a multitude of bright colours worn with a pair of leggings, accompanied by a large buckled belt pulled in tight to reveal her tiny waist. On top of her long blonde curls rested a pair of oversized black sunglasses and on her feet she still wore her kitten slippers. There was no doubt Dolores was still living her best life.

'I wouldn't say Hamish takes after his mother,' said Ella, making an observation.

'Not in his dress sense, but he's also very much down to earth, kind and considerate.'

Ella took another quick look over the balcony. Dolores had finished her cake and her arms now rested on her stomach, as she listened to a play on the radio.

'And how are you feeling about your new life so far?'

Ella felt a stirring in her own stomach, and realised it was a sense of relief. This was a new start for her in Heartcross. 'I'm feeling good. Don't get me wrong – even after six months, I still look for him in every street I walk down, but that crook is long gone… with my money.' Ella sighed, before continuing. 'However, I agreed that I'm not giving him any more head space. It's time to get on with my life,' she announced with vigour. Jumping up, she grabbed her trainers from the side of the sofa. 'Come on, let's explore!' Ella couldn't wait to see the rest of Heartcross and her brand-new place of work. She shot Callie her biggest grin and packed a picnic inside her rucksack.

'Alright, eager beaver, Heartcross will still be there in five minutes, you know.'

'I don't want to waste another second.'

As soon as Callie had her shoes on, Ella slung the backpack over her shoulders and linked arms with her.

'Honestly, you're like a little kid,' chuckled Callie, locking the door behind her and walking down the stairwell.

'No wonder – this is the first day of the rest of my life,' declared Ella. 'This is our time to shine and laugh again. We're going to be good for each other.' But even though Ella was trying with all of her might to be positive, there was still the constant worry of paying off all of her debts.

'Too right,' replied Callie, squeezing her arm. 'Heartcross, we are coming to get you!'

Chapter Four

L ater that day, with their stomachs full from their delicious picnic, Ella and Callie walked towards Flynn Carter's water taxis. They'd had fun on the paddleboards, but as the afternoon sun was fading, the weather was beginning to cool.

'That was fun, I bet this place is packed out in the height of summer,' said Ella, walking on to the wooden jetty and spotting the bright-yellow water taxi bobbing in the water with its engine humming away. There wasn't another soul in sight as they stepped on board.

Callie called out, 'Is there anyone there?'

Ella looked around and guessed the boat could take approximately fifty passengers. There was a tiny bar on board, a toilet and a sound system.

'It'll get a bit chilly on here in winter,' said Ella, thinking out loud, 'especially coming back from work on the late shift.'

'This is the summer boat. Flynn has winter boats too, fully enclosed, heating... all mod cons. Julia was telling me that they're planning to run boat tours too, narrated excursions, and apparently a tour of the historical places around here, as well as seeking out the mansions of the rich and famous that line the waterways. But the ones I'm interested in the most are the Christmas booze cruise along the river for the adults, and Santa's boat ride for the kids.'

'Flynn's definitely got it all worked out, hasn't he? Boats for every season.'

They heard a bang below deck and then the door opened. 'You!' exclaimed Ella, recognising Roman, who she'd nearly knocked off his bike earlier that day.

A wide grin spread over Roman's face. 'Well, if it isn't the woman with the dog that steals sausages.' He shut the door behind him and stepped on to the deck.

Ella got her second proper look at him that day. He had a very elegant look; his Stirling-blue eyes matched the colour of his uniform and he tipped his sailor's cap towards her. Roman's eyes flashed instant warmth.

Ella heartily shook his hand and couldn't help noticing that he was staring at her. 'Pleased to meet you, again.'

'Likewise.' Roman didn't take his eyes off her.

Ella turned and narrowed her eyes at Callie, who was grinning. 'When I mentioned Roman, why didn't you tell me he was the Captain of the boat?'

'I thought you'd find out soon enough.'

'And where are you from, with an accent like that?' asked Roman, leading the way to the front of the boat.

'Cheshire,' replied Ella.

'Wow! You've come mighty far for a ride on my vessel.'

Callie burst into fits of laughter. 'Maybe you need to rephrase that.'

Roman looked completely at ease walking along the deck towards the front of the boat, whereas Ella let out a tiny squeal and grabbed on to the seats at the side of her. Roman looked back in Ella's direction. 'Here, let me help you.' He grabbed her hand and caught her eye. Her whole body tingled at his touch, as she felt her pulse quicken and goose bumps rise to the surface of her skin. He led her to the seats just behind the wheel. 'It gets a little rocky at times, but thankfully the waters aren't that choppy today. The weather is in that in-between stage at the minute. Are you okay now?'

Ella sat down on the seat. 'Yes, thank you.'

'Where are we off to, ladies?' asked Roman, taking his place behind the wheel. He snagged a glance towards the jetty. 'It looks like you are my only passengers, so the world is your oyster. I can drop you at the bridge and it's just a short walk to Primrose Park, or you can enjoy an afternoon at the art galleries over at Glensheil – your wish is my command.'

'Over to The Lakehouse, please Roman. We need to pick up Ella's uniform.'

'Uniform? You're working at The Lakehouse?' Roman looked rather pleased as he started the engine.

'I am, my first shift is on Monday.'

'Great! I'll look forward to transporting you across the waters each day. It's my job to get you there and back safely every shift, and I'll have you know I take my job very seriously.'

'Glad to hear it,' replied Ella, wondering if they were actually flirting just a little.

'Sit back and enjoy the view,' he continued, in a professional manner but with a smile to die for. Roman began to steer the boat slowly away from the jetty, then as soon as they were in open water, he began to pick up speed.

With the wind in her hair, Ella took in her surroundings. 'This is just amazing. Look at this place!'

'It's something else, isn't it?' said Roman, looking over his shoulder. 'Are you staying in Heartcross or across the water at Glensheil?' he asked, his eyes fixed firmly back on the water ahead.

'I'm in Heartcross, staying with Callie... Just for six months initially, unless she has enough of me.'

'Why only six months?' He looked over his shoulder at her.

'I'm in between jobs at the moment, taking each day as it comes,' she replied, not giving much away.

'I know that feeling,' replied Roman, causing Ella to wonder what his story might be. 'This is the best place to get your life back on track, and I can confirm the rumour about this place. Once you arrive, no one ever wants to leave. That's you here for a long time.' He looked back over his shoulder at her again and smiled.

'Maybe,' she replied, biting down on her lip and holding his gaze. He really did have lovely eyes.

Watching the view sail past, everything looked picture perfect. With sweeping bays and sand dunes, gulls hovered over the white cliffs and Heartcross Mountain stretched towards the sky. Ella watched the waves overturn as the boat glided through them. 'How do you know where you're going? It's not as though there are any road signs,' she said, thinking out loud.

Roman laughed. 'That's probably because we're on the river, not the roads.' He gave her a mischievous look.

Ella chuckled, feeling like a bit of an idiot. What a stupid thing to say!

Roman smiled. 'I know this river like the back of my hand.'

'This bit gets a little choppy,' shared Callie, holding on to the safety rail at the side of her. 'Every time it gets me.'

'Eek, my stomach has literally flipped,' exclaimed Ella, mirroring Callie's actions and holding on. All of a sudden, she was beginning to feel a little queasy and her whole body felt warm. The last time she'd felt this way was when riding a rollercoaster at the local theme park. Unzipping her lightweight jacket, Ella felt the colour drain from her face.

'There's calmer waters up ahead. Do you normally get travel sick?' Roman asked with concern, slowing the boat down.

Ella thought back to when she was a child. She'd been on a ferry a couple of times, but couldn't remember feeling this queasy. 'Not that I can remember, but I'm going to have to get used to it, if I'm doing this journey twice a day.' Ella felt the churning in her stomach, and hoped she didn't look as green as she felt.

'Here, come and drive the boat. Sometimes it helps if you are in control. It'll take your mind off it.' Roman stepped sideward but kept his hand on the wheel.

Ella stood up and took the wheel. 'It's just like driving a car.' She gripped the wheel and Roman pointed in the direction they were heading.

'Over towards those trees... this lever slows the boat

down if you pull it towards you, like this.' Roman gently pulled down and the boat began to slow. 'Have a go.'

Ella's hand brushed against his as she took over the controls. She pulled back the lever and the boat slowed, then pushed it back up again to make the boat go faster. 'It's like driving a remote-control car, but on a bigger scale.'

'And not forgetting we are on the water… not the road,' kidded Callie.

'This is actually fun.' Ella kept her eyes on the water and successfully sailed the boat towards the trees. With the breeze in her face, she was already feeling better.

Jokingly, Roman took his cap off his head and placed it on Ella's head. 'You are a proper captain now. But there's a tricky part coming up.' Roman pointed to the small opening in between the trees. 'We need to slow the boat right down.'

Ella began to steer the boat into calmer waters, slowing it down gently.

'How are you feeling now?' asked Roman.

'The queasiness has subsided,' replied Ella, breathing in deeply and filling her lungs with fresh air.

'We're nearly there,' confirmed Callie. 'The Lakehouse is just around this corner.'

'Take a look over at the secret coves.' Roman pointed to the left of him. 'There's lots of stories about pirates hiding treasures in there.' He smiled. 'But are you ready for this? This will take your breath away.'

Roman stood right behind Ella and reached for the control. She could feel his presence behind her as he leant forward and placed his hand on top of hers. 'You need to pull this right back now, as far as it will go.'

He kept his hand on top of hers as Ella carefully steered the boat through the gorgeous weeping willows that hung over the water's edge, then around a cluster of rocks.

'Look at that!' exclaimed Ella, taking in the sight in front of her. 'Just – wow!'

'You haven't seen anything yet,' added Callie. 'It's amazing.'

When Ella took her eyes off the water for a moment, the boat gently bumped the bank and Roman placed his hand on the wheel.

'Sorry,' apologised Ella, letting Roman take over.

As the water taxi slowly sailed the calm water Ella gazed at the chalky-white rocks that overhung a tiny secluded beach of sparkling beige sand. 'It's absolutely stunning,' she breathed.

Roman guided the boat to the wooden jetty, where it bobbed on the water.

'This is your stop button.' Roman pointed to a round red button. 'Go on, press it. Just never press it if the boat is going at full speed, as it will catapult you forward at full force!'

Ella pushed the button and immediately the engine cut out. Still wearing Roman's cap, she glanced over towards The Lakehouse restaurant with its old-fashioned shutters, purple wisteria and pink roses twisting all around the doorway. Up on the roof there was a balcony with tables and chairs overlooking the secluded water.

'It's like something for the rich and famous,' murmured Ella.

'It's absolutely breath-taking.' Roman was looking directly at Ella, then turned his attention back towards The Lakehouse. Ella felt a flutter in her stomach. She was sure Roman wasn't just talking about the restaurant.

'It is... absolutely breath-taking,' she repeated, taking the cap from her head and placing it back on his head. 'Thank you for my driving lesson on water.'

'Anytime,' replied Roman, tipping his cap.

Ella couldn't take her eyes off The Lakehouse. 'It's like something out of a novel, a romantic hideaway for lunch.' She was in awe. She never imagined she'd be working at a restaurant hidden under a canopy of beautiful cliffs, but she would be from Monday.

'And the team are such a fantastic bunch,' added Callie.

'And here you are, delivered safe and sound.' The boat gently bumped against the jetty.

Ella watched as Roman jumped off and tied up the boat securely before pulling the gangplank forward. He stood to the side and saluted as they stepped off the boat, causing Ella to chuckle. 'I feel like royalty.'

'Are you coming in?' asked Callie, looking at Roman.

He shook his head. 'No, it's not my break time yet. And just remember the boat back to Heartcross leaves at half past the hour from here.'

Callie nodded. 'We'll catch you later then.'

'You sure will,' he replied, catching Ella's eye, and immediately her stomach gave a tiny flip.

'At least my motion sickness has subsided.'

'Sometimes it's mind over matter,' reassured Roman, stepping back on board.

As Ella began to walk down the jetty, she was sure she could feel him still watching her. Taking in the view all around, she hovered and watched the waterfall trickle down the side of the mountain. 'This place is so romantic.'

'Maybe you should be booking a romantic meal with Roman,' Callie came straight to the point and lightly nudged Ella's elbow. 'It might do you good to go and have some fun…'

'I couldn't afford to go out on a date. Every penny I earn goes towards those credit card bills.'

'There are dates that don't cost money – walking

along the river, picnics in Primrose Park... You could even sail out to the coast. Flynn has a selection of boats.'

'I've only just met the guy and, judging by my track record...'

'I get that,' replied Callie, linking her arm through Ella's. 'But I'd say, the way he was looking at you, he's already smitten. Mark my words.'

Ella was flattered, she really was. Roman was definitely her type – more her type than Alex had ever been, in fact. 'Never say never. Dolores predicted I would meet someone when I least expect it. And he wasn't wearing a wedding ring,' she added.

Callie's eyes widened. 'So you noticed that.'

They carried on walking towards the entrance of the restaurant.

'Just wait until you see inside.' Callie pushed open the door to the restaurant and Ella stepped through. 'What do you think?' Callie asked.

The inside of the building was just as breath-taking as the outside, with its shimmering central dining bar and signature large windows overlooking the bay. There was beautiful oak panelling and striking art hanging on the walls that gave it a warm and luxurious feel. The fifteen tables were spaced to allow a sense of privacy, and in the corner of the dining area stood an ebony baby grand piano. Each and every table was laid with a crisp white linen, cutlery and the finest crystal glasses. Ella was lost for words at its beauty.

'Come on, I'll take you through to the kitchen and introduce you to Gianni, the chef.' Callie led Ella through the dining area, which was mercifully quiet, unlike the kitchen, which was a hive of activity.

At the far end of the room Ella noticed four waiters gathered around a table.

'This is the daily briefing – it happens before every shift. Gianni hammers out the finer points from the menu,' whispered Callie, as they stood at the back of the room and observed.

Laid out on the table were a number of exquisite-looking dishes that the chef had already prepared. Ella watched as the staff began to line up. 'What are they doing?' her voice was low, and she couldn't help thinking how heavenly it all smelled.

'Those are today's specials. Gianni believes that to be able to talk about a dish with a passion, you need to savour the flavours, taste it. Each staff member samples the food. This way, if the diners ask any questions, they can answer them accurately. Gianni is passionate about his food and it's a team effort.' Ella could see he took his food very seriously and the rapport he had with the staff was commendable.

'Gianni can be a little hot-headed at times, but underneath he's as soft as a brush and as you can see, very easy on the eye,' added Callie, with a glint in her eye.

Gianni caught Callie's eye and waved, beckoning them over. 'Who have we here?'

Ella felt a little nervous walking towards them all, but even though she was the new girl, everyone gave her a welcoming smile.

'This is Ella,' presented Callie. 'She starts with us on Monday. Ella, this is the team.' Each and every one stepped forward and introduced themselves.

'Excellent, excellent,' said Gianni. 'Come,' he gestured for them to both come over. 'Have a try.' Gianni handed Ella a fork. 'Tell me what you think.'

All eyes were on Ella.

Feeling the pressure, she plunged the fork into the dish and took a mouthful. She did everything in her power not to groan with pleasure or go in for a second helping. She'd never tasted anything so delicious.

'That is amazing,' she praised, as the flavours exploded in her mouth.

Gianni looked impressed by her reaction. 'That is Scottish turbot, peas, razor clams, broad beans and lemon balm,' he triumphed. 'We have different foods each night – fish nights, comfort food nights – and we cater for a more discerning clientele on a Saturday night.'

Ella had never tasted turbot before. 'It's the best thing

I've tasted in a long time,' she admitted, going in for a sneaky second helping.

Gianni eyed her appraisingly. 'Welcome to the team.' He grinned, fixing his dark eyes on her.

Gianni had been the head chef at The Rose, in Manchester, a place where the rich and famous dined and which was booked up for months in advance. Flynn Carter had visited that restaurant on many occasions and head-hunted Gianni, who had been at a crossroads in his personal life. The offer of becoming the head chef in a secluded restaurant on the River Heart suited him down to the ground.

'Thank you,' replied Ella.

'Before you all disperse, this afternoon, Ryan, you are the host. And all of you,' Gianni swept his arm in front of everyone, 'don't forget to keep your uniforms clean and tidy. Any spillages, you change immediately.'

'Yes, Chef,' they all chorused, making Ella smile. The atmosphere was charged, and everyone seemed excited to get out into the restaurant and begin their shift.

'This restaurant's reputation not only depends on the food but on you too. We are family.' Gianni smiled, disappearing through a door at the far end of the kitchen.

'Come on, let's go and get your uniform,' Callie said, as she grabbed Ella's arm.

Ella followed Callie through the bar area into an office at the back of the restaurant, which boasted the inviting aroma of coffee. There were open French doors at the back of the room overlooking the sandy bay. The trees swayed in the wind and the gentle burbling of the river behind made the setting even more idyllic. The desk was large and impressive, oozing importance and Ella spun round the leather-bound chair and sat down. The wall was covered in figures and charts, meal plans and distributers. She noticed numerous framed photos lined up in front of her and picked up an old photo of a man and woman standing outside the entrance of The Lakehouse. The gentleman was wearing a double-breasted suit, in light grey with faint contrasting stripes. It spoke of individuality, with its three buttons, peaked lapel and cuff-bottom trousers. The woman was strikingly smart, in a gaily coloured futurist print that complemented the blouse of the attractive two-piece dress.

'Whoever they are, they look very important, like royalty,' exclaimed Ella, placing the photo carefully back on the desk.

Callie took a look over her shoulder. 'I reckon that's got to be Flynn's grandparents. This restaurant has been in the family for decades. Back in the day, it attracted the rich and famous, and Julia even suggested royalty used to eat here.'

Ella let out a low whistle. 'I bet this place has a few stories to tell.'

'Apparently Flynn used to spend his summers here with his brother as a small boy, but his grandfather closed the restaurant after his grandma passed away – he couldn't carry on without her. This place stood empty until Flynn stepped in to re-open it years later.'

'So, he's originally from around these parts?' queried Ella, looking at the rest of the photographs.

'That I am.' Startled by the voice, Ella immediately recognised Flynn Carter from the times she had googled him, and jumped out of his chair, quickly pushing it under the desk.

Flynn Carter was standing in the doorway of his office, looking at Ella in amusement, who felt mortified that she'd been caught sitting in the boss's chair.

'Sorry, sorry,' she said, 'I was just…'

'Don't worry about it. I thought maybe there was a new CEO running my business empire. You are…?'

'Ella, I'm a friend of Callie's, starting work here on Monday.'

'Ah, the girl from Cheshire who's been having a difficult time. Pleased to meet you.' Flynn stretched out his hand.

Ella felt a crimson blush to her cheeks. 'That'll be the one, and thank you for giving me a job. I won't let you down,' she blurted, wishing the words would stop gushing out of her mouth.

'We've all been there, and in need of a new start. A

change of scenery always helps, and if Callie thinks you're up to the job, then that's good enough for me.'

'Thanks,' answered Ella. 'We're just here to pick up my uniform.'

Flynn turned towards Callie and pointed to the top drawer. 'All the introductory packs are there, and we'll need Ella's bank details too.'

Ella stifled a sigh. She was already very much into her overdraft, which meant to start with all of her wages would be swallowed up, but beggars couldn't be choosers. She just needed to be extra careful with her money.

Callie nodded. 'I'll go through it all on Monday.' She headed over to the filing cabinet and picked up the uniform. 'Here you go.'

'Thanks,' said Ella, taking the white shirt and black skirt from Callie.

'If you're interested in photographs, you might want to look at the old photograph albums we found in the safe when we started renovations,' said Flynn. 'There are some amazing shots in there.'

'Really, can we take a look?' asked Ella.

'Of course. Dad was looking through them before – in fact, here he is now.'

An elderly gentleman was standing in the doorway leaning on his cane. 'Good afternoon,' he said, looking at Callie and Ella.

'Ella, meet my dad, Wilbur Carter. You'll see him around the place from time to time. Ella is a friend of Callie's and starts work in the restaurant on Monday.'

Ella smiled up at Wilbur, who was dressed in a burgundy velvet suit with a blue paisley shirt and a red cravat. He reminded her of an eccentric character from an old novel, and his wizened face smiled back at her.

'I was just talking about the photo albums we discovered. In fact, we've had some copied and have begun to hang them out on the wall in the corridor. Go and have a look,' suggested Flynn, before turning to Callie. 'Can I have a word with you for a second?' he said, his voice suddenly one of concern.

'Of course.' Callie turned towards Ella. 'Have a look at the photos, I'll be out in a second.'

As soon as Ella stepped outside with Wilbur, Flynn pushed the door closed. As Ella cast an eye over the photographs on the wall, she could hear Flynn and Ella speaking in hushed whispers. With one ear Ella was trying to listen in whilst holding her own conversation with Wilbur.

'These pictures are amazing – look at some of those outfits. It's like a different world,' Ella said as she stared at the photographs. Wilbur agreed with her and just as they made their way to the end of the corridor, Callie left Flynn's office and made her way towards Ella.

'Excuse me, ladies, I need to chat to Flynn about

something. Ella, it was lovely to meet you. Hope your first shift goes well on Monday.' Wilbur gave them both a little bow, before entering Flynn's office.

'You're quiet, what's wrong?' Ella asked, as she eyed Callie carefully.

Callie took a step backwards and looked up the corridor, then back towards Ella.

'There's no other way to dress this up, but The Lakehouse is in financial trouble.' She exhaled audibly. 'It's making a loss, and unless by some miracle we can get more diners in...'

Ella's mood slumped; after everything she'd been through, she was relying on this job. This just wasn't turning out to be her year.

'Flynn is worried but he's trying to put on a brave face.'

'Can we get the locals involved? Didn't you say they get discounts up at Starcross Manor? Maybe if Flynn does the same here...' suggested Ella.

'They already do get a discount. Maybe it's the fact that it's not accessible by walking or car? When The Lakehouse first opened up again there was an article in a hospitality magazine which Flynn perceived as bad press. This could have damaged the numbers a little, but with the amount of tourists in Heartcross, you'd expect the place to be full.'

'Maybe it's just that people don't know it's here. It's

okay trying to rely on word of mouth, but that isn't going to work unless people have something to talk about, or they've been here to dine. This place is unique. Look at its past. This restaurant is special, and Flynn needs to capitalise on that. It would be criminal for this place to close down.'

'Look at the business woman in you!' Callie was clearly impressed. 'You should talk to Flynn.'

'I've learnt so many valuable lessons from having my own little business, and as there was only me to rely on, sometimes I had to learn the hard way.'

'Come on, let's go and order a drink. Let's help the place look busy.'

They chose a table near the window overlooking the bay. Ella noticed Roman tying up the boat on the jetty. He was very charismatic even from afar, and she watched him as he acknowledged a couple of passengers as they ambled hand in hand towards The Lakehouse.

'There should be more diners, this is prime time,' remarked Ella, observing all the empty tables.

They both watched Ryan show the couple to their table, whilst the waiters hovered at the back of the restaurant waiting to hand out menus and take their drink orders.

Callie snagged a glance around the restaurant. 'There are more staff than diners, no wonder Flynn is worried.'

'This is a great location with a fabulous chef and a

really chilled-out atmosphere.' Ella was impressed with the whole set-up. It really did have a magical feel about the place. 'This restaurant needs to be shouted about.'

'Flynn has contacted the local news to see if they will do a feature and they've agreed,' said Callie, looking up as Wilbur appeared at the side of the table, followed by a waiter carrying their drinks.

'What have you got there?' asked Callie, watching Wilbur balance his cane against the table and place down a hefty photo album in front of them. 'This beauty was discovered in the safe when we reopened The Lakehouse. There's a whole lot of history in there. Some of these photos must go back many years. Thought you may want to take a look?'

'Yes please,' they answered in unison.

Ella pushed her drink to one side and moved the album between them both. Callie turned the first page. 'Look at this place,' she exclaimed, staring at the first black-and-white photo. The Lakehouse resembled the restaurant today, with a baby grand ebony piano, but the bar wasn't in the same place and the walls were covered in framed photographs, masses of them.

'I remember all those photographs, The Lakehouse wall of fame.' Wilbur pointed to the photos then the wall opposite. 'It was just over there. Anyone who was anyone had their photo taken, and it went up on that wall. It was full of extremely famous faces. Singers, models, even royalty. This place was their safe haven because my parents could control who came here and which diners could dine with whom – you couldn't just rock up without a reservation. Guests could dine in private, away from the fans and press. Some extremely famous faces became regulars.'

'These are amazing, look at their clothes.' Ella was mesmerised, turning the pages of the old photograph album. 'Vintage yet glamourous.'

'Everyone who came here dressed to impress, as you didn't know which famous face you would be dining next to. The dress code was always smart, and as a boy running round here, my mother used to always dress me as though it was Christmas Day.' Wilbur gave a little chuckle.

'Hence the reason Dad still dresses in these eccentric suits,' teased Flynn, tipping his father a wink as he passed their table to walk outside to speak to Roman.

'That actually may be so,' agreed Wilbur.

Callie and Ella were still turning the pages of the album. There were photos of the chef cooking up a storm in the kitchen, guests standing round the piano with a glass of wine in hand, the photos portraying everyone having a good time.

Wilbur continued. 'My father started out as a chef but also played in a jazz band. Any opportunity he got, he would be on the piano, and Thursday nights became regular music nights. The same diners would book time after time, and everyone used to stay till the early hours, singing and dancing. They used to put me to bed in the back office, but little did they know that I used to sneak out and watch the bands from under the table in the far corner of the room.' Wilbur smiled fondly at his memories.

'And who's that?' Ella pointed to a woman wearing the most elegant dress. The colourful printed silk oozed style and class. The collar, cuffs and jaunty tie were of contrasting colour to the black dress. Wearing a headscarf and black kitten heels, she was poised with the microphone, leaning against the piano, all the dinner guests staring in her direction.

'That's Dolores. She was a star – and I mean a superstar.'

'She's stunning! Look at those cheekbones, anyone would die for those cheekbones,' Ella scrutinised the photo.

'Everyone flocked in to see Dolores sing. There wasn't a spare table in the place the nights she performed, and look at it now.' Wilbur was saddened. 'Thursday nights became exclusive, a night for just the rich and famous.'

'I wish I'd been there,' Callie said. 'I bet these walls hold many secrets.'

'They certainly do. The press used to hover at the old boathouse just to get a photograph, but my parents would never let them on the boat. Some paparazzi obviously tried to overstep the mark and hire their own boats to try and get closer, just for that photo that might sell millions, but on the whole, back in the day, people respected other people's privacy more.' Wilbur turned the next page of the album.

'It seems Heartcross has always attracted the stars in one way or another,' chipped in Ella, remembering that Callie had told her all about heart-throb Zach Hudson visiting recently and enticing the local vet, Rory, off to work in Africa to film a documentary.

'Who's that?' asked Ella, pointing to the photo of Dolores having dinner with a handsome man dressed up in a very smart suit, with dimples to die for.

Wilbur raised an eyebrow. 'That is the prince.'

'A real-life prince?' questioned Ella, taking a small sip of her wine whilst running her eyes over the photograph once more.

'Absolutely a real-life prince. Dolores could have her pick of anyone. There were rumours he asked her to marry him, but who knows? The Lakehouse had magic back then. I just wish we could recreate a little bit of that now.'

'It's still early days,' reassured Ella with hope in her voice. 'Sometimes these new ventures take a while to build momentum.'

After they finished looking through the album,

Wilbur returned to the bar. Ella sipped on her drink, deep in thought. 'This restaurant has so much potential, and I can see why it was so special back in the day, with its exclusive club. There's got to be some marketing ploy Flynn can use to get people in through the door – buy one meal, get one free?' suggested Ella, looking out through the window. Flynn was still chatting to Roman, but Ella noticed the conversation looked quite serious. For a split second Flynn placed his hand on Roman's back before walking towards the restaurant. Roman appeared to look troubled as he blew out a breath and placed his cap back on his head, leaving Ella wondering what the conversation was about. He then checked his watch and stepped back on to the boat. Right on half past the hour he tooted the boat's horn, a sign to tell everyone who wanted to sail back to Heartcross that the boat would be leaving any minute. Ella's eyes were drawn to him again. She couldn't help it, there was something about him.

'Flynn doesn't want to go down that route, he wants to keep everything classy, upmarket.'

Ella didn't answer, she was still watching Roman.

'Earth to Ella.' Callie nudged her arm. 'Oh look, he's waving at you now,' mocked Callie, giving Roman a salute through the window. 'He must have realised you were watching him.'

'Give me strength, I was not watching him,' replied

Ella, shaking her head, but she knew she had been and was trying to play the situation down. Within seconds the boat had disappeared under the weeping willows and was now out of sight.

'Cocktails is what we need,' Callie looked over towards the bar and caught the eye of the waiter.

'Callie, we can't. I can't afford to be extravagant, I need to watch every penny,' Ella replied despondently.

'This one is on me,' insisted Callie and within minutes of choosing, they were halfway down their cocktails that were filled with crushed ice, squeezed fruit accompanied by fresh herbs and, of course, alcohol. Ella sucked on her straw; the alcohol zipped through her bloodstream only after a couple of sips. 'These are great cocktails, maybe Flynn needs to do a cocktail hour?'

'We've got a marketing meeting next week to put ideas forward, so why don't you suggest it? You'd have thought, with the tourist population in Heartcross, it would be packed to the rafters in here.'

'You'd think so, but maybe there's too much choice? There's the pub, the restaurants up at Starcross Manor, and the teashop… or maybe people think The Lakehouse is way too posh for them, or it's a place to come just for special occasions. You never know what anyone is thinking.'

'You might be right, and talking of the pub, Julia has

invited us for Sunday lunch, if you fancy it? It'll be a great way to meet the locals.'

Ella hesitated.

'Look, you have to eat. Please don't worry about paying your way at the minute. You'll be back up on your feet soon enough. And I'll let you into a little secret: most evenings Hamish leaves bags of vegetables and bread on the doorstep, free of charge.'

'Everyone really does look out for each other here, don't they?'

'Absolutely they do, and you are one of us now.'

Ella was grateful, Callie's words really warmed her heart. 'That means a lot, thank you.'

This was exactly what Ella needed, to be part of a community that looked out for each other. She was looking forward to seeing Julia again, and it was going to be great to meet a whole bunch of new people and immerse herself in village life.

'What do you know about Roman?' asked Ella.

'What do you want to know about Roman?'

'Come on, spill the beans.'

'Roman Docherty, handsome sailor, great smile, good sense of humour, but keeps his personal life very much private and lives over in the town. But recently he's been late for work on a few occasions – car trouble, apparently.'

'Single?'

'I've never heard him talk about anyone. He's an all-round friendly guy.' Callie watched the slight smile hitch on Ella's face before glancing over her shoulder and watching the staff hovering at the back of the restaurant with not much to do. 'Hopefully when the TV news report airs, that will generate more business,' said Callie, changing the subject whilst thinking out loud.

The waiter wandered back over to the table and asked if there was anything else he could get them as their cocktail glasses were empty. Callie looked towards Ella. 'The boat has only just left, we have time to kill.' But before they made a decision Callie heard her phone ringing.

Quickly rummaging inside her bag, she looked at the screen. 'It's Hamish, I wonder what he wants?' she said, immediately taking the call.

Ella watched as Callie's smile disappeared from her face and she concentrated on what Hamish was saying.

'Callie, what's up?' Ella whispered. She waited patiently for Callie to hang up the call but could quite clearly see that something was wrong.

'It's Dolores.' Callie was still staring at the phone, placing it on the table before meeting Ella's gaze.

'What's happened?' asked Ella, not liking the sound of that.

'I don't know. Hamish took her some lunch and discovered her lying on the living-room floor. She's been taken to hospital and he's asked if we could look after McCartney and Fred until he gets back. He doesn't know how long he's going to be there.'

'Is she okay? Any broken bones?'

'I don't know, that's all he said.' Callie stood up and took out her purse. 'Wilbur,' she called out, 'can we have the bill, please? We have to go. Oh damn... there's no boat, it's literally just left.'

Wilbur looked up from behind the bar. 'Everything okay?'

'Unfortunately not,' shared Callie, explaining that Dolores was in hospital.

'The boat has only just left, let me see if I can catch Roman,' replied Wilbur, picking up the phone at the back of the bar. Wilbur waited patiently for Roman to pick up. 'Roman, how far have you got? Is it possible to turn around?'

As soon as Wilbur placed the phone back on the hook, he confirmed that Roman was turning the boat around and that he'd be back at the jetty in approximately five minutes.

'Thanks, Wilbur,' said Callie, unzipping her purse, but Wilbur was having none of it. 'Don't worry about that. Get yourself back to Heartcross, and if you hear any news, do let us know.'

Roman arrived quickly, and he reminded Ella of James Bond as he stood up straight at the helm, looking like he was on a mission. As soon as he'd docked the boat and safely unfolded the gangplank he looked across at the girls with worry. 'Is everything okay?' he asked as they climbed on board. 'Wilbur asked me to come straight back.'

'It's Dolores, she's in hospital,' replied Callie, sitting down on a seat. 'We're looking after her animals until we know what's going on.'

Roman gave a salute. 'I'll get you back as quickly as possible.'

As Ella started walking up to the front of the boat, she noticed Roman take a call on his phone and move out of earshot. She sat down next to Callie, who was chatting away to another passenger and was oblivious to the fact that Ella was watching Roman. She'd noticed that his whole aura had changed in a matter of seconds, and as he hung up the call and took his place behind the wheel, Ella felt a slight tension in the air. Roman looked pensive, like he suddenly had the weight of the world on his shoulders.

Callie was now scrolling through the photos on her phone, giving Ella a running commentary and showing her pictures from Julia's fortieth birthday. 'We took her ghost hunting, but she wasn't impressed. I believe old Marley up at Heartcross Castle is in hospital. Have you heard anything, Roman?'

'No sorry, I haven't,' he answered, but kept his eyes firmly on the water.

'I wonder what will happen to that place when Marley passes away. That's Heartcross Castle over there.' Callie pointed in the distance.

'It looks stunning,' replied Ella, glancing over, then back towards Roman, who was participating in the conversation, but the faraway look in his eye suggested his mind was elsewhere.

'It's a huge place to stay empty. Has Marley got any relatives?' he asked.

'I'm not entirely sure, but I think I heard Wilbur talking about a daughter, but she doesn't live round here,' answered Callie.

Five minutes later Roman slowed the boat down and pulled in alongside the jetty outside The Boathouse. After he'd secured the boat Callie and Ellie stepped on to dry land.

They thanked Roman before ambling down the jetty towards the rocky path. Ella cast a glance back in his direction and saw he was standing in the middle of the boat with his phone pressed to his ear again.

'Don't you think that was a little strange?' asked Ella.

'What's a little strange?' replied Callie, linking her arm through Ella's.

'On the way there, Roman is over-chatty, shows me how to drive the boat, he's laughing and joking. But on the way back, he barely looks at us, his conversation is minimal and he didn't seem quite there.'

'I didn't notice at all. Maybe you're over-thinking it. He was just doing his job.'

But Ella had noticed. There was no mistaking the fact that the easy-going, jovial atmosphere she'd enjoyed on the journey over to The Lakehouse had somewhat plummeted on the return journey. Something was bothering Roman, she just knew it.

Chapter Five

The following morning, as soon as Ella opened her eyes, she felt like she was being watched. She bolted upright to discover McCartney sitting on her bed, his eyes firmly fixed on her.

'Good morning, McCartney,' she said, reaching forward to stroke him.

As soon as Ella moved, his tail began to wag and he leapt forward, trying to lick her face before waggling his bum and rolling over on the bed, waving his back legs in the air. Ella tapped his nose then ruffled his tummy.

'You must be missing Dolores, staying here must feel a little strange,' she guessed, scooping him up in her arms and swinging her legs out of bed. 'Let's hope Dolores has had a comfortable night in hospital and hopefully will be home soon.' Walking into the living room with McCartney in her arms, she popped a kiss on his head.

Callie was walking through to the living room from the kitchen, and placing McCartney down on the floor, Ella swiped a piece of toast from Callie's plate.

'Oi!' exclaimed Callie, holding her plate up high, but it was too late.

'Good morning,' sang Ella, sinking her teeth into the hot, buttery slice of granary bread. 'Any news on Dolores?' she asked, looking over at Fred, who was busy pecking at his food, his cage placed in the middle of the coffee table.

'I was up with the larks, so I nipped down to see Hamish. The poor man looks exhausted. I offered to sort out the morning papers, but he assured me it was all under control. I think he wants to stay busy.' Callie poured them both a mug of tea and sat down at the table outside on the balcony. 'I'm not sure how many more mornings we can brave sitting outside.' She pulled her cardigan tightly around her shoulders. 'But Dolores has had a comfortable night,' Callie continued. 'Hamish said she'd undergone numerous tests and it turns out her blood pressure was low.'

'Has she suffered from low blood pressure before?' asked Ella, knowing that her own grandma suffered with her blood pressure.

Callie shook her head. 'Not from what I know of, but

Hamish put it down to old age. He got quite upset when he was talking to me this morning, choked up.'

'Bless him! Does he need any help in the shop at all? I don't mind helping out. You're at work today, aren't you?'

'I am, and I already offered your services, but he's roped in Aggie and Martha this morning; you've not met them yet. Pop down and say hello. Martha is Isla's grandma and lives up at Foxglove Farm with them, and Aggie is Fergus's mum. Fergus goes out with Felicity and works at the farm...'

'I've met Felicity, the girl in the teashop.'

'That's the one. You'll like them both.' Callie glanced up at the clock. 'I'm due at work just after lunch, there's a couple of meetings I have to be present at. I think Flynn is going to throw some more marketing ideas on the table.'

'Fingers crossed that whatever Flynn comes up with, helps to boost business. Is Roman at work today?' Ella's thoughts turned back to his change in mood yesterday.

'Day off today, I think.'

Ella tucked into another piece of toast and flicked through the newspaper on the table. Every news article she read was depressing; there didn't seem to be anything good going on in the world at all. 'They should just print a happy paper,' Ella suggested as she leaned over the balcony. 'It's so quiet without Dolores downstairs.'

'I was thinking the very same,' agreed Callie.

'Has Dolores ever married?' Ella was thinking about the photo of Dolores with the prince, and the handwritten letter she'd received yesterday. Maybe she still had someone special in her life.

'I'm not entirely sure. I've never heard her talk about anyone, but I know she's very close to Hamish. And he thinks the world of her.'

'I miss my parents.' As soon as Ella mentioned them, tears sprang to her eyes. 'How does that happen?' She flapped her hand in front of her face. 'The second I mention them… the tears.'

Callie reached over and gently touched her arm. 'It's normal.'

'It's hard, all the things you take for granted, and then the next minute they've gone forever.' Ella took a swig of her drink. 'And Dolores reminds me a lot of my own grandmother, she has a very good heart.'

'She has indeed.'

'How far away is the hospital?' asked Ella, thinking if she had the whole day to herself she could visit Dolores there. 'I could go and keep her company.'

'Good plan, she'll love that. The hospital is over in Glensheil. It's not far at all. I think the buses are every hour on a Sunday, or a taxi would drop you off straight at the door. I'll check the bus times,' she said, scooping up McCartney after he'd finished his own breakfast and wandering out on to the balcony. She placed him on her lap. 'I bet this little one wonders where she is.'

'Don't worry, McCartney. Dolores will be home as soon as possible,' Ella soothed, leaning across and lightly patting his back.

'He can't hear, you know.'

Ella chuckled. 'I keep forgetting he's deaf.'

They sat and chatted for the next ten minutes and were just about to clear away the breakfast dishes when the doorbell rang. Callie looked over towards Ella. 'Are we expecting anyone?'

Ella shrugged and headed towards the door. She was surprised to find Roman standing on the other side.

'We were just talking about you,' she said, opening the door wide. 'Were your ears burning?'

'What do they say? "Right for spite, left for love"?' He touched both ears. 'All good, I hope.'

'Now that would be telling,' she joked. 'Are you coming in?'

'As long as I'm not intruding. I've just come to check up on Dolores. Any news?' he asked, stepping inside the hallway.

Whatever had put him in his reflective mood yesterday, seemed to have passed as Roman was all smiles and in a very chatty mood.

'Coffee?' asked Ella.

'That would be great.'

Callie leant back on her chair and clocked eyes with Roman. 'Good morning, you're up early.'

As Roman headed out towards the balcony, his woody aftershave filled the room, leaving Ella briefly closing her eyes and inhaling the aroma as he walked past her. Roman fussed over McCartney. 'Sausage stealer,' he joked, ruffling the top of his head. Immediately McCartney rolled on his back with his four stumpy legs sticking up in the air, causing everyone to laugh. 'See, he's got no shame. Steals my food, and for the privilege I get to tickle his tummy.'

'Ha, funny,' replied Ella, thinking if she didn't know any better, McCartney actually looked like he was smiling. 'I'll get your coffee.'

'Thanks.' He clocked the breakfast laid out on the table. 'I didn't mean to intrude, I was just checking up on Dolores.'

'Here,' said Ella, handing over the drink. 'I'm going to head over to the hospital this morning, when I've worked out where exactly it is.'

'That's easy, I can take you.' Roman waggled his car keys in the air. 'It's my day off and I've nothing else planned. The car's outside.'

'Really? Only if you don't mind?' Ella knew that would certainly be easier than trying to juggle the bus times.

'Honestly, it's no trouble. All I've got to do today is a

supermarket shop, which doesn't take long when you're shopping for one, so it will be my pleasure.'

'Perfect, as long as it's no trouble.'

Roman drank his coffee and then reached into his pocket and looked at his vibrating phone. He hesitated for a second, then was up on his feet. 'I've got to take this. Shall I meet you outside in around an hour? I've got a couple of errands to run first.'

Was it Ella's imagination, or did Roman just bristle? Whoever was calling him, it was clear that Roman was reluctant to answer. Ella witnessed the same distressed look he'd had in his eye yesterday.

'That will be great,' replied Ella.

They watched him hurry to the door, still staring at the vibrating phone. Roman presumably answered the call as soon as the front door had shut behind him.

'What do you make of that?' asked Ella, moving to the window and watching Roman as he crossed over the street.

'What do you mean?' queried Callie. 'He's just answering a call. Maybe he wants some privacy.'

As soon as Callie mentioned the word 'privacy' it triggered something inside Ella. For some strange reason, she felt a slight sense of panic. 'I've just had one of those moments... déjà vu.'

'Huh?'

'It's just, that's exactly what Alex used to do and say.

"I need my privacy." Sometimes he'd go to the bottom of the garden to take phone calls. He used to say it was to do with work, patient confidentiality, which of course we now know was all lies…'

'Are you trying to tell me that Roman is a fraudster and pretending to be a doctor on the side?'

Ella stood up and cleared away the dishes. 'Call it woman's intuition, but there's something going on in Roman's life – he's hiding something. Gut feelings are always right. Anyway, I need to go and get showered.' She began walking towards her bedroom, when Callie shouted after her.

'I know one thing. When he threw in that comment about shopping for one, that wasn't for my benefit. He was letting you know that he's single. That's *my* woman's intuition!'

'You're reading way too much into it. He's a friend, and we've only just met,' protested Ella.

'No one needs extra friends at our time of life.'

'Actually, I do, and I'm not listening to you.' Ella was chuckling when she closed the bedroom door behind her. This was exactly how she imagined life would be, living with Callie – fun days and full of laugher.

After a quick shower, Ella swiped her clothes from the wardrobe and plumped for a pair of baggy ripped jeans, a Levi's T-shirt and an over-sized cardigan. As she pulled a brush through her hair, she sat down at the dressing table and stared at herself in the mirror. How things had changed in such a short time. Even though she'd only been in Heartcross a matter of days, her old life was beginning to feel like a lifetime ago. The flat already felt like home, she felt settled, and that's when Ella realised she could count her good friends on one hand – Callie.

She thought back to when she'd started to date Alex. As he became a permanent fixture in her life, her friends began to dwindle away. Looking back, Ella had come to realise that Alex had manipulated situations and isolated her from her friends. Every time she'd arranged to go out with a girlfriend, Alex would turn up, sporting a huge bouquet of flowers with a posh restaurant booking under his belt. Each time he made out that she must have forgotten their arrangement and, in the end, she started to believe it and doubt herself, but it was all part of the game. Alex was a professional narcissistic fraudster. Her friends had warned her, but of course she didn't want to hear it. She was in love and each time she'd put him first. One thing she'd learnt from the whole situation was, that was never going to happen again. Friends were important.

After applying her make-up and a squirt of her perfume, Ella pulled on her Converse and wandered into the living room to find Callie rummaging in the overstuffed drawer in the kitchen that was full of knickknacks. 'Here it is,' she said, holding up a key. 'The spare front-door key. You may be needing this.'

'Thanks. I feel important, having a key,' Ella grinned, grasping it in her hand. 'Will you be gone by the time I get back?'

'I'm not sure, but say hello to Dolores from me and keep those fingers crossed. Hopefully this afternoon we'll come up with the best plan to keep The Lakehouse afloat.'

'I've got everything crossed,' Ella said before grabbing her bag. 'Right, I'm off. I'll catch you later.' When she reached the bottom of the stairwell, she closed the door behind her and watched Roman for a second. He was leaning against an old battered green Land Rover, reading a newspaper.

She coughed lightly and he looked up. A huge smile hitched on his face as he closed his newspaper and stood up straight.

'There you are… meet Bette!' Roman patted the Land Rover with such affection that Ella burst out laughing. 'She's reliable,' he continued. 'Never failed to start, in all the years I've owned her.'

'Bette? You've named your car Bette?' Ella walked around the battered old car, which had seen better days.

'After Bette Davis, my grandma's favourite actress, and as my grandparents bought me the car, they got to name her.' With a gentlemanly confidence Roman went to open the door, but struggled with the lock. 'However, she can be a little temperamental at times.' He tried again. Finally, he proudly opened the door.

'Temperamental, eh? Just like any woman.' Ella bit down on her lip to suppress her smile. Climbing into the passenger seat, she was surprised to see how immaculate Bette was inside. She was cleaned and polished to within an inch of her life.

Roman whizzed around to the driver's side and slipped into the seat beside Ella. He adjusted the mirror and put the key in the ignition while Ella pulled on the seatbelt, but it wouldn't move. She tried again. 'I think Bette is having a moment.'

'Mmm, she's playing up at the minute.' Leaning across Ella, Roman pushed his wild fringe out of his face before grabbing the seatbelt, which he gave an extra-hard tug.

'Here you go. Don't worry, she's as safe as houses,' he reassured, pulling at his own seatbelt. 'If you fancy putting on some tunes, all we have is an old-fashioned tape deck.' He waved his hand towards the glove compartment. 'It's full of tapes.'

Ella opened it up to find it stuffed to the brim with old cassette tapes. 'Mix tape?' She waggled it in the air. 'What's this one?'

'A little bit of everything – they came with Bette when I got her. History is what those are,' replied Roman, starting the engine. He looked over his shoulder to check the road was clear. 'Oh, and we don't believe in mod cons, do we Bette? Which means we have no air con and the heaters play up too, which means she's not so great in summer and not so great in winter.'

'So you're telling me, Bette is not so great.'

'Shh, she'll hear you.'

Ella threw back her head and laughed as Roman kangarooed Bette into the middle of the road.

'And sometimes, Bette does exactly what she wants.'

'It may be time to trade Bette in for a newer model,' suggested Ella, grinning and holding on to her seat until Bette had calmed herself down. 'I'm thinking it would have been safer to take the bus.'

'We've been on so many adventures together, and I really can't bear to part with her. Everyone should have a Bette in their life.' Roman clunked the gears as he made his way over the track at the bottom of Love Heart Lane, then headed towards the bridge that took them over into Glensheil.

Feeling relaxed and at ease in Roman's company, Ella sat back and watched Heartcross whiz by through the window. He pointed to the rowing boats that were bobbing about on the river and Ella spotted Flynn Carter's water taxi in the distance. 'Who drives the boat when you're not there?'

'Would you believe Wilbur! He loves it. However, he

refuses to wear the sailor suit! I don't know what the problem is. I love a good uniform – I think I pull it off well,' he joked. 'And it also saves me thinking about what I need to wear to work.'

'Most women like a man in a uniform,' agreed Ella, with a glint in her eye, before her thoughts immediately turned to Alex. She couldn't quite believe that Alex had had the audacity to turn up, day after day, wearing a white doctor's coat, and often with a stethoscope hanging around his neck, when he wasn't even a doctor. But she shook the image from her mind. She was learning to give him less and less head space each day. 'And yes, you do pull it off well.' Changing the subject, she said, 'Let's just hope today's emergency meeting throws up some good marketing plans.'

'Emergency?' queried Roman, slowing down at the traffic lights and looking sideward at her.

'If they don't get more diners on seats soon, things won't be looking good for The Lakehouse.'

'How do you know this?' he asked, with a concerned look on his face as he slowed down at the roundabout.

'Callie. That's where she is today.' Ella suddenly wasn't sure it was common knowledge, if Roman was unaware of the situation. She hoped she hadn't gone and put her foot in it.

'I'm amazed! I didn't see that coming. I thought Flynn had all these wonderful ideas to re-open the exclusive club, famous people on Thursdays etc. The restaurant has already had a couple of famous faces eating there. I honestly thought it was doing okay.'

'Think about the number of diners you take across the river each day.'

Roman thought for a minute. 'Yes, I suppose you're right. I've never really thought about it. I assumed, with Flynn being the multi-millionaire businessman he is, that it was dead cert that it would be successful. So does that mean I should be looking for another job?'

'I'm in exactly the same boat – no pun intended.' She smiled, but Ella had to admit, the last thing she wanted to do was look for another job when she hadn't even started work there yet. And jobs were hard enough to come by as it was, never mind in a small place like Heartcross – and she really didn't fancy moving back to the city. She was enjoying the slower pace of life and actually talking to people.

'Let's hope our jobs are safe,' she said. 'Sometimes business ventures take their time to get off the ground.' She pointed to the cassette player. 'I know this one, top tune.'

'This is one of my absolute favourites. It must be about twenty years old,' replied Roman, keeping his eyes on the road. 'The music of today isn't a patch on the olden days.'

'The olden days,' she repeated, laughing, noticing the red hospital signs as they drove through the main town of Glensheil. 'This place is just like I imagined it too,' remarked Ella, thinking it was such a pretty town with its outstanding coastal views and surrounding countryside. There was a small sailing club based on this side of the estuary which was already a hive of activity. The streets were lined with boutique shops, art galleries – this was the sort of place Ella could spend hours mooching around in. The restaurants looked amazing, there were carts selling seafood on the street corners, and Ella noticed a sign for delicious ice-cream and a whole shop dedicated to Glensheil Gin.

'It's a great town and complements Heartcross perfectly if you want a change of scenery.' Roman slowed down at the traffic lights and indicated left. 'That's my place just there,' he pointed, as he drove up a quieter road that ran parallel with the River Heart. 'I can't imagine living anywhere else. I mean, look at that view – its peaceful, tranquil, walking distance to the shops and the pub, everything you need.'

Roman's house was not what Ella was expecting. She'd pictured him in a trendy one-bedroom apartment filled with the latest technology, overlooking the High Street with a balcony – but here she was, driving past a period semi-detached cottage built in a gorgeous traditional stone. The garden was charming – an area of lawn with a shrub border and a sunken paved terrace which provided a wonderful place for outside dining.

'I have fishing rights and a boat dock, so if I've forgotten anything I can sail across the river and moor the boat outside my house, even though I've had a few funny looks from the neighbours.'

'How long have you been there? It's a beautiful property.' Roman's house was the kind of place she'd imagined herself living in one day, but thanks to Alex, she'd be lucky to be able to just pay rent on a place one day.

'A little over six months. I moved in when I started the job on the river.'

'You have the best of both worlds – the tranquillity of the water and the local town for bars and restaurants. Just perfect. So where were you before?'

Roman was slowing down and concentrating on the cars in front of him. 'Edinburgh.'

Ella was surprised. Her geography wasn't up to much, but that must be around two hundred miles or so. 'That's a hell of move,' she said, sharing her thoughts. 'Edinburgh must be around three hours away, at a guess.' Ella took a sideward glance towards Roman.

'Yes, about that,' he replied, not adding any more to the conversation.

Ella was curious. What had brought Roman over to Heartcross? 'Have you always sailed boats?' she asked.

Roman kept his eyes on the road ahead. 'No, it's a fairly new thing. I was a tour manager, making sure concert tours run smoothly. I looked after the finances, the road crew, and made sure everyone was where they were supposed to be and were on task.'

'That sounds like an amazing job. You must have met some very famous people.'

Roman nodded. 'That I did.'

'So why the change?' Ella was genuinely interested.

Roman paused. 'Sometimes things happen.' His answer felt quite guarded, he didn't elaborate and kept his cards very close to his chest.

Ella felt that Roman was holding back; there was something he didn't want to talk about. But she knew better than most that life sometimes throws you curveballs when you least expect them, and things in your life change and you have no control over them. She only had to look at herself. One minute she was a business woman with her own property and a hefty inheritance in the bank, and the next she was living with her friend and working as a waitress and was broke.

'And what about you?' he asked, swiftly changing the conversation back to Ella. 'What brings you to Heartcross?'

'Callie, saving my life... That sounded quite dramatic!'

Roman glanced across at her and Ella continued. 'If

I'm honest, I was struggling with life, I needed help and Callie came to my rescue. I lost my parents, my home and my business. I think it's safe to say the last twelve months of my life have been the worst ever.' Ella swallowed down a lump in her throat. She turned towards the window while she blinked away the tears.

'I'm sorry to hear about your parents.' Roman's voice was soft, and he turned down the volume on the cassette deck.

'Tragic accident,' added Ella. 'Carbon monoxide poisoning, and to add to everything, I lost my inheritance and my fiancé, when he went to work one day and never came home. I've not seen him or my money since.'

'You *are* kidding me, right?' Roman narrowed his eyes. He really wasn't sure whether Ella was being serious.

Ella shook her head. 'I kid you not. It's so far-fetched, you'd never believe it in a million years.'

'I'm absolutely shocked! It's like something you'd read in a magazine. Is he still missing, your fiancé?'

Ella nodded. 'Yes, my guess is he's living it up with my inheritance. You see, Dr Alex James wasn't even a doctor – who knows what his actual name is! But I was conned and he took my heart, my money and left me with a parting gift that I wasn't expecting... He'd maxed my credit cards up to the limit, leaving me with thousands to pay off.'

Roman looked shocked to the core. 'How could anyone do that? He literally went to work and never came back?'

'Exactly that. I spent a short time thinking he was dead, lying at the bottom of a river, but when the police investigated, they discovered everything. It all sounds so stupid when I say it out loud. Although we were together twelve months, it wasn't me he was interested in – he was just interested in stealing everything I owned, including my self-worth.'

'I'm actually lost for words. I'm so sorry you've had to go through all this!'

'I've spent the last six months sinking so low that I thought there was no way out, pretending I could manage when I couldn't. The only friend I have left in the world is Callie, who has literally saved me. Sometimes you've just got to let people help and swallow your pride. Good friends are hard to find, but if it wasn't for her...' Ella's voice faltered. 'There you go, that's me in a nutshell.' It had been a long time since she really opened up like this and was surprised at how good it felt to talk to Roman.

'Ella, I really don't know what to say.'

'There's nothing to say. I'm here, and hopefully getting my life back on track. Heartcross is my brand-new start.'

'And from what it sounds like, you deserve your new

start and happiness.' Roman turned into the hospital carpark, which was already busy with cars lined up, waiting to grab the first space available. He drove around a couple of times until he was lucky enough to spot a space and park up. 'I don't mind waiting here for you. I have a few phone calls I need to catch up on.'

'You can't do that! I really don't know how long I'm going to be.'

'That's okay, honestly – take your time.'

For a second, Ella hesitated. 'Okay, thank you. As long as you are sure?'

'Absolutely sure.'

'Thank you,' she said again, stepping out of the car.

'And pass on my best to Dolores.'

Heading towards the main entrance, Ella walked past the line of ambulances and through the revolving doors. A fleeting thought of Alex passed through her mind. She'd waited so many times in the hospital carpark to pick him up after work, and she wondered now what the hell he'd actually done all day with his time? She gave a little shudder. Every time she thought of him now she was angry.

Hovering in the hospital entrance, Ella stared up at the white signs hanging above her head and slowly made her way to Ward 17, situated on the second floor. Within five minutes she'd arrived, to find a nurse sitting at the desk outside the ward talking to a doctor. As soon as they finished their conversation the doctor smiled at Ella before disappearing down the corridor. 'Can I help you?' asked the nurse, shuffling a pile of papers in front of her.

'I'm looking for Dolores Henderson,' replied Ella. 'I've come to visit.'

'Dolores is in the bed on the right, closest to the window. She'll be pleased to see you.'

Ella stepped on to the ward and noticed many of the cubicles had the curtains pulled around the bed to give a little privacy. She walked towards the windows; the sun was shining through the cracks in the blinds, painting narrow, vertical bands of light on the magnolia walls. There were other visitors sitting at patients' beds, but Ella noticed everyone seemed to be talking in a whisper.

'Dolores, it's me… Ella,' she said, slowly pulling back the curtain. Dolores was lying underneath a white cotton sheet with a blue blanket tucked in around her chest, fast asleep. Ella couldn't help but smile. Even though Dolores was in hospital, her hair was just so, her blonde curls framing her face and resting over her shoulders, and she had a full face of makeup. She looked peaceful lying there, even though she was hooked up to a machine at the side of her bed, the wires protruding from a gap in her nightie. It bleeped every few seconds.

Slipping quietly on to the chair at the side of her bed, Ella switched her phone to silent. She watched Dolores sleeping. The map of wrinkles on her face showed a life of experience, her eyebrows were immaculately shaped, and Ella was a teeny bit jealous that her eyelashes looked better than her own. She wondered what sort of life Dolores had lived. Thinking back to the star-studded line-up in the photograph album over at The Lakehouse, that was certainly a different world to today's. These days the world was full of reality-TV stars that had no real talent, their careers based on their looks or their love life. Whereas Dolores was an actual singer with fans who followed her career. From what Wilbur had said, she had lived life to the max and fulfilled ambitions others could only dream of, and her career had started at The Lakehouse. Ella wanted to know all about it.

For a moment she watched Dolores sleep before reaching for the well-thumbed magazine on the table next to the bed. She flicked from page to page until Dolores began to stir. The second she opened her eyes, Dolores smiled at Ella and was in good spirits.

'A visitor... It's lovely to see you... They can't get rid of me just yet,' she joked, sitting up straighter. 'I'm destined to receive my letter from the Queen.'

Ella leant forward and gave her hand a little squeeze. She couldn't help thinking that must be something you think about a lot when you reach that time of your life. 'It's lovely to see you too. You gave everyone a little scare there for a minute. Please don't do it again.'

Dolores gave a chuckle. 'I'll try not to. How's my brood, are they behaving? I'm missing them.'

'McCartney and Fred are just fine, don't worry about them. McCartney slept on my bed, he's made himself at home. How are you feeling?'

'Bored is what I am. The conversation isn't up to much in here, and this bed is the most uncomfortable thing I've slept on in a long time. I just want to go home.'

'You'll be home soon enough, I'm sure of it.'

'So what have I missed?'

Ella smiled. 'Dolores, you've been in here less than twenty-four hours, there's nothing to miss!'

'There's always something to miss. Did you go and pick up your uniform at The Lakehouse?'

Ella nodded. 'Yes I did!'

'And what did you think of the place?'

Ella brought her hands up to her heart. 'What an absolutely stunning location, the whole place has a magical feel about it.'

'I'm going to book and Hamish can take me for lunch. I can't wait to see the place again, it holds such very special memories for me. I can picture it now, packed to the rafters, the pianist playing on the grand piano, exquisite food, and does it still have the separate roof terrace? Many glasses of champagne have been drunk on that roof terrace!'

'It sure does, and I can't wait to start work there, even

though I'm not sure how long I will be there.' Ella scrunched up her face.

'Why, are you planning on moving on so soon?' Dolores reached for the glass of water at the side of her bed, but her eyes were still on Ella.

'I wasn't intending to, but the way things are going, that pianist will be playing to himself.' Ella shared with Dolores the news that The Lakehouse wasn't doing as well as Flynn had hoped, and that it was already losing money.

'Word of mouth... reputation. The Lakehouse never had to advertise. Anyone who was anyone knew it was there.' Dolores was thinking out loud. 'That place is full of history, it's an iconic establishment, it can't shut again. That place launched my career. Anyone who was anyone performed there on a Thursday evening. It was a club for the rich and famous. I still have my little black book...' Dolores gave Ella a knowing look. 'I have the phone number of every person who ever performed there. Sadly, now some have passed away, but the majority of us are still hanging on for dear life.'

'Tell me how you started out. We saw a photo of you in an old album over at The Lakehouse.' Ella was loving this conversation. She could picture Dolores hanging out with the rich and famous back in the day.

'By accident!' chuckled Dolores.

'Tell me more?' Ella was genuinely interested.

Dolores patted Ella's hand and laughed heartily. 'That night, I should have been somewhere else, but rumour had it that Frank Divine was making a special appearance at The Lakehouse. Frank was huge, a household name, a sex symbol with amazing talent. The guest list was by invitation only, but that wasn't going to stop me and my best friend Blossom Rose sneaking on to the boat and pretending we were someone we weren't. The pair of us used to have so much fun. Cutting a very long story short, we talked our way into The Lakehouse. Honestly, we just couldn't believe it, champagne was being handed out like it was water, and we were surrounded by some of the most famous people in the world.

'Then Frank Divine took to the stage by the baby grand piano. The tables were pushed to one side and everyone was dancing. Blossom and I were having a ball. Frank noticed us and he kept giving me the eye. Then all of a sudden, his hand reached forward, and he pulled me up next to him. Everyone was watching, but I didn't feel nervous – just excited, my whole body was buzzing. Then without warning, he held the microphone towards me and I sang back to him the song he was singing. He stopped dead in his tracks, and I carried on singing. The whole room erupted in applause, and it was a feeling I'll never forget.

'Then we began to sing together. I took a bow at the

end and Frank kissed me on both cheeks and asked my name. Then, within seconds, there was a guy at the side of me with a huge bucket of champagne and he introduced himself as Richie Kirk. He was Frank's manager and he signed me on the spot. The rest is history. The Lakehouse signed me up to sing every Thursday night alongside other artists and before I knew it, everywhere I went people recognised me. If it wasn't for The Lakehouse and that night, goodness knows what I would have ended up doing as a career.'

'What an amazing story! That place has so much history. Surely Flynn has some way of using its reputation from the past to make it a success again?' Ella's mind was ticking over.

'From what I know, Flynn Carter is an intelligent and successful businessman. He'll come up with a strategy to make the place work. But anyway, enough of that, how are you? Tell me how you are settling in,' Dolores commanded. 'Have you made any other new friends yet?'

Immediately Ella thought of Roman. 'Thanks to McCartney, I've met Roman.' Ella told Dolores the story of McCartney eating his sausages, which made Dolores chuckle. 'He may be deaf, but that dog can smell a sausage a mile off, and I told you you would meet someone when you least expect it.'

'I haven't met him… well, I *have* met him, but not like

that; we've only just met. Actually, he brought me here today.'

'He brought you here today?' Dolores gave Ella a knowing look. 'I know you've not had an easy time of it, but just take each day as it comes and live for the moment. And remember that not everyone is out for what they can get.'

Listening to Dolores' words of wisdom, Ella knew that she was right. Maybe she should ask Roman out for a drink, just as friends? He could show her around. She found him attractive, but Ella always had that nervous niggle in the back of her mind – could she let anyone get close to her again?

'Sometimes this world is cruel, and you have to grab every bit of happiness whilst you can.' Dolores' tone was suddenly sad and Ella sensed that Dolores had a story of her own to tell, but before she could say any more, the nurse appeared at the end of her bed.

'How are you feeling Dolores?' she asked warmly, picking up her arm and taking her pulse.

'The machine is still beeping, so I must still be alive.'

'Every cloud,' The nurse winked jokingly.

Whilst Dolores was distracted by the timely arrival of the nurse, Ella's thoughts drifted back to Roman. Maybe she could ask him out for a drink as a thank-you for bringing her here today. After all, that was the least she could do.

As soon as the nurse left, Dolores waggled her finger at Ella. 'Ask him out – friendships that blossom are wonderful things.' It was like Dolores had just read her mind. 'What's the worst that could happen?' joked Dolores. 'You'll have to swim to work if you two fall out.'

'I'm not a strong swimmer, so let's hope that doesn't happen!' Looking down at her watch, Ella realised that they had been chatting away for over an hour and was conscious that Roman was just sitting in the carpark waiting for her. It was probably time to make a move.

'And one more thing. Would you be kind enough to have a slice of cake waiting for me when I get home?' Dolores lowered her voice and looked towards the curtain. 'The food in here isn't up to much. I wouldn't feed it to my worst enemy. Creamed potatoes,' she whispered, wrinkling up her nose.

Ella grinned. 'I think I can manage that,' she said, standing, 'and I'll see you tomorrow after I've finished my shift.'

'Fingers crossed, I'll be home.' Dolores gave Ella a warm smile.

Bette hadn't moved a muscle when Ella returned to the car. She peeped at Roman through the window and his eyes were closed. She rapped loudly on the window, causing him to bolt upright.

'Sorry, I couldn't resist.' Ella grinned, flinging open the door and climbing into the passenger seat. Roman's eyes were wide. 'You frightened the life out of me!' He quickly ruffled the front of his hair whilst checking his appearance in the mirror.

'Don't worry, you weren't dribbling.'

'That's a bonus, but more importantly, how's Dolores?'

'Hopefully home by tomorrow, fingers crossed. She's going to be just fine, and I've had a very interesting history lesson. Did you know that The Lakehouse was the start of Dolores' career? Back in the day that restaurant was a gold mine.'

'Mmm, let's hope this marketing meeting today can produce some ideas to turn the place around and make it into a gold mine again.'

'I'm sure Flynn won't go down without a fight.'

'Here,' Roman reached to the dashboard and held up a cardboard cup. 'I've only just closed my eyes after getting you a skinny latte from the coffee van. It should still be hot.'

'Skinny… are you trying to tell me something?' Ella jested, putting her hand to her chest, pretending to be hurt. 'Do I need to go on a diet?' she teased with a glint in her eyes.

'Hell no,' replied Roman over-enthusiastically, causing Ella to laugh. 'You look mighty fine to me.'

'I'm only winding you up.' She grinned, about to take the drink from him.

'Good job I'm winding you up, then, isn't it? I got you a luxury hot chocolate with all the trimmings, mine is the skinny latte,' Roman patted his stomach. 'I really need to lose a few pounds... unlike some.'

Ella's eyes widened as Roman produced the most scrumptious-looking drink in a cup from the drinks holder. 'Wow! Look at that!'

'You have marshmallows, cream, chocolate flakes and enough calories to sink the titanic, and I hope it tastes as good as it looks.'

'Now that's more like it.' Ella was impressed by his kindness. 'Thank you!' she said, taking a sip of the hot chocolate, leaving a moustache of cream above her lip.

'You're welcome,' he replied, bursting into laughter as he put the key in the ignition.

'What? What are you laughing at?'

Roman looked at her in amusement and gestured to her top lip, which Ella immediately wiped clean with the back of her hand, then quickly checked her reflection in the mirror on the back of the sun visor.

'Right, let's get you home.'

Luckily, Bette was playing ball when Ella reached for her seatbelt and clunked it in place, but when Roman attempted to turn over the engine, nothing happened. Thankfully she started on the third attempt. He patted the steering wheel. 'That's my girl.'

'Do you always talk to Bette like she's a person?'

asked Ella, studying his profile as Roman looked over his shoulder before reversing Bette out of the space. His wild hair really did have a mind of its own. His eyes were piercing, and his stubble glistened in the sunshine. His navy-blue polo shirt clung to his abs and his skinny jeans were a different look from his sailor's outfit.

Would asking Roman out for a drink be such a bad thing?

Roman was just about to put Bette into first gear when he locked eyes with Ella. 'What, why are you staring at me?'

Damn, he'd caught her watching and Ella lost her nerve.

'Nothing,' she replied, fixing her gaze forward but still smiling.

As the car began to move, Roman pushed the cassette tape into the player and Simple Minds blurted out of the crackly speaker. 'Great tune,' he said, driving towards the barrier. 'I need coins,' he muttered, patting his pockets. 'I forgot about the car park.' He quickly rummaged around inside the glove compartment, but Ella came to his rescue, emptying the silver coins from her purse on to her lap and counting out the change.

As the barrier lifted, Ella was plucking up the courage to ask out Roman for a drink but he was saved by the bell: his phone began to ring.

Immediately, Roman indicated to pull over into the

layby a little further up the road. 'Sorry, Ella, I need to take this call.' As soon as Roman pulled on the handbrake he was up out of his seat with the car door firmly shut behind him. He began pacing up the embankment with the phone to his ear like his life depended on it. He was deep in conversation and Ella watched his frantic hand movements as he threw his arm up in the air. Ella could see from the car that he looked like he was in turmoil. Finally, he finished the call and sat back in the car. Without speaking, he started the engine and began driving. For a moment a heavy silence settled over them, the tension uneasy.

'Is everything okay?' asked Ella, breaking the silence. She noticed that Roman shifted uncomfortably in his seat.

For a split second Roman looked like he was going to say something but changed his mind. He kept his eyes firmly on the road as he drove across the bridge towards Heartcross.

'Sometimes talking about things can help. A problem shared…'

'It's nothing, just family business.'

'I can see that family business is causing you some upset. I hope you can sort out whatever it is soon.'

Roman looked her way. 'I'm just struggling with a situation at the minute, but there's only me who can sort it out. I'll get there, but thank you.' Roman didn't say anything else as he pulled up on the kerb outside the entrance to the village shop and pulled on the handbrake.

Like the gentleman he was, he jumped out of the car and opened Ella's door for her. 'Back safe and sound.'

'Thank you,' she replied, attempting to press down the red button to release her seatbelt, but nothing happened. 'Bette doesn't seem to want to let me go.'

Roman reached over and brushed his hand against hers. The feel of his touch sent an unexpected shiver down her spine as she sat back against the seat. He unclipped the seatbelt with ease. 'There must be a knack to it,' she said and climbed out of the car.

'I'll see you at work tomorrow, and Roman...' Ella paused. 'I know you don't know me that well, but sometimes it's good to talk. If Callie hadn't rescued me at such a difficult time, goodness knows where I would have ended up, but it wouldn't have been Heartcross.'

Roman nodded and held her gaze. 'Thank you. I hear you, and I'll see you tomorrow.'

Ella watched as he clambered back into the car, leaving her wondering what was going on in his life. She'd opened up to Roman about Alex, but Roman hadn't felt able to do the same. Whatever was going on for him, she knew it must be more than run-of-the-mill stuff. She didn't like to see anyone struggling, especially when she knew first-hand that having a friend to talk things through with and support you was worth its weight in gold.

After Bette disappeared at the end of the road Ella opened the door to the stairwell and heard footsteps thumping down the stairs. She was met by Callie bounding towards her, her arms full of files and notepads. 'I'm late, I've got to hurry to make the boat. How's Dolores?' she asked, still walking but talking.

'Hopefully home tomorrow.'

'Good, fantastic news! McCartney hasn't been for a walk yet, so if you have time... I've really got to run, but don't forget Sunday dinner at the pub... The gang will be there – Julia, Eleni, Felicity and Isla. You'll love them.'

'Fab! I look forward to it, and good luck with the marketing meeting,' Ella bellowed after Callie, but the stairwell door had already shut firmly behind her.

Looking for the flat key in her bag, Ella thought about sharing her concerns about Roman, but what was that going to achieve? And she didn't want Roman thinking she was talking out of school. She was torn. Maybe if things got tougher for him he'd realise he could open up to her, and she was there to help.

After kicking off her shoes and hanging up her coat Ella had her afternoon mapped out: a walk with McCartney, followed by a spot of housework, a long soak in the bath and tea at the pub, but first she fired up her laptop and immediately logged on to Facebook, then typed in Roman's name.

He came up straight away and she admired his profile photo. His privacy setting were watertight, his friends list not accessible, but Ella clicked on to his profile pictures. There were three altogether. The first one was of Roman pictured backstage with a band, wearing a T-shirt sporting the words *Tour Manager*, with all the band members pointing towards it. The second was Roman's current photo and in the third Roman had his arm draped around a beautiful girl who wouldn't look out of place on the cover of *Vogue*. A slim size eight with long brunette hair that hung below her waist. Her make-up was immaculate, her eyebrows pencilled to perfection, and over her shoulder she clutched a Louis Vuitton bag. The girl was tagged in the photograph and Ella clicked on her name… Megan Docherty. Ella was amazed to discover that this stunning young woman was Roman's daughter. She was shocked to discover that he was a dad because he'd never given the slightest hint that he had a daughter. Ella wondered if Megan was an only child, and where was her mother?

Carefully clicking through Megan's profile, Ella discovered she was nineteen years old, which meant Roman must have had Megan when he was just sixteen years of age. Ella was surprised. She knew at that age she had barely been able to look after herself, never mind being responsible for another human being, and wondered if Roman had found fatherhood difficult at that age. After looking through a few more images there seemed no trace of Megan's mother – was she still in Roman's life? Ella wasn't sure and after searching for a couple more minutes, she uncovered very little. Why hadn't Callie mentioned he had a daughter? Ella quickly pinged her a text:

Did you know Roman has a daughter?

Immediately the text delivered and seconds later the reply came back: *No, has he?*

Ella was a little astonished by the reply. Surely Roman would have dropped Megan into conversation at some point. He had been sailing the boat since The Lakehouse reopened, and six months was a long time not to bring up the fact that he had a child – that seemed a little strange to her.

Next Ella searched for Dolores Henderson on Google. Immediately up popped numerous articles on Dolores, taking her completely by surprise. Ella read headlines about fans queueing for hours along the riverbank to try and secure Dolores Henderson tickets. There was a picture of Dolores on the roof terrace at The Lakehouse whilst a select crowd of fifty watched from the sandy bay below.

Ella carried on reading. There were hundreds of articles describing Dolores as a sex symbol who regularly sold out concert halls, and there were pictures of her hanging out with all the rich and famous in the most magnificent dresses. She carried on clicking, then hovered over one dramatic headline: 'Will Dolores Henderson Be a Future Princess?' Wilbur had been right, Dolores could have been royalty.

The newspaper reported how Dolores had spent the summer with Prince George under the scorching sun in St Tropez. They'd enjoyed time on his yacht and were photographed together from a distance diving off the boat, swimming under the most spectacular waterfalls, and Dolores looked stunning.

Ella read on and was taken aback by the next headline: 'Dolores Dumps the Prince!' The article described how it was believed that the prince had proposed to Dolores in the South of France, but on their return they had gone their separate ways. From what Ella could find on online, Dolores had stayed out of the limelight for the rest of the year before returning to sell-out gigs across the United Kingdom. Ella searched but she couldn't ever find anyone romantically linked to Dolores at all after the prince. It felt like the whole of Dolores' personal life had simply disappeared from public scrutiny.

Shutting the lid of the laptop, Ella ruffled the top of McCartney's head. 'Right then, McCartney, it looks like it's me and you.' He opened one eye. 'Let's go for a walk.

I've not been up to Starcross Manor yet. You can lead the way.' Ella jumped up and grabbed McCartney's lead. He may be deaf, but he wasn't blind and the second he saw his lead, he was off the sofa and weaving in and out of Ella's legs with his tail wagging madly.

They set off and ten minutes later Ella walked up towards the grand entrance of Starcross Manor and took in the beauty all around her. 'Amazing,' she murmured, staring out across the lake. It was stunning and the whole place took her breath away. She carried on walking up the driveway that swept into a wide circle with an ornate fountain in the centre, with the impressive manor house standing proudly behind it. The whole place reminded Ella of a royal palace. Huge stone steps led to the large double oak doors within a broad porch of stone pillars and ivy clung to the walls of the building. She followed the path at the side of the lake which led her and McCartney through lush green grass which incorporated formal gardens, a deer park, woodlands and a wildflower meadow. The woodland path led her towards Primrose Park where Ella acknowledged a couple of dog walkers before climbing over the stile and following the lane back towards the main High Street. Everywhere was peaceful and calm and this was exactly what Ella needed in her life right now.

As she turned the corner and could see the village shop in the distance, Ella spotted Roman in Bette, slowly driving up the High Street towards her. Taking her hand out of her pocket, she was about to wave to him when the Land Rover came to an abrupt halt. She watched as the same girl in the photograph that she'd just seen on Facebook flung open the passenger-side door and started screaming at Roman. 'It's you who has the problem. You need to sort yourself out. Leave me alone!'

Megan began to walk away and Ella watched her stumble on her high heels, before leaning against the wall and whipping her shoes off her feet. It was strange to see a young woman striding along the High Street in the early afternoon barefoot. Roman was up and out of Bette, looking fraught, but Megan was gone, disappeared within seconds, leaving Roman throwing his hands up in the air. A moment later he was back in the driver's seat and Bette took off like a rocket up the High Street in Ella's direction. She quickly shielded herself behind the red post-box in the street, suddenly not wanting to be seen. Roman's face was like thunder as he drove past, his eyes firmly fixed on the road in front of him.

Ella turned Megan's words over in her head… 'It's you who has the problem.' What did she mean by that?

As Bette disappeared at the end the road Ella stepped out from behind the letter-box and began to walk towards the village shop. McCartney pulled on the lead and as Ella looked down, he promptly cocked his leg against the lamp-post without a care in the world. As

Ella waited patiently for McCartney to finish his business, something caught her eye in the middle of the road, the same place where Roman had just pulled up. Stepping out into the road, Ella picked up an appointment card with Roman's name on it. The appointment was for Wednesday, at Oasis Lodge. Ella had no clue what Oasis Lodge was, but it looked like some sort of medical card. For the time being Ella slipped the card into her bag and planned to hand it back over to Roman in the morning on the way to work.

Chapter Six

Ella was collapsed on the sofa when Callie returned from work. She'd busied herself for the rest of the afternoon by cleaning the flat before snuggling up on the settee watching a Frank Sinatra movie alongside McCartney whilst snacking on a packet of biscuits.

Callie threw her coat over the chair and poured them both a glass of wine. 'And why are you eating biscuits? We are about to go and devour one of Meredith's roast dinners and you're stuffing biscuits into your mouth,' questioned Callie, kicking her shoes off her feet and wiggling her toes. 'And the flat looks amazing by the way,' she said, snagging an impressed glance around the room.

'You're very welcome. I want to do my bit, and believe me, I'll have room for a roast dinner, I can assure you of that,' said Ella, scrunching up the top of the packet and laying them down on the table.

Callie held up her wine glass. 'I needed this,' she claimed. 'What an afternoon. Mentally I'm exhausted. We've thrown a few marketing ideas around but we seem to be missing that spark, that idea that would just put The Lakehouse back on the map. Flynn still wants to keep it classy, so doesn't wasn't any cheesy gimmicks, but the rest of the staff are suggesting two-for-one cocktails etc. etc., but he doesn't want this restaurant to become like any other on the High Street.'

'Surely, it's worth thinking about it, even if it's only in the short term.'

'We'll get there, we have to.' Callie took a gulp of her wine. 'However, we have good news! The TV news crew have confirmed and they are coming tomorrow. Flynn is hoping the coverage will generate bookings.'

'Well, it can't do any harm, and all this is happening on my first day. How exciting!'

'Very, and what about your day? What was the text all about... Roman has a daughter?'

'Apparently so. I discovered her on Facebook but I'm a little surprised he's never mentioned her to you before now.'

'No, not to me, but thinking about it, all we ever seem talk about is work,' said Callie.

Ella didn't share that she'd witnessed some sort of

argument between Roman and Megan in the street when she was taking McCartney for a walk. Whatever was going on in his personal life at the minute, he didn't need her adding to the mix. She had no clue what was going on in his life, so assuming or judging wasn't going to help anyone.

However, Ella asked the question that had been on her mind since finding Roman's appointment card. 'What's Oasis Lodge?'

Callie's face looked a little surprised. 'Why do you want to know that?'

'It popped up on an advert in my homepage. Just wondered whether it was bar or something?' she replied, even though she felt a twinge of guilt telling Callie a white lie.

'Hmm, it's definitely not a bar, in fact quite the opposite, and it makes me wonder what you've been googling if that's coming up on your homepage. It's a rehab centre.'

Ella nearly chocked on her wine. 'Are you serious?'

'Yes, it's well known in the area,' confirmed Callie. 'So whatever you're googling, you need to stop.'

Ella gave a false laugh but couldn't help wondering why Roman would have an appointment at a rehab clinic. There was no way he was an alcoholic, she'd spent enough time with him to know that, yet Megan's words were whirling around her head:, *It's you who has the problem.* It didn't make sense and, from this morning's conversation, Ella knew that Roman liked keeping things to himself. For a split second Ella thought about telling Callie about the appointment card but quickly changed her mind. Roman sailed the boat for a living and it could have a detrimental effect on his livelihood if Flynn found out and began to question why he was attending a rehab centre. Ella didn't want to add to his troubles, as it seemed he already had enough on his plate.

The best thing to do was to hand the appointment card discreetly back to Roman first thing in the morning and again let him know she was there if he needed a friend to talk to. That's all she could do. 'What time are we going across to the pub?' asked Ella, her eyes firmly back on the packet of chocolate biscuits.

Callie leapt to her feet. 'Fifteen minutes. I'm going to freshen up whilst you slide a hot iron over your uniform, and don't even think about eating any more of those.' Callie pointed to her eyes and then to Ella. 'I'm watching you.'

Whilst Callie freshened up Ella quickly ironed over her uniform and thought about the day ahead tomorrow. She felt a little nervous that the TV crew would be filming but she was looking forward to it. According to Callie, Gianni was already panicking over the dishes for tomorrow, whereas Flynn had brought in extra staff from Starcross Manor to make sure the place looked as good as could be. There were fresh flowers in every corner of the restaurant, on the piano and at each end of the bar. Flynn had pulled out all the stops.

'Right, I'm ready.' Callie appeared whilst Ella was hanging up her uniform ready for the morning.

'I might even get my fifteen minutes of fame. What a way to begin a new job,' remarked Ella.

'You might indeed. Come on, I'm starving.'

On her way out Ella ruffled McCartney's head and topped up Fred's food, then followed Callie down the stairwell. As they shut the stairwell door behind them they spotted Roman walking out of Hamish's shop swinging a carrier bag and whistling. His mood had certainly lifted from a few hours ago. Ella couldn't help but admire his appearance; he was a vision of gorgeousness dressed in black skinny jeans and a tight white T-shirt.

'Good evening, Roman,' Callie called out.

Roman spun round. 'Hi, how was work?' he asked, looking at Callie, then turning his attention towards Ella. 'You look lovely, Ella, that colour suits you.'

Ella felt herself blush.

'Thanks, this old thing?' she said, trying to play down his compliment. Ella couldn't remember the last time she'd treated herself to any new clothes. With all the credit card debts hanging over her head, it would be a long time before she could go on a shopping spree.

'We are just off for a Sunday roast at the pub. Would you like to join us?'

Roman held up the carrier bag in his hand. 'Vegetables! Even though I believe Meredith serves up the best roasts. But I'm making a vegetable curry. I heard Hamish grows the best veggies from his allotment. But thank you for the invite. I'll see you both tomorrow.' Roman gave Ella a warm smile and clambered into Bette and with only two attempts, got the engine started.

Ella clutched the appointment card inside her bag. Roman was kind, polite, he'd stopped and made conversation. He dressed immaculately and he seemed a genuinely nice guy. There was no way he had an alcohol problem, it just didn't stack up.

Callie's eyes swept from Bette then towards Ella. 'And that contraption got you to the hospital?'

'That contraption is a treasured member of Roman's family and he loves her.'

'Someone has to,' Callie joked, opening the door to the pub. 'Welcome to the Grouse and Haggis, it's the best pub around.'

Ella stepped into a room that was packed to the rafters. Fraser and Meredith were famous for their Sunday roast with all the trimmings, and since the increase in tourism to the area booking a table was an absolute must.

Meredith smiled up from behind the bar. 'Good

evening, how are you both doing?' She placed a beer mat down in front of them both. 'Julia's in, she's over the far side with Eleni.'

Callie looked over her shoulder and waved at her cousin. 'Meredith, can I introduce you to Ella, she's staying with me for the foreseeable.'

Meredith gave Ella a warm welcoming smile. 'Of course, pleased to meet you.' She extended her hand across the bar. 'Your very first drink is on the house. Welcome to Heartcross! What would you like?'

'That's very kind, I'll have a glass of Pinot Grigio, please, and thank you so much for the homemade lasagne the other day, it was just what we needed after our long journey.'

'It was my pleasure, and the same for you?' Meredith glanced towards Callie. 'Wine?'

'Perfect, thank you.'

As Meredith reached up for the wine glasses that were on the high shelf she shouted over to Fraser who was stocking up the crisps at the other end of the bar.

'Fraser, come and meet Ella, a friend of Callie's. She's staying over the road.'

Fraser walked over and stretched his hand across the bar. 'Welcome to the Grouse and Haggis.'

'You've probably heard me talking about Allie in the past, she's Fraser and Meredith's daughter,' informed Callie.

'Yes! And her boyfriend is the supervet! How cool is that. I watched the programme on the telly.'

Fraser and Meredith beamed. 'Yes Rory, he's currently over in Africa, still working with Zach Hudson.'

'Zach Hudson!' swooned Ella. 'I've watched every Netflix film he's been in.'

'Me too, if I'm really honest.' Meredith lowered her voice, 'Very easy on the eye.'

'I can hear you, you know. I'm only standing here.' Fraser swiped Meredith playfully with the bar towel, and she chuckled.

Ella admired the familiarity between them, and could tell they adored each other and knew each other inside and out, they radiated such warmth. That's exactly what she thought she'd had with Alex, before he'd revealed himself to be a liar and a cheat.

'When is Rory home, Julia was saying he must be due any time now?' asked Callie.

Meredith placed the two glasses of wine in front of them. 'Stuart and Alana were in earlier and they said his arrival is imminent. I think Stuart is counting the days. Molly has been covering Rory's shifts at the practice and as far as I know, the new surgery is nearly ready over at Clover Cottage, but he's ready to hang up his scrubs and spend his time with Alana.'

Callie quickly explained to Ella that Stuart and Alana were Rory's parents and Stuart and Rory were partners in the local veterinary practice. 'Alana has dementia, and Stuart is retiring so the surgery is closing shortly.'

'And hopefully when Allie returns from Glasgow they can start planning the wedding,' continued Meredith with hope in her voice. 'I love a good wedding.'

'Exciting!' remarked Callie, taking the wine glass from the bar. 'We've made a reservation as well. Ella has come to sample your famous roast dinner.'

'And we hope you won't be disappointed.' Meredith smiled up at Ella before checking the list of bookings in the diary at the side of the till. 'Fraser has put you on the table next to Julia, number twelve. Feel free to push the tables together.'

'What lovely people,' exclaimed Ella, following Callie over to the table where Julia and Eleni were deep in conversation and scribbling on a pad in front of them.

'Good evening,' chirped Callie, pulling out a chair and sitting at the table next to them.

Julia looked up with a big beam on her face, before standing and enveloping Ella in a huge hug. 'It's been too long, welcome to Heartcross!'

Callie quickly rescued the glass of wine which was spilling over from Ella's hand and placed it safely on the table.

Julia stood and held Ella's hands. 'You look fabulous, how are you settling in?'

'I'm feeling very settled already, like I belong,' admitted Ella.

'Let me introduce you to Eleni,' Julia gestured towards Eleni who was looking up smiling. 'Eleni, my right-hand woman, works at the B&B, and we are just racking our brains.'

'About what?' quizzed Callie, looking at them with intrigue.

'Trying to help Flynn. You've had a meeting this afternoon, haven't you?' But before she could say any more Ella hit Callie's arm. 'OMG that looks like that chef off the TV.' Ella's jaw had hit the floor as she stared towards Andrew Glossop who was enjoying a pint on the other side of the bar.

Julia laughed and started to explain, 'That's Andrew, he's the chef up at Starcross Manor and has been a rival of Gianni up at The Lakehouse for many years. Secretly I think they are very fond of each other. They've been in many competitions against each other. Andrew took part in the cooking show—'

'The Road Trip Around Italy,' interrupted Ella, still staring at him. 'I L-O-V-E-D that programme,' she trilled, stringing out the word. 'He is my absolute favourite. Is everyone famous in Heartcross?'

'Well, don't be saying that to Gianni if you're working at The Lakehouse,' chipped in Callie, 'as he is your boss.' She grinned. 'And you need that job!'

'I won't be saying a word!'

Meredith came over to the table and took the girls' orders as Isla and Felicity walked into the pub and headed straight towards their table. Ella had met Felicity and was soon introduced to Isla, who she instantly clicked with.

'You're the owner of the alpaca farm.' Ella had noticed the comical creatures grazing in the field. 'They are gorgeous things.'

'That's me, tired housewife to one, mother to two, with my mad granny living with us.'

'Sounds like fun to me,' replied Ella, thinking everyone was so welcoming and that Isla was lucky to have a family.

'So tell me what brings you to Heartcross?' asked Isla innocently, taking a seat at the table.

Ella and Callie looked between each other.

Silence.

'What have I said?' asked Isla, looking around the table. 'Have I said something I shouldn't?'

'It's not you,' reassured Ella. 'I've just come out of a really difficult relationship, that's all.'

'Tell us more,' chipped in Felicity. All eyes were on Ella.

Ella had already opened up to Roman and getting it all out in the open was like her own form of therapy. She felt better talking about it and having the support of the people around her. The more she voiced what had happened between her and Alex, the more it made her determined to make something of her life, pay off those debts and get her life back on track.

'Well, in a nutshell… after my parents passed away, I fell in love with a doctor at the local hospital who helped me through all my grief. He was the love of my life and moved into my home. We talked marriage, kids and even started to look for a place together. Then one day he went to work and never came back…'

Everyone's jaw hit the floor at the same time, trying to take in exactly what Ella was telling them. 'This is awful – and is he still missing? What have the police said?' asked Isla tentatively.

'Oh, he's still missing, alright… along with Ella's inheritance and a brand-new Range Rover! It turns out he's not a doctor, he never worked at the hospital and we have no clue who the man was,' chipped in Callie.

'Shit! No way, are you serious?' asked Eleni, not mincing her words. 'This is the type of stuff you read about in the newspaper.'

'It's all true, I've no clue who this man is, what his real name is…' Ella blew out a breath. 'It turns out everything was a lie.'

Felicity raised an eyebrow. 'And I bet you're spending your whole life looking over your shoulder and scrutinising everyone you pass in the street.'

Ella nodded. 'I was... I did, but somehow I don't think I'll be bumping into him in Heartcross.'

'Let's hope not, because we would all run him out of town. You chose well coming here, Heartcross is like no other place, the magic draws you in and we all look out for each other,' confirmed Isla, in a voice that sounded like she was the voiceover for a TV advert, causing everyone to laugh.

Ella already knew of the fantastic community spirit, everyone had gone out of their way to make her feel welcome and strangely enough, she was already beginning to feel like she was part of the gang. Sharing her story put her at ease. The truth was out, and she knew if she was struggling or having a bad day, there was someone she could talk to. 'These people are professionals, it's a type of grooming, preying on the vulnerable. You think these things can't happen to you, but they can and I'm sorry this happened to you,' said Isla with such warmth.

'I watched a documentary once and these type of people scour the obituaries looking for their next victim – these tributes always tell them more information then we should share. It's then easy to track anyone down these days with social media,' chipped in Felicity.

Ella knew Felicity was absolutely right. Anyone could find out anyone's worth in a matter of seconds. She thought back to her own parents' obituary, in the write-up they talked about their successful business and the fact they were leaving behind one daughter… Ella Johnson, age 35. Dr Alex James had had everything handed to him on a plate.

'That was exactly my life,' confirmed Ella. 'And what a fool I feel.'

'Well don't. Look how courageous you are. You've taken the plunge and moved miles away to get yourself back on track. You might have no material possessions, but you have us and we'll do everything we can to get some sort of normality back in your life. I just can't imagine what you've been through…' sympathised Julia. 'But you are here in Heartcross, and we won't let anything happen to you.'

One by one the girls stretched out their arms and put their hands on top of each other in the middle of the table, then wiggled their fingers before sweeping their arms above their heads. 'Us girls stick together, and you can be in our club,' announced Felicity and the rest of them chorused, 'Hear, hear!'

Ella felt gladdened at being welcomed into the fold. She felt a good caring vibe from each and every one of them and was glad she'd trusted them with her past. They hadn't judged her, or thought she was stupid, they'd just been there for her. Callie had been right about this village, it was a very special place.

'We've all been out on a limb at some time or another

but there's always someone to talk to or hang out with. There's something about this place and the people...' Julia looked between all the girls.

'And you never want to leave!' everyone chorused, causing Ella to laugh.

'Anyway, what's all this?' Felicity pointed towards the pad in front of Julia.

Julia tapped her pen on the pad. 'Brainstorming... The Lakehouse. Flynn is stressing. Look at this place, packed out. This is what we need at The Lakehouse.' Eleni twizzled the notepad towards them all. 'So far, we've got a big fat nothing.'

Callie and Ella glanced at the blank page.

'Flynn needs to buy the front page of the Scottish *Daily Mail* and print a voucher for a free meal,' joked Ella. 'Just imagine how many readers will see that ad.' She sipped on her wine whilst everyone around the table stared at her.

'Ella, you might be on to something there,' Julia looked impressed and jotted down Ella's idea. 'I'm going to mention that to Flynn.'

'Swot!' teased Callie. 'Ella saves The Lakehouse.'

'And I've not even officially worked my first shift yet.' Ella grinned, putting a smug look on her face. 'And maybe he could organise for a couple of well-known faces to dine at The Lakehouse.' Ella was on a roll. 'A few photos on Instagram and people will start rolling in.

Zach Hudson for instance,' Ella almost tripped over her words. 'He would be perfect to attract the diners.'

'Exactly, but Zach is still in Africa with Rory,' replied Julia.

Ella was tugging on Callie's jumper. 'Zach Hudson is not in Africa, he's just walked into the pub alongside Rory!'

They all spun round to witness Meredith screaming as she set eyes on her future son-in-law for the first time in months. 'Fraser, Fraser,' she bellowed. 'Quick! Rory's home, he's back and Zach, Zach's here too.'

With a wide grin and a suntan to die for, Rory held out his arms and Meredith fell into them and hugged him tight. The whole of the pub erupted in applause, leaving Rory to raise his hand in the air and wave at everyone around.

'I can't believe you're back,' Meredith was stumbling over her words with excitement. 'Why didn't you say you were coming?'

'Any chance of a pint from my favourite landlady?' He grinned, heaving the rucksack from his back and leaning it against the bar. 'It's been a long journey home.'

'Fraser, get the boys a pint,' ordered Meredith, her voice still shaking with excitement. 'Look at you,' she held his hands before turning towards Zach. 'Welcome back to Heartcross.' Taking Zach by surprise, she hugged him too.

'When Rory invited me back for a few days, how could I resist?' He grinned, shaking hands with Fraser who was completely flabbergasted by their sudden arrival.

'Well, we weren't expecting this.' Fraser slapped Rory on the back. 'But it's good to have you home, son. Let me get you both a pint.'

'That's music to my ears.' Rory laughed, taking a swift glance around the pub and waving towards Julia, Felicity and Isla who were up on their feet and heading towards him. Ella and Callie watched as the old friends reunited.

After hugging Rory to death, Felicity and Isla came back to the table. 'All we need now is for Allie to come home and all the gang is back together.' Isla looked happy as she sat back down.

'And here's Flynn now and Gianni,' Julia noticed them walking in the back door. Immediately Flynn made his way over to Julia and kissed her. He turned back to say something to Gianni when everyone noticed Zach, with a wide grin on his face, welcoming Gianni like a long-lost friend. 'Gianni!'

'I can't believe it,' chimed Gianni in a loud Italian accent. 'What are you doing here?'

'Never mind me, what are you doing here?' replied Zach, thumping him on his back. As thick as thieves, they disappeared over towards the bar whilst Flynn pulled up a chair next to Julia.

'Honestly, I feel like I'm in a weird dream, just pinch me.' Ella offered her arm to Callie. 'I'm dreaming I'm in this quaint pub in the Scottish Highlands with a legendary actor, a TV supervet and a famous chef.'

Callie pinched her arm.

'Ow! That hurt!' Ella rubbed her arm.

Everyone laughed.

'This is so surreal.' Ella was still staring over at Zach.

'Welcome to Heartcross!' exclaimed Julia, holding up her glass as they all clinked them together.

'How's Dolores?' asked Flynn. 'Callie mentioned you'd been to visit her at lunchtime.'

'Low blood pressure, doing good and hopefully home tomorrow, and I had the best history lesson about The Lakehouse, which was apparently the place that launched her career. Do you know Dolores still has a little black book full of all the artists' telephone numbers that performed at The Lakehouse, including some of their sons and daughters who followed suit?'

'That woman has a remarkable talent,' replied Flynn, accepting a drink from Fraser who'd just brought him a pint over. 'Dad was telling me the Dolores Dinner evenings were always packed out. First your meal, then you watched your favourite artist perform. Win–win.'

Ella slapped the table, and everyone looked at her. 'I

think I've just had a light-bulb moment.' Ella's eyes were wide, which matched the grin on her face. 'This afternoon Dolores was telling me how she would love to perform at The Lakehouse one last time, so with the TV crew coming in tomorrow and reporting on the history of The Lakehouse, why don't we have a trip down memory lane?'

Flynn was listening intently to every word as Ella continued. 'Let's use Dolores' little black book. She can headline the evening, be the main star… "A Trip Down Memory Lane with Dolores Henderson". There could be a competition to win tickets, the locals obviously get a special discount and we can have numerous artists leading up to the grand finale.' Ella paused. 'I know it's probable that some of the artists may have passed away but Dolores mentioned she's up to date with family members of theirs who followed in their footsteps. If Dolores is in involved, surely everyone will want to be involved, we may be able to pull in a few recent artists.' Immediately Ella thought of Roman, surely he had contacts, especially as he used to be in that line of work. 'Gianni can cook up a delicious menu, we could even dress up just like the olden days if we wish to take it that far?'

Ella was watching Flynn's reaction, a huge smile hitched on his face. 'What do you think?' she asked, waiting with bated breath.

Flynn picked his pint up off the table and held it towards Ella. 'I think you, Ella Johnson, are a genius. This could absolutely get The Lakehouse back on the map. Think of the media coverage,' he looked around at everyone. 'What do you all think? I think this is an excellent idea.'

Callie spoke up first. 'I think you're on to something with "A Trip Down Memory Lane with Dolores Henderson". But we need to make sure she's willing and able. Don't forget, she is currently in hospital,' Callie reminded everyone.

'I think she will be more than in. This has success written all over it,' trilled Ella, with excitement in her voice, knowing that Dolores loved The Lakehouse.

'This could lead to our own celebrity club launching again, but let's include the locals in that too,' suggested Flynn, much to everyone's delight. 'But one step at a time. Ella, do you think you can pull this off?'

Ella was taken aback. 'What do you mean?'

'I'm saying this is your call. You talk to Dolores, find out if you can have access to her little black book. Would she be up for a star-studded night dedicated to her and the past... "A Trip Down Memory Lane" has such a great ring to it.'

'Are you asking me to organise this event?' Ella's voice trembled and she moved her hands to her heart, her eyes glistening and her smile broad.

Flynn pointed at her. 'Exactly that.'

She grabbed on to Callie for support who whispered, 'You can do this.'

Pressing her lips together, Ella tried to contain her emotion. Could she actually do this? Flynn was putting The Lakehouse in her hands, hoping that her idea was going to save the restaurant from going under. This was a huge ask. She didn't know a thing about event management or putting acts on stage.

'Do you think you could pull it off? We can talk to the TV crew tomorrow and try and get them involved?'

Ella was thinking fast on her feet; could she do this? She'd run her own business and organised sale evenings and special events in the shop to bring in the customers, but this was on another scale. But surely, she could just do what she did before and just magnify everything to the next level? Ella knew she had a natural affinity with Dolores, who would do anything to help make The Lakehouse succeed. She looked over at Callie again, who was still nodding and encouraging her every step of the way. 'Say yes,' she mouthed.

'If Dolores is in agreement, then… yes!'

'Fabulous, we can chat tomorrow at work.' Flynn held his glass up towards Ella.

Callie mirrored his action. 'Ella Johnson saves The Lakehouse.'

'Ella Johnson saves The Lakehouse,' repeated everyone else around the table.

'No pressure,' whispered Ella to Callie. 'I can do this, can't I?'

'You can, and that's because you're absolutely fabulous,' exclaimed Callie, bumping her shoulder against Ella's.

Ella gave a broad grin. She felt honoured to have been given the chance, and already felt like part of the community of Heartcross. Ella wasn't going to let Flynn down. If Dolores agreed, this was going to be the best night The Lakehouse had ever seen – she'd make sure of that.

Chapter Seven

Ella jolted awake from a nightmare where she was being chased by a lion with the head of Alex over the bridge into Heartcross. He was shouting at her to give him all of her money and although she was running as fast as she could, he was gaining on her. Feeling panicky, Ella wiped the sweat from her forehead and pulled at the neck of her pyjama top, allowing herself to breathe easier.

'Damn you Alex, stop haunting me,' she murmured, sitting up in bed. After calming her breathing she reached out for McCartney, who was curled up at her side. He'd slept on Ella's bed for the second night and she was getting rather used to having him by her side.

'It's today McCartney, my first shift at The

Lakehouse.' But McCartney was oblivious, he was too busy waggling his legs in the air, hoping for a tummy tickle. 'And then I have to talk to Dolores. Fingers crossed.' She picked up McCartney in her arms and gave him a huge squeeze before wandering out into the living room to find Callie talking on the phone. As soon as she finished her call, she sang good morning and handed Ella a cup of tea.

'I don't think we'll be sitting out on the balcony this morning.'

The rain was lashing down, and it sounded like pellets firing against the windowpanes. 'According to the weather forecast it's going to clear up in the next hour. Let's hope it stops before we head over to the boat. How are you feeling about your first day?'

'I'm really looking forward to it. It should be a fun day. Who was on the phone?'

'Flynn,' replied Callie, 'asking where Roman is. He gave him an early shift to ferry the TV crew across the river, but he's failed to turn up.'

'Really?' Ella was surprised, he really didn't seem like the unreliable type.

'It's not the first time and I know Flynn has got enough on his plate without any added pressures at the minute.'

'There's got to be a reasonable explanation,' replied

Ella, trying to smooth the way, even though the appointment at Oasis Lodge had just popped back into her head. Maybe Roman really was recovering from an addiction of some kind, but then Ella scorned herself for jumping to conclusions. 'Something must have happened because he said he'd see me at work today. Bette has probably broken down, it will be something simple.'

'There's things called phones.' Callie waggled her own phone in the air. 'This was the last thing that Flynn needed this morning. Wilbur should be inside the restaurant, not sailing the boat. We need all bums on seats to make the restaurant look busy, but I'm just about to rope in a few more of the gang. Julia and Eleni will hopefully get over to the restaurant once everything is sorted at the B&B.'

'Today will run smoothly, I'm sure. Roman will have an explanation, the TV news report will bring in more diners and as soon as I've talked to Dolores, hopefully we can all go on "A Trip Down Memory Lane". I still can't quite believe Flynn has faith in me to organise it, when I've only just arrived. I'm still a little nervous – can I organise such a star-studded bash?'

'Without a doubt you can. Think about how you turned your own little business around. You tripled those profits with your browse-and-biscuit mornings, and the wreath-making classes, and I even remember your furniture-painting mornings were a huge success. When you put your mind to something you make things a success. You are amazing, and this is going to be amazing.'

'Yes, I did do that, didn't I?' Ella felt proud, thinking how she'd turned her own business around to make a profit. 'It's all about believing in yourself.'

'Exactly that! And I believe in you and Flynn believes in you.'

Ella was smiling. 'Eek, let's hope Dolores agrees. I wonder what names she has in her little black book?'

An hour later, they set off to work. It took a little over ten minutes to reach The Boathouse along the riverbank under the wide dark sky, but thankfully for the time being the rain had stopped and the buffeting winds had calmed down a little. This was the perfect walk to work for Ella, the view of the cliffs and the river tumbling over the rocks beat fighting for a seat on a hot and over-packed bus that took twenty minutes to ride into the city centre each day. There was something enchanting about travelling to work by a boat.

'There's Bette.' Ella pointed to the Land Rover parked at the side of The Boathouse. 'And there's Roman.'

They witnessed Roman stepping out of the driver's side of the car whilst buttoning up his shirt. He thrust his arms into his jacket then checked his hair in the wing mirror before pulling his cap on his head. Then he hurried down the jetty to the water taxi that had just docked, and stepped on board. For a moment he was in conversation with Wilbur before taking the helm behind the wheel.

'Good morning,' Ella chirped as they stepped on board, looking towards Wilbur and Roman.

'Good morning,' replied Roman with a smile, quickly tucking his shirt into his trousers.

Ella noticed that he looked exhausted, not to mention a little dishevelled. His tie was wayward, his shirt wasn't pressed and he didn't quite look his usual immaculate self.

Hearing voices in the distance, Ella turned around to see Isla and Felicity leading the gang to help support Flynn and put bums on the seats. Isla waved over towards the boat and within seconds they were joining them on the deck.

'The cavalry has arrived!' trilled Felicity.

Callie had a big smile on her face. 'You lot are stars, Flynn will really appreciate this.'

'I hope so,' replied Drew. 'I should be over at the markets, but,' he said, straightening his tie, 'you never know when your fifteen minutes of fame is going to happen!'

'Ella, meet Drew, my husband,' said Isla. 'He's only here to try and get his mug on the telly.' Isla gave him an adoring smile, but Drew was rolling his eyes.

'Whatever the reason, I'm sure Flynn appreciates all the community support.' Ella stretched out her hand and shook Drew's. 'Pleased to meet you.'

'Oooh, it's your first day,' remembered Isla, 'and with all this going on too!'

'I know, and I'm really looking forward to it,' replied Ella, moving towards the front of the boat. As the boat began to rock Roman held out his hand to steady her. Even though he was putting on a smile, Ella noticed his eyes looked troubled.

'We're going to perch in the middle,' Callie told Ella. 'It's less rocky.'

Ella nodded. 'I'm going to catch the breeze up at the front.' She sat down just at the side of Roman. Wilbur had taken a seat next to Drew and everyone was chatting away as Roman readjusted his seat and carried out the safety checks.

'Aren't you sitting with your friends?' asked Roman, casting a glance over his shoulder towards the rest of them.

'I quite fancied a seat up the front and thought I'd

come and keep you company, if that's okay?' Ella knew this would be the perfect opportunity to hand back the appointment card and once more offer any help she could. She was just waiting for the right moment.

'Of course,' he replied, tipping his cap. 'Let's get you all across this river. Thankfully the rain has stopped for the moment. It's definitely the finest views up front.'

'And the best way to travel to work,' said Ella. 'So different from the city life. You must find that too, coming from Edinburgh,' she continued. 'Which do you prefer?'

'They both have their pros and cons,' he replied, sitting down and placing the key in the ignition. 'Pull on that lever… go on!'

Ella leant forwards and pulled the lever. She jumped out of her skin as the horn hollered out across the water.

Everyone behind her laughed.

'We are ready to set sail,' declared Roman, giving her a smile.

The journey across to The Lakehouse was blissfully therapeutic even though a little rocky today, bobbing along the river with the breeze in her hair, compared to her old commute to her gift shop in the city. The sky was dark and no doubt more rain was on the way. Ella could hear nothing but the slapping of the waves against the boat and the gulls circling above the whitewashed cliffs.

She took in the magnificent view and knew she would never tire of it. In the distance there were a number of speed boats crashing through the water further along and a handful of bikers riding along the coastal path.

'How's the travel sickness today?' asked Roman, casting a sideward glance towards Ella who thankfully wasn't feeling queasy at all.

'I'm actually doing okay. How are you doing today?' Ella felt a tiny trickle of nerves as she glanced backwards at the others who were in deep conversation. This was the perfect opportunity to hand back the appointment card that was stored safely in her bag, but she had no clue how Roman was going to react.

'Just the same as normal,' he replied, looking out over the spectacular scenery.

'Roman.' She blew out a silent breath and he looked towards her.

'Is everything okay?' he asked.

'I am, but are you?' Ella reached into her bag and pulled out the card.

Immediately Roman's smile disappeared. 'Where did you get that?' His voice was low, not wanting to draw any attention to himself.

'I found it in the street, you must have dropped it. I saw you arguing with your daughter – Megan, is it?'

Roman stared, expressionless, at Ella, his face slightly reddened. 'You've been doing your research, haven't you?' He didn't look best pleased and Ella knew he had every right to be upset if he thought she'd gone delving into his business, but it wasn't like that. She knew something was wrong and genuinely wanted to help.

'What's going on, Roman? This place is a rehab centre and my educated guess, judging by the way you conduct yourself, hold down your job and the fact that you are usually dressed immaculately, is that you haven't got an addiction.'

Roman looked down at his creased shirt and quickly straightened his tie.

'But something is going on, because you've been late for work, and today of all days you aren't looking your usual self. Is there anything I can do to help?' she asked tentatively, watching Roman slip the appointment card into his inside pocket without saying a word. 'Is there something wrong, Roman?'

Roman nodded. 'But I really can't talk about it, I just can't.'

'Please let me help you,' she continued. 'If it wasn't for Callie helping me when I was in a mess... Don't struggle on your own. If you continue being late, what's going to happen to your job?'

'I never intended to be late this morning. I was up early but sometimes things are taken out of your hands.'

'What things?' probed Ella softly. 'Everything is fixable, you only have to look at my life. It hasn't at all been plain sailing, but I didn't have to struggle by myself. I had a friend who cared, and you have friends who care.'

Roman looked like he was going to share something with her, but instead said, 'No one can help me, I just can't talk about it, Ella. Please just leave it.'

Ella had no alternative except to leave the conversation there. She'd offered her help and Roman had turned her down. What more could she do? Except be there if he changed his mind.

'What are you pair chatting about?' Callie appeared behind them, causing Ella to jump and turn around. 'First-day nerves, is what we are talking about. I was just telling Roman how I'm feeling nervous yet a little excited, but I can't wait to become part of the team.'

Roman glanced across at Ella and gave her a look of appreciation. Ella knew the conversation between them was private, and even though she had got very little out of Roman she wasn't going to share his business with anyone. She just hoped whatever was going on, he got some help from somewhere, because Ella recognised the signs. Roman was on a downwards spiral, and things must be proving too much to handle, especially as he had started being late for work.

Roman fixed his eyes back on the water ahead as he began to steer the boat through the weeping willows, leaving Isla and Felicity gasping at the view as the restaurant came into sight.

'The beauty of the place gets them every time.' Roman smiled warmly towards Ella.

'It is a magical place,' agreed Ella, suddenly thinking of Dolores. In her mind she could picture Dolores stepping off the boat dressed up to the nines and mingling with the rich and famous. 'A Trip Down Memory Lane' was what this place needed and hopefully Dolores would agree.

'Who's that?' asked Felicity, now joining them at the front of the boat. She pointed to the huddle of people standing on the sandy bay outside the restaurant along with Flynn.

'That's the TV crew,' observed Isla, clapping her hands together. 'It's all go!'

They all stood up as Roman slowly sailed the boat alongside the jetty and cut the engine. He turned towards everyone. 'Here we are folks, please step on to the jetty with care. The boat sails back half past the hour, every hour.'

Like a gentleman, Roman held out a steady hand and helped each and every one of them off the boat. Ella was the last to leave. 'Thank you for keeping my business between ourselves,' whispered Roman as he helped her down.

'You're welcome,' she replied, 'and you know where I am.'

Ella followed the gang towards the entrance to The Lakehouse, but she quickly glanced back over her shoulder. Roman was watching her and Ella saluted, leaving him grinning at her. She could only hope that, in time, he would begin to open up.

Chapter Eight

F lynn greeted everyone inside the restaurant with a huge smile. 'Thank you for coming, I know you are all busy and I really do appreciate it.' He guided them all to the reception area, where a member of staff showed them to their tables.

Ella noticed that after a short private conversation with Callie, Flynn headed outside towards the boat. Within a couple of minutes Roman, looking sheepish, followed Flynn towards his office. Ella guessed he was going to have to explain why he was late for work and hoped he'd be okay. If Roman wouldn't open up to her, he would hopefully confide in Flynn.

'Let's get started – your very first shift!' trilled Callie, appearing at her side.

Ella had to admit, her confidence had wavered a little

since she'd stepped inside The Lakehouse. Everywhere was a hive of activity and she didn't know which way to turn. 'Now I'm here, I'm actually feeling a little nervous.'

'You'll be brilliant,' reassured Callie. 'Come on.'

Whilst Ella and Callie walked towards the back of the restaurant, Ella noticed that Wilbur had changed into yet another bright flamboyant jacket and was now serving behind the bar, whilst Gianni peered around the kitchen door looking harassed. He waved a tea towel in Callie's direction, who hurried over to him, and after a short conversation she began walking back towards Ella.

'That man's blood pressure must be through the roof,' exclaimed Callie. 'Gianni is having kittens.'

Ella couldn't imagine the strapping Italian chef having kittens about anything. He always looked cool and collected and in charge.

Callie leant in and lowered her voice. 'Don't make it obvious, but see the woman sitting by the window overlooking the bay...?'

Immediately, Ella swung her head round and looked in that direction.

'I said don't make it obvious!' Callie slapped Ella's arm then rolled her eyes.

'You know when someone says that I'm bound to look straight away.' Ella laughed, turning back towards Callie.

'Apparently she's a food critic for a very well-known

food magazine, and what a day to turn up, with the TV crew here too.'

'How do you know she's a food critic?' asked Ella, taking another quick look at the woman who was busily scribbling away on a notepad. Her burnt-orange hair fell below her shoulders, her make-up was just so and she looked very business-like sitting there in a navy-blue pinstriped suit. 'She looks very serious.'

'She's notorious, well known in the field. Apparently, she and Gianni have come to blows in the past after she gave him a bad review.'

'Yikes, no wonder he's feeling the heat.'

'I'm counting on you to charm her.' Callie tilted her eyebrow challengingly.

Ella looked horrified.

'I'm joking! We wouldn't do that to you on your first day.'

Once their coats were hung up and their bags stowed away safely in the lockers, Callie led the way towards the film crew who were standing in the corner of the restaurant surrounded by wires, microphones and a man with a huge TV camera on a swingy tripod.

'Hi, I'm Callie, restaurant manager, and this is Ella, one of our waitresses for today.' The director introduced herself as Nancy. Her eyes were framed by brown-rimmed spectacles, her magnified hazel eyes looking straight at Ella. She was a tiny voluptuous woman – five foot, if that – and her blonde curls were tinged with purple dye that ran through the ends. Ella couldn't even hazard a guess how old Nancy was, but dimples appeared in her blushed cheeks as she gave them both a warm smile and extended her hand, which they both promptly shook.

'We're going to start filming in a minute, we will be wandering around and taking some sweeping shots over the restaurant, so just carry on your business and pretend we aren't here. We'll do our best not to get in anyone's way.'

Ella noticed Wilbur being interview behind the bar as they headed towards the kitchen. 'There's a real sense of community here at The Lakehouse. What does being a part of this community mean to you and your team here?' asked the interviewer, firing questions at Wilbur, who seemed at ease with a microphone held in front of his mouth and a camera pointing in his face.

'We source all our food locally…' The sound of Wilbur's voice trailed off as Ella and Callie wandered back into the staff-only area and closed the door behind them.

'Gosh, it's all go, isn't it. What time is break time?' joked Ella.

'That's a good thing – being busy and all this going on makes the day go quicker. You need one of those.' Callie pointed to some brand-new notepads sporting The

Lakehouse logo. 'Pick one up at the start of each shift, ready to take your orders.'

Ella took one and placed it in the pocket of her apron.

'Come on, I'll take you through.'

After Callie had introduced Ella to everyone, she checked with Gianni that he was ready for them and then led them into the main kitchen. Breathing in the kitchen's unique aroma – a mixture of coffee, sweet desserts and pots of herbs scattered about the worktops – Ella noticed Gianni piling up profiteroles on top of each other. He looked up and quickly wiped his hands on a small white towel stuffed in the front of his apron, then beckoned everyone over to the tasting table. 'Come, come...'

Callie touched Ella's arm. 'Good luck, you'll do just fine.'

Everyone lined up as Gianni began to lay numerous dishes out in front of them. 'The restaurant is busier than normal, especially with the TV crew in. Each and every one of you needs to act professional and courteous at all times, nothing is too much trouble for the diner, and remember – what the customer wants, the customer gets. And smile.'

'Yes, Chef!' they all replied in unison without any prompting, causing them all to look at each other and grin.

'Get your pads and pens out ready in case you need

to take notes,' ordered Gianni. 'Today's specialities are laid out in front of you.'

Gianni was talking so fast that Ella had to concentrate to understand his accent. Her pen was poised on her pad as Gianni began reeling off the day's dishes, which Ella had to admit looked amazing. He handed each of them a fork. 'Taste,' he ordered as everyone delved in before he fired questions at them. Thankfully everyone had written down the key ingredients and once Gianni was satisfied they knew their stuff, he ushered them over to the whiteboard in the corner of the kitchen. 'The area of the restaurant you are covering is up on the board, take a look and get out there... Oh, but this is important.'

All the waiters stopped and looked at Gianni. 'Tiffany Down is in the restaurant. She is a restaurant and food critic so please have your wits about you. The food is down to me, but the customer service is down to you.' Gianni pointed at a waitress whose name was Amy, according to her name badge. 'Tiffany is in your section of the restaurant, you have been here the longest, so make sure she leaves here a happy critic.'

Amy looked petrified but nodded.

'Now get out there,' Gianni clapped his hands then ushered them out of the kitchen.

'Yes, Chef!' they all replied, filtering into the restaurant. Ella noticed a slight smile on Gianni's face as she spun round on one foot and followed the rest of them.

Pushing open the door into the restaurant, Ella smoothed down her skirt and took a deep breath. She spotted the TV crew bunched together in front of the bar, the camera scanning the restaurant.

In Ella's section of the restaurant were Isla and Felicity, which she was relieved about as that took some pressure off her if she wasn't sure what to do. As she walked towards their table, Ella noticed that Amy, despite painting a smile on her face, actually looked petrified of Tiffany Down, and she saw Tiffany glowering at Amy.

'Good afternoon, I'm Amy and I will be your waitress today.'

Ella followed suit and, armed with menus, she handed them out to everyone who was sat at the table with Isla and Felicity. Drew was sat opposite Isla and then there were two others sitting at the table that Ella didn't know.

'Good afternoon, I'm Ella and I will be your waitress today.'

'Oh she's good,' joked Felicity, 'and sounds the part.'

'We're so glad you're our waitress!' said Isla. 'Let me introduce you to Martha and Aggie. Martha is my grandmother and Aggie is Fergus's mum. They came across on the boat before us.'

Ella greeted everyone then began to take their drinks orders. She felt a sense of importance as she jotted their order on her brand-new pad in her best handwriting, which was silly, but Ella desperately wanted to give a good impression.

Once the orders were taken, she noticed that Tiffany's voice was carrying across the restaurant. It seemed she was already rattled about something.

'I've been waiting a while to be served and I don't appear to have a drinks menu.' Tiffany's tone was short and sharp.

Whilst Amy was apologising profusely, Ella hurried over. 'Sorry for the delay, Amy! I've just printed an up-to-date drinks menu, here you go.' Ella handed a drinks menu over to Amy, who looked relieved.

'Thank you,' replied Amy, handing over the list to Tiffany, who immediately began to look it over.

'What would you recommend for a Monday lunchtime?' asked Tiffany, staring up at them both before Ella could escape.

Ella noticed that Amy looked a little flustered but didn't want to step on her toes. 'I do like a glass of Chablis – how about you, Amy?' shared Ella, who had a little bit of wine knowledge after spending nearly a year with Alex. He was always buying expensive wines which, of course, she'd now discovered, had been paid for mainly with her credit card.

'I love a good Chablis too,' joined in Amy, taking Ella's lead.

Ella noticed that on the wine list there was a short description next to each drink listing the ingredients and the origin. Ella held the menu in her hand and discreetly pointed to the next one on the list, so Amy could see that all Ella was doing was reading what was printed. 'Or we have Sancerre,' suggested Ella.

'Produced in the eastern part of the Loire Valley in France,' continued Amy. Between them they talked their way through the bulk of the wine list, leaving Tiffany looking suitably impressed.

'You pair seem to know your stuff. I think I'll go for your first recommendation – a small glass of Chablis.'

'That's the perfect choice,' acknowledged Ella, who thought for a fleeting moment that Tiffany had actually cracked a slight smile.

'I'll get that for you right away,' replied Amy, writing it down on her pad and hurrying towards the bar.

Ella was just about to walk away when Tiffany picked up the food menu. 'Can you talk me through today's specials too, please?'

Ella looked over towards the bar, but now Amy seemed to have disappeared out of sight. She didn't want to step on anyone's toes, but it would have looked unprofessional if she'd called Amy back over to cover her own table, and Ella didn't want to leave Tiffany waiting longer than necessary.

'Certainly,' replied Ella, who had to admit she was secretly enjoying herself. She felt her confidence building by the second as she opened up her notepad and sang her way through the delicious meals that she'd tasted only a few moments ago.

'Which would you recommend?' Tiffany was once again putting Ella on the spot but she answered immediately.

'Without a doubt, the escalope of Pork à la Milanese garnished with fresh rocket, piccolo tomatoes, shaved pecorino and fresh lemon,' replied Ella, not knowing why she'd just spoken in a French accent, leaving Tiffany to raise an eyebrow and Isla and Felicity stifling their laughter at their nearby table.

'And what is pecorino?' quizzed Tiffany, testing Ella's knowledge.

'The most delicious Italian cheese,' replied Ella confidently, thankful she had listened to Gianni and had jotted that information down on her pad, otherwise she wouldn't have had a clue. 'I think you'll love it.'

'Okay, I'll take your word for it.' Tiffany plumped for the pork and handed the menu back to Ella, who turned around to discover Felicity and Isla giving her a thumbs up and Callie watching her from the back of the restaurant.

With a spring in her step, she spotted Amy coming back through the double doors. 'Amy, I'm so sorry. Tiffany collared me about the food, so I just took the order. I hope that's okay?'

'Of course it's okay! And thank you for coming to my rescue with the wine menu – it was my fault, I'd forgotten to put them out on the table.'

'I think we got away with it. I'll put her food order into the kitchen, but I didn't mean to take over.'

'You didn't, don't worry.' Amy was thankful. 'You're such a natural with the customers. Happy first day!'

Ella smiled brightly as she tore Tiffany's order from her pad and handed it over to the kitchen. Callie placed her hand on her shoulder. 'Look at you! Keeping Tiffany happy. Flynn will be pleased, not to mention Gianni.'

'I hope so. Is Roman still in with Flynn?' Ella had just realised she hadn't seen him leave the office yet and the boat was due to leave soon.

'It appears that way. Wilbur is going to take the boat back to Heartcross and I'm going to cover the bar. Don't stand around, go and work those tables. Amy can take carry on with her section now.'

'Okey dokey,' Ella replied. Even though she hadn't quite worked a full hour yet, she loved being surrounded by people, the hustle and bustle of the kitchen and doing the best she could to please the customers. It was so different from her last job, sitting all day by herself in her shop, waiting for customers to walk through the door.

Once Ella was back on the floor she flitted between her tables, taking down orders and serving drinks. She never knew work could actually be so enjoyable. Apart from a couple of tables, the restaurant was actually full. Everyone had come together to support Flynn, the restaurant looked busy and the atmosphere was jolly.

Nancy directed the team as the food began to make its way to the customers and the camera was rolling inside the restaurant. For the next five minutes everything went swimmingly, with a mouth-watering aroma from Gianni's delightful dishes wafting through the restaurant and The Lakehouse looking very much alive.

Hearing a tut from the next table, Ella looked over towards Tiffany, who promptly scrawled something on her notepad then tapped her watch. 'Have they gone to France to crush the grapes to produce my Chablis?' She turned towards Ella, who quickly looked over towards the bar. Amy had put the drinks order in and Ella the food order, but they both must have automatically assumed the other one would have served the drink from the bar.

Facing a stony-looking Tiffany, Ella hitched the biggest smile on her face and collected Tiffany's drink before placing it on the table. 'I'm so sorry for the delay, and I have to say, I've just been admiring your handbag, it really does match your suit. You have exquisite style. You must turn heads wherever you go.'

For a split second Tiffany looked perplexed, maybe she wasn't used to people being nice to her? After the initial shock had worn off, she brushed the lapel of her jacket and said, 'What, this old thing?' but Ella could tell that Tiffany was secretly delighted. She thanked Ella for the Chablis without making any further fuss.

'You've got her eating out of your hand – good work,' whispered Callie as she walked past carrying a tray of drinks. 'Management team next for you.' She winked.

'Kill them with kindness,' replied Ella, but thinking about what Callie had just said. She knew that Callie was only joking but it definitely gave her food for thought. Why couldn't she work her way up to the management team? There was absolutely nothing stopping her from reaching the top if that's what she decided she wanted to do.

Ella quickly returned to the kitchen. There was something smelling delicious as she walked up to the serving pass but the atmosphere felt charged and reminded Ella of the programmes she'd watched on TV. The sous chef and kitchen assistants were running around preparing meals so fast that Ella felt dizzy watching them. Gianni was shouting orders and everyone else looked frazzled and this was only at the start of the shift. Ella handed over another order when she spotted Amy.

'Is that Tiffany's food? We left her drink on the bar by mistake, but I think I've smoothed the way.'

Amy put her hand up to her chest. 'That's my fault – I just thought you'd serve the drink, but it is *my* table. Tiffany's meal is just coming on the pass now. I'll take it out.'

Gianni's voice boomed over his sous-chef and assistants. 'Will you two stop chatting and get the food out? Table four is ready.' Gianni sounded stressed as he wiped his forehead with a tea towel. That was Isla's table. Ella didn't take Gianni's comment to heart – that was also part of the job. Knowing his bark was worse than his bite, she gave Gianni a smile and his expression softened as he shook his head with a slight smile on his face.

Walking towards Isla's table, Ella spotted Roman for the first time since he'd been summoned into Flynn's office. Looking at her watch, she saw he'd been in there for nearly an hour. The TV crew had moved outside and Ella could see Flynn had gone to join them. Just as she was about to walk through the doors towards the kitchen, Roman caught her eye. Ella gave him a little wave and he tried to smile but didn't look happy at all. Ella guessed he'd had a dressing down from Flynn for being late this morning. She watched as he walked off up the stairs to the rooftop terrace. After Ella grabbed the rest of the food for Isla's table she too headed towards the rooftop. When she reached the top of the steps she found Roman was staring out at the white chalky cliffs towering over the water and watching the spectacular waterfall trickling down the mountainside. Hearing someone behind him, he spun round to face her. Immediately Ella noticed his face was almost as white as the envelope he was holding in his hand.

'Are you okay?' she asked. 'What happened?'

'Not really,' he replied, his voice shaky. He held up the envelope. 'This is what happened, my official written warning for being late today. I really can't afford to lose this job, but Flynn's right – I'm not being reliable and he can't have someone on his team who's a liability.' He gave Ella the envelope and she cast a quick glance over the letter inside.

'He'd already given me a couple of chances and this morning, of all mornings, I let him down. He's right, he doesn't need me adding to his stress.'

Ella handed the letter back. 'Why were you late today? What's going on here, Roman? Because Flynn is a decent guy, and if you had a good reason, he would understand and I know he'd help you in any way possible.'

Roman turned his back on Ella and stared out over

the water. They could see Wilbur in the distance heading towards Heartcross.

'I need this job because it's easy, not mentally taxing. I have the wind in my face, and it helps to keep my head in a good place.'

Ella stood by his side and also looked out over the water. 'Have you told Flynn what's going on?'

Roman didn't look at her. 'I can't. I just can't, Ella.'

For a moment the words hung in the air. 'If you are not going to let us help you, we can't do anything. You will end up losing this job, and for the sake of not talking to someone about it, is it worth it? You will end up losing everyone around you who cares – take it from someone who knows. All this secrecy is no good for anyone, it will eat away at you, and then it's going to eat away at every relationship you have, and possibly that will include ours.'

Roman took a sideward glance at her. 'Why, what do you mean?'

'I lost all my friends, Roman, because of Alex, and I know this isn't the same situation, but my friends warned me against him, they could see he was manipulating me, isolating me, and they wanted to help but I didn't listen. I didn't accept their help. Do you know what I did?'

'No, what did you do?' He turned to face her.

'I cut myself off from everyone, I thought I was

superwoman, I could handle it on my own, but there were days that I didn't get out of bed, I lay there with the curtains drawn, my phone switched off. I never ate, barely washed and if it wasn't for Callie I'd probably still be there. Whatever is going on, surely it can't be as bad as that.'

He looked at her again.

'People can help you, but if you push everyone away and keep it all to yourself, there will be consequences.' Ella looked towards the letter.

'I'm already living with the consequences. I'm sorry Ella, but I really can't talk about this.'

But Ella wasn't going to give up on Roman that easily. 'Look, I've been hurt by secrets in the past and I would never go down that path again. Just for the record, I haven't told a soul about the appointment card and I won't. It's your business, but please take the help whilst it's being offered.' Ella wished he'd open up, she could see he was hurting.

'And who's this now?' he said, hearing someone coming up the stairs. They both looked towards the doorway and to their amazement, the TV crew and Callie walked on to the rooftop.

'Here you both are… this is perfect,' said Callie, looking towards Nancy who was nodding approvingly.

Ella and Roman shared a look that said they both had no clue what was going on. 'I've just finished my break and need to get back to work,' said Ella, remembering she'd just abandoned Isla's table, and it may be her getting her marching orders at this rate. She took a step towards the stairs.

'Stop right there! You aren't going anywhere. What do you think?' asked Callie, looking at Nancy again who was beaming.

'Yes, they are both perfect,' confirmed Nancy, looking through the lens of the camera.

'Perfect for what?' asked Ella, stringing out the words slowly.

'A romantic meal for two!'

Roman and Ella looked at each other then back towards Nancy, who pointed to the table that was laid out on the balcony overlooking the bay, which neither of them had noticed. All the tables had been pushed to one side except this one, which was laid with a crisp white cotton cloth, champagne flutes and a tea-light candle in a silver holder flickering away.

'This is the perfect backdrop for the news report. All you have to do is sit down at the table, enjoy a meal and look like you're in love.'

'And they call this work?' joked Ella, grinning at Roman. 'So you're telling me I'm getting paid to go on a pretend romantic date with a gorgeous man and eat the best food prepared by Gianni. I think I can do that!'

'I'll second that.' Roman smiled, thankfully looking a

little more relaxed. He folded up the envelope and slipped it into his pocket.

'I knew they would be up for it.' Callie clapped her hands together. 'I've cleared everything with Flynn too, so you don't need to worry, Roman. Wilbur has already set sail to Heartcross and we should be all finished here by the time the boat is due to leave again.'

Even though Roman had received a written warning, Ella could see no one was treating him any differently. They were all so fond of him and he was part of The Lakehouse community, but if Roman wouldn't open up to Flynn about why he was late for work, Flynn really had no alternative, he had to put his business first.

'Okay, let's get you seated,' announced Nancy. 'And look happy. I want you dreamy-eyed and pretend the cameras aren't there. It's as easy as that.'

Ella beamed as a make-up artist appeared from nowhere and began to powder her face. 'Just taking away the shine for the cameras,' she said, turning towards Roman who immediately put up his hand.

'Not for me, I really don't mind looking shiny,' he said, clearly horrified by the idea of wearing make-up.

'I think a little bit of blusher to those cheeks would do you the world of good,' teased Ella, making her way to the table.

'I think you shouldn't think,' he joked, pulling out a chair for Ella to sit down on.

'And what impeccable manners you have. Thank you.' As they both sat down Roman seemed a little more chilled out. Ella was hoping he'd at least have a think about what she'd told him and about the support she had received from Callie – and of course Flynn, who had given her this job. 'What a way to start my first day!'

'A date with me! I'm not sure who's the lucky one – me or you.' Roman's eyes sparkled as Ella caught his eye.

The rooftop terrace was the perfect romantic location. The scenery was breath-taking and the table was all set up for luxury dining. Once the segment aired on the news, surely it would bring in some extra diners.

'We are going to be on the TV,' Ella whispered excitedly. 'Our fifteen minutes of fame… Oh my God, look!' Ella's eyes swept towards the waiter who'd appeared at the top of the stairs holding a silver tray with a colourful array of food. He walked over towards them and placed the tray down on the table. Ella noticed he was dressed in a black suit with a bow-tie and was wearing white gloves. Suddenly she was feeling very regal to be waited on in this way.

'Wow!' Ella's gaze dropped to the food in front of her.

'You have lobster, langoustine, salmon and sorrel ravioli. All the tastes from The Lakehouse bay,' revealed Callie, 'and a bottle of champagne to wash it down with.'

'Perfect,' replied Ella. 'Everything's perfect.' Without thinking, she reached across the table and took Roman's hand. He entwined his fingers with hers and held Ella's gaze and she knew she had a goofy grin on her face.

'I'm not sure we needed to hold hands just yet, the cameras haven't started rolling,' teased Roman.

Ella was caught off guard, it had just felt so natural to reach across the table, and she immediately went to pull back, but Roman kept hold of her hand as they smiled at each other.

'And roll,' ordered Nancy. 'Roman, are you able to pop the champagne cork? Oh, and don't worry about your conversation – that will all be edited out. We just need to see the romantic chemistry fizzing over, just like those champagne bubbles.'

Ella knew they didn't have to pretend – there really was chemistry because the air was charged between them. Roman picked up the bottle of champagne and popped the cork, which launched over the balcony and landed on the golden sand below. Ella giggled, she felt extremely relaxed and comfortable in Roman's company. This actually felt like a proper date and Ella was enjoying every moment.

'I'm having a fantastic time on our pretend date.' Ella tasted the delicious food and brought her hand up to her mouth. 'This tastes amazing.'

With the most gorgeous smile, Roman leant over and filled up her glass. 'Glass of champagne, just for you.' Ella watched him fill up his own glass then clink it against hers. 'Here's to fabulous food, great company and the best date.'

With a pounding heartbeat, Ella knew she had a silly grin on her face, the eye contact between them was strong, their legs touching under the table. The electricity was fizzing between them and Ella wasn't quite sure if they were still pretending, as this all seemed very real to her.

'This footage is amazing,' threw in Nancy from the side-line.

'And this food is the best I've tasted in a while.' Roman made a few approving noises as he waved his fork over his dish.

Ella agreed with Roman – the food was delicious. She remembered her own reaction when she'd first tasted Gianni's food: all the flavours had zinged her taste buds and she'd delved in for a second helping. 'Let's have a toast… to us, a blossoming new friendship,' suggested Ella, holding up her glass.

'To our first date,' replied Roman without hesitation.

Ella scrunched up her face and tilted her head to one side. Either Roman was acting this part well and could possibly be nominated for an Oscar or he actually meant it. 'To our first date,' she repeated, sipping her champagne and placing the flute back on the table, but fully aware that not one drop of alcohol had passed Roman's lips – his glass of champagne was untouched.

After Roman had devoured his food, he placed his knife and fork in the centre of his plate and gave Ella the most adoring smile as he sat back on his chair. When she'd arrived in Heartcross dating had been the last thing on her mind, but now Roman was breaking down those barriers and she really wished she could break down his.

'I'm having the best time,' she said.

'Glad to hear it. My day has definitely improved in the last thirty minutes.' He leant forward and took her hand again, sending shivers down Ella's spine.

'And cut,' shouted Nancy. Immediately Roman dropped Ella's hand as they both looked towards Nancy. 'I think we nearly have what we need,' continued Nancy, hovering at the side of the table. 'What a lovely couple you are! You two represent what this restaurant is all about: fine dining, the best champagne and romance on the roof terrace, but we just need one last shot...' Nancy pointed to the cameraman. 'Alf is going to capture the stunning backdrop, so we would like you to stand up from the table and walk over to the balcony. Roman, if you could stand behind Ella and wrap your arms around her waist and look out over the beautiful bay that would be the perfect frame.'

'I think I can do that,' replied Roman, looking across the table at Ella.

'Okay, on the count of three, if you can stand up,

Roman, pull out Ella's chair and walk over to the balcony, hand in hand. 'One... two... three...'

Looking out to the bay, Roman stood behind Ella. Feeling his presence so close to her, Ella's whole body was trembling. She could feel his breath on her neck and every inch of her body erupted in goose bumps. As she looked upwards over her shoulder, their eyes stayed locked, neither of them faltered. Roman dipped his head slightly, their lips were centimetres apart.

'Cut! It's a wrap!' shouted Nancy, causing Ella and Roman to jump.

'And that's that, our pretend date is over,' she murmured, still staring into his eyes. They pulled away from each other slowly then turned round and walked towards Nancy and Callie.

'All the footage looks amazing, so natural,' announced Nancy, 'there's so much we can use on the news reports. Thank you both. Tune in tonight at six o'clock.' And with that Nancy and the TV crew headed back down the stairs.

Callie was looking at them both in amusement.

'What?' asked Ella, knowing exactly why Callie was looking at them in that way.

'I'm saying absolutely nothing, and it sounds like you will both get your fifteen minutes of fame, but in the meantime, we need to bring you back down to planet earth and get you back on the restaurant floor,' said

Callie, checking her watch, 'and Roman, if you can take over from Wilbur, the boat is due back soon.'

After Callie had disappeared down the stairs back into the restaurant, Ella turned towards Roman. 'I have to say, that was the best pretend date I've ever been on.'

'Me too, and I wasn't even stung for the bill.'

Ella swiped his arm playfully.

'You better get back to work before we're both on a written warning.'

Even though Roman was making a joke, Ella could hear the worry etched in his voice. 'Back to reality.'

'Unfortunately,' he replied.

When Ella was halfway down the stairs she remembered she'd left her apron on the spare table and quickly hurried back up to the balcony. As she stepped back on to the rooftop, she saw Roman was staring out over the bay holding his glass of champagne in his hand, which surprised Ella. Roman hadn't even attempted to drink it at the table. She watched in silence as he poured the drink away into the plant pot in the corner of the balcony whilst muttering something under his breath.

Without a sound she reached for her apron and quietly padded back down the stairs. Why would he do that? He could have just left it on the table. Ella thought back to the appointment card and began to wonder. Maybe Roman was a recovering alcoholic and didn't want the world and their wife to know his business, especially his employers, but she wouldn't know as Ella still had no clue about his life or how he ended up in Heartcross. All she could do was hope that Roman would open up about his past before it affected his future.

Chapter Nine

'Dolores, you're home!'

After being tipped off by Hamish that Dolores had arrived back from hospital that afternoon, Ella knocked on her front door then let herself in. As Ella stepped into the hallway she was relieved to hear the music filtering from the record player and Dolores belting out a tune. Things were back to normal.

'Dolores, it's me!' Ella called out again. Stepping into the living room, she could see McCartney was back where he belonged, curled up on his favourite armchair, whilst Fred looked comical bobbing his head to the beat of the music.

Dolores was far from taking it easy. There she was, standing in the middle of her living room, with her kitten heels on and her hair bouncing down her back, holding a broomstick whilst miming to Freddie Mercury.

'There's nothing like taking it easy when you've just come out of hospital.' Ella laughed, standing in the doorway.

'Live every day like it's your last!' exclaimed Dolores, smiling and walking over towards the record player to turn the volume down.

'I wish I had your energy, it's been a busy day,' admired Ella, feeling her feet swelling inside her shoes. Her first day at The Lakehouse had whizzed by, but not without drama. 'But I received my very first tip today, and praise from the boss.'

'That's good going, tell me all about it.'

'I saved The Lakehouse's reputation by killing the food critic with kindness.'

'Better than food poisoning, I suppose,' chuckled Dolores.

'And she went out of her way to give a glowing report to my boss regarding my excellent knowledge on wines and customer service... Between you and me, I had a little knowledge on good wines thanks to my time with Dr Alex James...'

'So it wasn't all bad then,' joked Dolores.

'Dolores! For most of them, I just read out the descriptions from the wine menu, but I must have been convincing.'

'Good girl! Fake it till you make it, has always been one of my favourite sayings... act confident and people believe you know what you're doing.'

'Then I was filmed having a so-called pretend date for the news report going out tonight on the six o'clock news.'

'A pretend date?' quizzed Dolores.

'Yes, a pretend date with Roman, and all I want now is a glass of wine. It's been really hard work today.'

'Sounds like it,' teased Dolores. Walking over to the dresser, she picked up the decanter alongside two glasses and placed them on a tray. 'All I have is sherry.'

'Sherry it is,' replied Ella, watching Dolores pour the drinks then taking a glass of the dark-brown liquid from her. 'Yikes, that has got a kick to it.'

'One glass of the good stuff always makes things seem a little better. Now tell me, who was this food critic?' Dolores settled back in her armchair and rested her feet on the footstool in front of her.

After Ella had told her story about Tiffany, she shared that later that afternoon Flynn had called her into his office to congratulate her on the way she'd handled her.

'She is a difficult critic and customer. Tiffany has crossed Gianni's path many times and usually she has the staff tied up in knots, but the way you handled her was a credit to yourself and to us at The Lakehouse. Your customer service skills were an example to the rest of the staff, and I'm delighted you are on the team. Keep up the good work.' Ella's impression of Flynn made Dolores chuckle as she reached for the remote control.

'It's nearly six o'clock,' said Dolores, switching on the TV.

As usual the news was all doom and gloom. 'And that is the reason I don't watch the news at my time of life, it's depressing. I think at least one day a week it should be law that only joyous news stories can be shared, to give the country a lift,' declared Dolores.

'I think you should run for Prime Minister, you'd get my vote,' replied Ella with a smile, thinking Dolores really did have a point.

'I think I'd do a better job at it too.' Dolores took a swig of her sherry. 'These politicians have no clue these days. They make up the rules, then break them themselves.' She tutted. They watched a couple more reports before the local news was aired, Ella recognising the reporter as soon as she flashed on to the TV screen. 'This is it,' shared Ella excitedly, waving her hand at the TV and wondering whether she was actually going to see herself on the screen.

'Oooh, look at The Lakehouse, it hasn't changed a bit,' Dolores sat up straight and shuffled forward on her chair. The reporter was standing on the jetty with the impressive restaurant behind. 'This place was once full of the rich and famous and often frequented by royalty, and has now been re-opened by property tycoon Flynn Carter. There's only one way in and one way out – by water taxi. The mouth-watering dishes are devoured by diners, and no wonder – cooking up a storm in the kitchen is world-famous chef Gianni... but first, let's take a look back in history.'

They both stared at the screen as a number of old photographs of The Lakehouse flashed up. 'Oh, my days!' exclaimed Dolores. 'I used to know all those people.'

There were images of elegant men and woman sipping cocktails at the bar, others were dining, and then Dolores let out a squeal: 'There's me!' A short clip was shown of Dolores singing on the stage next to the piano. 'I look so... young.'

'You look amazing!' remarked Ella, her eyes wide. The reporter returned to the screen. 'The Lakehouse used to be an exclusive dining experience, with reservations booked for months. And new owner Flynn Carter is well on his way to re-creating the past in the present.'

They cut towards the bar where Flynn was being interviewed about his plans for the future, before the report switched to the stunning scenery outside, the golden sand, the bay with striking white jagged cliffs. The reporter described The Lakehouse as a place of romance and the perfect venue for that special dinner.

Dolores pointed at the screen. 'Look!'

'Oh, my days… there's me!' exclaimed Ella, as she appeared on the screen holding hands across the table with Roman.

'This is the perfect setting for romance,' continued the reporter. 'The Lakehouse has everything, the perfect rooftop terrace, the best champagne and all the food is sourced locally.'

'And that's Roman, the guy who brought you to the hospital?'

Ella nodded, noticing the way he lit up the screen, which didn't go unnoticed by Dolores either.

Dolores raised a perfectly arched eyebrow. 'He is rather handsome too.'

After the news report finished, Ella noticed that Dolores looked a little saddened. 'Those were the days, just the best days.'

'Do you miss those days?' asked Ella, pulling her legs up on the sofa and tucking her feet under herself.

'When you get to my age you miss yesterday… every day.'

'Dolores, I need to ask you something and I'm hoping you'll say yes.'

Dolores placed her glass down on the table. 'Go on.'

'Despite the news report just now, The Lakehouse is actually in trouble… financially. Hopefully, this might generate some business, but Flynn really wants to recreate those days, from the footage we just saw. We need to bring something special to the table to put The Lakehouse back on the map.' Ella had Dolores' full attention. 'I've suggested we hold a very special evening called "A Trip Down Memory Lane with Dolores Henderson". Gianni could prepare the most delicious dishes and after a three-course meal, you and some of the artists from your little black book could come along and perform. The locals could get involved, and maybe we could have a couple of current artists too, and I'm sure Nancy, the director we met today, would get involved with maybe another follow-up feature. Flynn would really love to get the exclusive Thursday nights back. But at the moment the word isn't spreading quickly enough. What do you think?'

Dolores was listening to every word and when Ella had finished there was silence.

'You think it's a bad idea, don't you?'

Much to Ella's relief a huge smile began to spread across Dolores' face. 'Young lady, you had me at "A Trip Down Memory Lane with Dolores Henderson"!'

Ella let out a squeal. 'Are you serious, are you in?' She waited with bated breath.

'Of course I'm in! This is where my career started and, sad as it may be, this is where my career can end… and who doesn't want an opportunity to dress up and perform?'

Ella clapped her hands like a demented sea-lion. 'This is brilliant, are you absolutely sure?'

Dolores held up her glass of sherry. 'Here's to "A Trip Down Memory Lane".'

Ella was up on her feet, engulfing Dolores in a heartfelt hug, before she rang Callie who answered within a couple of rings.

'Everything okay, Ella?' she asked.

'Where are you?'

'I'm still at the restaurant. Why?'

'Is Flynn with you?'

'He is.'

'Put me on speaker,' insisted Ella, feeling her heart pound.

'Done, you're on speaker.'

'I've got news! I'm sitting with Dolores and she has agreed to do "A Trip Down Memory Lane".'

Ella held the phone away from her ear while Callie squealed. 'Thank you, Dolores!'

While Ella was on the phone Dolores stood up and walked over to the bookshelves. She pulled a black book out from the second shelf and then walked back to the armchair and handed it to Ella. 'Everything you need to know is in there, guard it with your life.'

'Dolores, we can't thank you enough, you are a huge part of the history of this place,' chipped in Flynn.

'You're very welcome.' Dolores looked like the cat that had got the cream, her smile was huge.

'What date are we looking at?' asked Ella, knowing this was going to take some organisation to pull it all together.

'How about two weeks, Saturday?' said Flynn. 'Do you think you can pull it off by then? Callie and I will get on to the TV news people, we can upload news about the event on Facebook, Twitter and all the social media channels. If you can organise the artists, you will need to think about timings, how long is each one going to perform?'

Ella gulped, two weeks on Saturday – that was going to take some organising.

'Two weeks?' Ella was suddenly feeling overwhelmed and was looking for reassurance.

Which she received immediately from Callie: 'Yes, two weeks – you can do this!'

Ella was on a roll. 'Flynn, I've just had another idea, how about getting the locals involved? Maybe throughout the night they can share their own memories of The Lakehouse, making them feel more connected to the place? I can ask them for any old photos, maybe video footage? It shouldn't be too hard to organise.' Ella knew she was babbling but she had lots of ideas whizzing around in her mind and couldn't wait to get started.

'Ella, you're a genius!' bellowed Flynn. 'Let's get this show on the road.'

As soon as Ella hung up the phone, she had mixed feelings of excitement and trepidation. It was going to take a lot of hard work to pull this off, but she was going to give it everything she'd got.

'You've made their day.' Dolores grinned at Ella, opening the black book. 'All the names no longer with us are crossed out and the rest are still contactable.'

Ella's eyes widened. 'Dolores, look at all the famous names in here!'

'My whole life is in that book.' She held up the decanter. 'Another tipple?'

Ella shook her head. 'I'd best not, I've got a lot of organising to do.' She gripped the book. 'And I will guard this with my life.'

'You have, and I've only got two weeks to pick my outfit, and that will take a lot of planning.'

The last thing on Ella's mind was her own outfit. She had a star-studded bash to organise and she knew just the man who could help her... Roman. Ella knew she had brilliant organisational skills and could pull the night together, but what she was unsure about was all the technical stuff – microphones, amplifiers and instruments. She knew she had a lot to learn in the next two weeks, but she was ready for it.

Slipping the black book into her bag, Ella thanked

Dolores and stood outside on the pavement whilst she rang for a taxi. She was going to take the bull by the horns and go over and see Roman straight away. She was eager to get the ball rolling and knew she was capable of making this the best night ever. She kept her fingers crossed that Roman would agree to help.

Eloise had stood outside the reception whilst she waited for a reply. She was going to take the lead and go back and go over and see Rochford until soon. She was aside from the ball where and knew she would shortly be matron but she had motioned and sent her messages at that Rochford would meet to help.

Chapter Ten

Climbing into the taxi, Ella wished she'd had Roman's number. Now she was travelling through the streets of Glensheil, she wasn't sure how he was going to react to her turning up unannounced, but she was just too excited to wait until tomorrow. Ella took in the view as the taxi turned off the main road and before she knew it, the river was back in sight. She could see the water taxi in the distance and knew Roman wasn't on shift tonight. Ella smiled as she recognised the road and she was hoping Roman would be as excited as she was about the event.

'If you could just drop me here please,' asked Ella, feeling the taxi slow down as the driver indicated and pulled up at the side of the road. After paying, she stood for a moment and took a breath. Arriving outside his beautiful home, her feet echoed over the wooden bridge that led to the path of his garden, which Ella noticed was very well maintained. The property had such stunning views, and for a second she watched a couple of swans gliding through the water, and a mallard with its brown speckled plumage, bobbing its head under the water. It was all so very peaceful. 'What an amazing view to wake up to each day,' she murmured.

Walking up to the duck-egg blue wooden back door, she rapped lightly and waited. Through the panes of glass, she noticed two suitcases with a small holdall placed on top. Ella heard a door shut inside followed by footsteps, and she locked eyes with Roman through the glass as he walked through the kitchen towards her. Immediately Ella noticed his bloodshot eyes and knew he was upset.

'What are you doing here? Is everything alright?' he asked, staring at Ella as he turned the key and opened the door.

'I'm just about to ask you the same thing. Are you okay? You look kind of distressed.'

'Far from okay – end of my tether, to be honest.' Roman sounded fraught. 'And I just don't know what to do anymore.'

Ella could see that Roman was nearly at breaking

point. 'It looks like I've arrived at the right time, a friend in need and all that.'

Roman opened the door wide and Ella immediately noticed that he was wearing a wedding ring, and that really was a shock to her system. Not once had Roman ever hinted he was married, and she'd only discovered Megan existed by accident. She felt hurt that he'd kept such an important piece of information from her, especially when she thought they had a connection and she knew that hadn't been all one-sided. Almost immediately she felt that slumping sensation in the pit of her stomach... uncertainty about everything. A feeling she just couldn't cope with anymore. Then her eyes veered back to the two suitcases standing in the hallway.

'Are you going somewhere?'

'No, I'm not,' he replied, immediately picking up his phone as it rang. 'Have you seen her?' he asked the caller. 'Do you know where she is?' Roman was frantic, raking a hand through his hair. He seemed at his wits' end, and the second he hung up the call he began to pace up and down the hallway.

Ella took hold of his arm. 'I'm going to make you a drink,' she said, taking control and shutting the door behind her.

'Tea is really not going to help me.' He blew out a breath. 'I've just got no one left to call now. No one has seen her.'

'Seen who?'

Roman stared into Ella's eyes.

'Roman, who?'

'Megan, she's gone again.'

'Gone where?'

'I don't know, probably Edinburgh, but I can't take much more. The way she's going, she'll end up dead.'

'Let's go and sit down,' Ella said with authority and Roman didn't object. She followed him down the hallway into an impressive living room that looked like it could be featured in *Scottish Life*.

In each alcove at the side of the striking fireplace were shelves spilling over with books. There was a cosy two-seat settee and leather wingback armchairs placed at either end of the coffee table in front of the log fire, which was currently kicking out some heat. There was also a dresser full of photographs.

Ella swallowed down a lump as she picked up a photograph of a younger-looking Roman with his arms around a girl. 'I didn't know you were married.' Ella cast a glance towards his ring and put the photograph back. 'Why would you keep that from me? I've not got a clue what's going on here, Roman, but I felt something between us and I thought you did too. There's something going on in your life that you won't talk about, but after everything I've been through, you just need to be honest because I've had a bellyful of lies and secrecy – enough to last me a lifetime. I just don't understand why you wouldn't have said you have a wife, a daughter. I actually came here to ask you to work on a new project with me, but all this is just a little too much.' Ella stood up.

'Please don't go. I'm not married. I'm really not. Please sit down.'

Ella sat back down and watched Roman remove the ring from his finger and place it in the middle of the table.

'I'm not making a fool out of you; you are the first person who has brought a smile to my face and made me think about life again in a really long time. I don't go buying hot chocolate with all the trimmings just for anyone, you know.' Ella knew that Roman was trying to lighten the mood. 'But you were right, I'm at breaking point and I need help. I just can't hold it together anymore, and today is really not a good day for me.'

There was a calmness to Roman's voice which Ella wasn't expecting. 'Heartcross was a new start for me too.' He took a breath. 'But it's all spiralling out of control now.' Roman stood up and picked up the same photograph that Ella had looked at and placed it down on the table next to his wedding ring. Ella could see his hand shaking as he brushed away a tear from his eye.

She didn't say a word but she leant forward and put a hand on his knee.

'What is it, Roman?' Her voice was soft.

He blew out a breath. 'I was getting married, hence the ring, but we never quite made it to the altar.' Roman's voice faltered but he carried on. 'Hattie and I met at school, we were childhood sweethearts, inseparable. We had grand plans to live in a mansion with an army of children running around our ankles. Hattie got pregnant at sixteen, before we'd even started college. At first our parents were mortified, telling us how stupid we were, how our lives were ruined, but Hattie and I stuck to our guns and we had a beautiful baby girl, Megan.' He took a breath. 'At first we lived with Hattie's parents who were worth their weight in gold. They helped us with the baby and when we were eighteen I proposed. We couldn't afford a lavish wedding, just a small group of family and best friends. I forfeited my stag do to look after Megan and encouraged Hattie to go out with her friends, as her favourite local band was playing at the pub. I didn't mind – I just wanted her to have fun, as she worked so hard looking after our daughter.'

Ella was still listening intently and could see that Roman was building up to something. He picked up the wedding ring and put it in the palm of his hand then squeezed it tight.

'That night, Hattie got drunk, and I mean drunk like I'd never seen from her before. She rolled in and literally collapsed in bed. We were all staying at her parents' house but that night I took Megan to the spare room so we didn't disturb Hattie. In the morning, Hattie's mum was cursing her for being late getting up, and I had to go to work, but I was hanging on just to give Hattie another five minutes, as I knew she would have the hangover from hell, and looking after a two-year-old all day wasn't going to be any fun.'

Roman squeezed his eyes shut. 'I was changing Megan when I heard her mum scream. I'll never ever forget that moment. I walked into the room…' The tears were freefalling down Roman's face now, but he took a breath and continued. 'Hattie was lying on the bed, still wearing her clothes from the night before. During the night she'd vomited and must have choked. She was already gone when we found her… If I had stayed in the same room as her that night, I could have helped her. She might still be here today.' Roman was distraught. 'It never gets any easier talking about it. And I didn't want to talk about it, but today's just brought all those memories back to the surface again.'

Ella was stunned. The knot in her stomach was twisting. She could see the bottom had fallen out of Roman's world, and she didn't know what to do or say. She moved closer to him and held him tightly as he cried.

'I'm so sorry, this is awful,' she murmured. There were just no words that could make this situation any better, it was so utterly heart-breaking. She held him until he pulled away,

'And that's the reason I don't drink. Not a drop has passed my lips since that day. Alcohol killed Hattie.'

'I saw you pour the champagne away… into the pot plant, of all places.' Ella squeezed his knee. 'But what I don't understand is what's happening now.'

'Megan is what's happening now and she's out of control. I feel a failure as her dad, just saying that.'

'You aren't a failure, I'm sure you're a wonderful dad.'

'I wanted to handle it on my own. What's happening now is Megan's business but I'm at a loss as to how to support her. I have got outside help… from Oasis Lodge. It's Megan who has the problem with alcohol, not me – and that's probably all my fault too. I brought Megan up as a single father and with my job, we were on the road a lot. She was surrounded mostly by hard-drinking men, no mother figure in her life; and yes, she skipped a lot of school, but I had no choice.

'I was good at my job and it paid well, but on the road, Megan started pinching booze backstage from as early as thirteen, and I had no clue. She technically left school at sixteen and came on the road with me full time, wanting to learn about the business, but that environment wasn't good for her and soon the booze became her life. She wouldn't listen to me when I told her how booze killed her mother, she just rebelled even more.

'That's why I gave up the job and moved here. I brought her with me, but the situation has got worse, she's blaming me for leaving her friends behind, she can't even hold down a job, due to drink. The boat job is perfect, it's a steady income, and I'm off the road and can keep a closer eye on Megan. But that's proving rather difficult when she gives me the run-around, and that's exactly what she did today. That's why I was late for work.'

'What happened this morning?' asked Ella.

'Today, she should have gone into rehab for four weeks. Between myself and her counsellor, she finally acknowledged that she has an unhealthy relationship with alcohol, and I managed to secure a place at the Lodge for her, but then I woke up and she'd gone AWOL. She's stolen money from me, my iPad has gone, and I spent all morning looking for her and lost track of time.'

'And you've not heard from her since?'

Roman shook his head. 'I've rung everyone I know and no one has seen her. Usually I would have heard something by now from someone.'

'So what can we do?'

'We?'

'Exactly that, *we* – a problem shared and… and I really don't know what to say. We've both been through the mill, but what I would suggest is, be open with Flynn. Tell him what's going on. He's not going to judge you, and you need that job. Then we'll make a plan to find Megan.'

Roman didn't speak. He picked up the ring and the photograph and walked over to the dresser. For a second he stared at the ring in his hand, then placed it safely back in a drawer alongside the photograph.

'I will talk to Flynn. I suppose I felt ashamed – I wasn't in control and I felt a failure. I love Megan so much and she reminds me a lot of her mother, and all I want to do is protect her – which is ironic, really, when it was me who put her in an environment that was laden with booze.'

'You were just trying to survive, be a single father, earn a salary with a job that you loved.'

'I'm so sorry, Ella,' Roman sat back down next to her.

'You have nothing to be sorry for.'

'When you stood up before and were about to leave, I couldn't let you. I knew I had to swallow my pride and let down my guard. There was something about you that morning when we met, an instant connection. I knew we were going to be good friends, and hearing your story, I knew it must be hard to open up. But it made me see you were trustworthy, and it's been a long time since I've trusted anyone or been close to anyone. I never thought I was worthy.'

Ella was close to tears. Roman was wearing his heart on his sleeve and it had taken a lot for him to open up. 'You *are* worthy – more than worthy – and we are both here for the same reasons, to move on and have a fresh start. I'm here to help, and I know it's difficult for you, but with a father as good as you, Megan will come good. Just believe.'

Ella held out her arms and they hugged each other tightly. 'We're a right pair,' she said.

'And I mean it when I say thanks – you've talked some sense into me. Something had to give.'

'You don't need to thank me.'

'Why did you come tonight?' Roman asked, checking his phone, but he had no new messages.

'Because I need your help.'

Roman raised an eyebrow. 'That sounds intriguing. Shall I make us a drink and you can tell me all about it? It'll keep my mind occupied.'

Ella knew his thoughts had turned back to Megan. 'How long does she normally go missing for?'

'It depends. Usually days, but today I hoped we would get up and I'd drive her to the centre and in four weeks' time we would all be in a better place. I know it's selfish to say, but it would give me a rest too. I would know exactly where she is, and more than likely I'd get a good night's sleep. The other problem is, she's classed as an adult, so as much as I love her, she is her own person and I have no control over that. She's more than likely gone back to Edinburgh. She worries me sick.'

Hearing her phone ring, Ella saw Callie's name flashing up on the screen. 'I'll just take this. It's only Callie, she's probably telling me she's staying at work a little longer.'

'Hi Cal,' answered Ella, taking the call. 'The news report was fab, wasn't it?… Yes. I'm actually with Roman now… why?'

Ella looked towards Roman. 'Okay, we are on our way. It looks like Roman has the speedboat docked outside, we can use that.'

Ella hung up and looked at Roman. 'Don't panic, but Megan isn't in Edinburgh. She's been drinking and has been a little loud over at The Lakehouse.'

'You're kidding me?!' Roman was up on his feet. 'That's my livelihood! I'm hanging on to my job by a thread as it is.'

'Apparently, according to Callie, she's gone in shouting the odds and has upset a few diners, and Flynn was about to ring the police when she made a comment about her dad working there.'

Roman was already reaching for his house keys. 'This is typical of Megan, doesn't give a damn about anyone…'

Ella could see that Roman was getting angry and she

took hold of his hands. 'And breathe… Don't go shouting or losing your temper, she needs our help. Let's stay calm, get Megan calm, and fingers crossed, her place is still available at Oasis Lodge. This isn't Megan, it's the alcohol. It's an addiction. Okay?'

Roman nodded. 'I just want my girl back, I just don't recognise her at all.'

'And she will come back, but what she needs is support, not anger. Let's stay calm.'

Roman exhaled loudly. 'I'll do my best.'

'Good, because that's all any of us can do.'

———————————

As the speedboat bounced over the waves, they arrived at The Lakehouse in record time. Callie was looking out at the entrance of the restaurant and hurried down the jetty towards them.

'What's going on? Where's Megan?' asked Ella.

'We aren't quite sure. Flynn asked her to leave because she was causing a scene. Honestly, we weren't aware she was your daughter, Roman. The boat was about to leave so Wilbur agreed to sail her back to Heartcross, but then she started shouting in the restaurant, staggering between the tables, and a couple of glasses were broken. Flynn was in the middle of an important business meeting when Megan started shouting about her dad working here, and that's when we realised.'

Roman exhaled loudly. 'I'm so sorry Callie, I don't know what to say, I really don't.'

'All I can say is Flynn's not best pleased; he can't have scenes like this in restaurant. We are trying to build up the reputation of The Lakehouse, not cause any more bad press. He wants to see you.'

Ella looked towards Roman. 'You go and see Flynn and explain the situation – and I mean the *whole* situation.'

'What's going on?' asked Callie, looking between the pair of them. 'What situation?'

'Roman just needs to speak to Flynn first,' Ella placed her hand in the small of his back. 'You go.' She looked back towards Callie. 'So did Megan get on the boat?'

Callie shook her head. 'No, I got a glimpse of her literally a moment ago over the far end of the bay. I was about to go after her when I saw you arrive.'

'I'll go and see if I can find her, and Roman – go and talk to Flynn!'

Roman hesitated. 'Sometimes she may be a little aggressive, I'm not sure…'

'I'll be fine, honestly,' reassured Ella.

Ella watched as Roman and Callie disappeared back inside The Lakehouse before she set off walking to the far end of the bay. Feeling a little apprehensive, she didn't know what she was going to say or how Megan was going to react. Ella had never been in a situation like this before. As she turned the next corner, she immediately spotted Megan sitting on a rock. She was leaning on her knees, hunched over.

'Megan, hi. I'm Ella, I've just come to see if you're okay,' Ella said softly, slowly walking towards her.

Megan looked up, startled. There was a pool of sick splattered on the rock in front of her and she started to heave again.

'I'm here to help you, I'm a friend of your dad's.'

Megan didn't say a word, just carried on retching. Her cheeks were blackened by her mascara, her eyes were bloodshot, and she really didn't look in the best way.

'Here.' Ella handed Megan a clean tissue from her bag. Megan took it without making any eye contact with her.

Ella crouched not far from the side of her. 'I hear you're not having the best of days. I've been having one of those years until recently. I think you and I have a lot in common. Do you mind if I sit?'

Megan looked up for a brief moment. 'If you want.'

Ella kept her voice calm, but inside she was on tenterhooks and her heart was racing as she sat on a nearby rock. 'I miss my parents,' shared Ella, 'every day, like you wouldn't believe. Both of them died the same day. One minute they were here, and the next...' Ella swallowed down a lump in her throat and noticed Megan looking over in her direction. 'What I would give to see them one last time, have one more conversation with them. At first there was only one way to block out the pain, and that was drink.' She took a breath. 'One drink, turned into two, then three... and before I knew it, it just became the norm, until I met a man who I thought cared for me. I began to feel happier in my life because I had something... someone... to focus on, and I was lucky that the drink took a back seat. However, that's only the start of my story.'

'Why, what happened to you?' asked Megan, engaging in the conversation for the first time.

'Well, the man I thought cared for me was a crook; he stole my inheritance from my deceased parents. After he left I rotted away in bed for six months, I didn't get dressed, didn't bother to look after myself, and it was only when I knew I couldn't keep on punishing myself and I swallowed my pride, that I got the help I needed.'

'Help?'

'Heartcross... Callie. I think you've just met Callie, she's the restaurant manager. She brought me here for a fresh start, and so I moved miles, all the way from Cheshire. She gave me a home and a job and helped me to pick myself up. You moved too, didn't you? That must have been difficult.'

Megan nodded and tilted her face upwards. She didn't speak but Ella noticed her eyes gleamed with tears. 'It was,' she said finally.

'I know it doesn't seem like it now, but your dad brought you here for all the right reasons. He loves you and wants to help you. Just think about letting him help you. You still have each other, and what I would give to have my parents still with me.'

Megan looked over again and wiped the tears with the back of her hand. 'I don't even like myself when I drink.' She retched once more and Ella moved closer and gathered up her hair as Megan vomited again. Ella gently rubbed her back and noticed movement behind her. She looked over her shoulder to see Roman walking towards them. Ella gave him a reassuring smile that said everything was okay and calm.

'Here's your dad now. I'll leave you two alone.' Ella stood up and took a step towards Roman. 'How did it go?'

'I told Flynn everything and he was really understanding. He's told me to do what I need to do and my job is still there.'

'See, I told you, being honest and open is always the best policy. I'll meet you back at the restaurant. Megan is calm but feels a little sick. Take it easy on her.'

'Thank you, Ella – I mean that.' He touched her arm before walking towards Megan.

Ella watched from afar as Roman bent down next to his daughter and opened his arms wide. Megan fell into them. Somehow she'd lost her way, but looking at the way they were hugging each other tight, Ella was sure everything was going to be okay.

Chapter Eleven

'How are you doing?' asked Ella, handing Roman a cup of tea. 'Did you sleep?'

Roman sat down on the settee. 'It's the first night I've slept well in ages. When I woke, I felt a sense of calm – and that's all down to you.'

Flynn had given Roman a couple of days off work to get himself rested and gather his own thoughts. Roman was relieved at how understanding Flynn was when he'd shared his life story with him, and Roman wished he'd been honest from the start.

'But what I want to know is, what did you say to Megan?'

'Nothing much, I just pointed out the obvious.'

'You mean you aren't going to tell me? What

happened to being honest and open at all time?' he teased.

Ella knew she'd struck a chord with Megan when she'd shared her own story. They had something in common, yet they were worlds apart. Ella had memories of her own parents which helped her to get through the grieving process. She could remember their smiles, their laughter, their scents – but then everything was taken away from her in an instant. She couldn't have one last conversation, she couldn't tell them how much she loved them, she was all on her own and she would do anything to spend one more day with them.

Megan was hurting and though she didn't have any memories of her mother to cling on to, her grief still tortured her every day. The only way she could find to block out that pain was to drink. Ella thought about Roman, how much he loved her but how much he was also hurting, blaming himself for the past, tormenting himself that he wasn't a good father. What if something happened to either of them and they were the only one left in the world? Each of them needed to see their own self-worth. Roman needed to stop feeling guilty about the night Hattie died, and Megan needed to learn to love herself again. Both of them had agreed to have joint counselling, after Megan's stay in the Oasis Lodge was completed, to help each other.

'Sometimes, when someone who isn't close to the

situation gives advice, people listen.'

'I just hope these next four weeks work their magic and the programme is successful.'

'It will be – have faith,' Ella said gently.

'I just need to keep myself distracted, sail my boat, but I'll be doomed if The Lakehouse doesn't pick up business soon,' Roman said with a weary sigh.

'Well, I have the very thing to keep you distracted.' Ella grinned. With everything that had happened last night, she hadn't got round to telling Roman about the star-studded bash at The Lakehouse. And with everything Roman was going through, Ella was even more determined to make this event a success. He was relying on his job and what he needed right now was a break. Ella was just about to tell Roman all about 'A Trip Down Memory Lane' when her mobile rang.

'Do you need to get that?' he asked.

It was only Callie. If it was important, she'd leave a message. 'It's fine – my voicemail will catch it.'

The phone rang off then almost immediately rang again.

'Someone wants you. Honestly, take the call.'

Her conversation with Callie left Ella feeling breathless with a flutter of excitement. This week was really turning into a week of highs and lows. She closed her eyes briefly to digest the information.

'What is it?' asked Roman. 'Is it good news?'

Ella sucked in a huge breath. 'Oh my God, it's very good news. Nancy the TV director is coming back to The Lakehouse tomorrow to interview me.' She was talking so fast, she was tripping over her own words.

Roman looked puzzled. 'Why?

Quickly rummaging in her bag, Ella took out Dolores' little black book and handed it over to Roman. 'Take a look – go on, open it.'

Ella watched his face as he opened it up. The book went back years, naming every artist that had ever performed at The Lakehouse, alongside nearly every famous person in the music industry.

'Bloody hell, Ella, where did you find this?'

'It's Dolores'. She kept it for all these years and in two weeks' time The Lakehouse is going to hold the most prestige event... "A Trip Down Memory Lane with Dolores Henderson and Guests", and I am organising the whole event.'

Roman looked as excited as Ella felt. 'Tell me more.'

Ella told Roman all about Dolores being discovered at The Lakehouse, and how it had launched her career. 'Flynn is hoping, with the publicity regarding Dolores, he can turn The Lakehouse around, remind people about the history of the place and jog people's memories about how fabulous the restaurant is, and fingers crossed, word will spread like wildfire. Everyone loves to star-spot whilst they're out and about, and if Joe Blogs off the street thinks he might see his idol… well, hopefully they will book The Lakehouse.'

'I think you are all on to something.' Roman looked impressed. 'This could put The Lakehouse back on the map.'

'The locals are also going to get involved with their own memories, maybe a screen in the background with old photos etc. There's just one catch, though…'

'Which is?'

'It's in two weeks' time.' Roman let out a low whistle. 'Good luck with that, it's a huge job that'll take some doing, but you'll be great.'

'I don't want to be just great; I would prefer to be brilliant, but I could only see that happening if I had someone on board who actually knows what they're doing.' Ella scrunched up her eyes and put her hands together in a prayer-like gesture. Daring to peep through one eye, she saw Roman smiling back at her.

'Is that a yes? Please tell me it's a yes! It will be a very good distraction for you too.' Ella tilted her head to one side and waited with bated breath.

'This is a difficult event to pull off in such a short amount of time. These artists have busy lives, schedules etc. and some may need to reshuffle. There are sound checks, the dress rehearsal… I could go on.'

'Most of them will be retired, if not all.'

'And these are the artists' direct numbers?'

'I'm assuming they are... So is that a yes then? Will you help me? Please!'

Roman flicked through the book and looked towards Ella. 'This could be the greatest star-studded event ever. Have you seen the contacts in this book?'

Ella was liking the sound of that. 'I have... so...' She circled her hand to hurry up Roman's answer.

'I'm in,' he confirmed, with a wide smile.

Ella squealed and flung her arms around him and hugged him tight. 'Thank you, thank you. I can't believe this. Eek! Where do we begin?'

Roman rolled his eyes. 'You won't be this excited when the hard work begins. First things first, let's celebrate. Have you got any lemonade?'

'I have indeed,' replied Ella, fetching a bottle from the fridge and two glasses.

'Then let's get to work, the clock is ticking. Firstly, we need to work out timings. What time will the first artist take to the stage etc., and what time Flynn wants the night to end? Have you eaten?' Roman asked, thinking out loud and looking at his watch. 'I skipped breakfast.'

It was fast approaching midday and Ella shook her head. 'I can prepare my signature dish and then we can get cracking. Let's see if we can secure any names before my interview with Nancy tomorrow, that'll help to create a buzz.' Ella stood up and headed towards the door. 'There's a pen and pad over on the desk, grab those and we can start looking through the names and making a few calls.'

Ella couldn't believe this was happening. She'd literally only just arrived in Heartcross and now she was being given the responsibility of organising this event. Even though it was completely throwing her in at the deep end, she was going to take this opportunity with both hands and show everyone that Ella Johnson could pull this off. She was going to make sure this night would go down in history.

'By the way, what is your signature dish?' Roman shouted after her.

'Beans on toast,' she replied.

'My absolute favourite!'

They caught each other laughing as Ella popped her head back around the door.

'Oh, and Ella…'

'Yes?'

'Thank you, this is just what I need to see me through the next few weeks.'

As she disappeared back into the kitchen, Ella felt a kind of warmth flush through her body. She had one agenda for the next two weeks – organising the star-studded event and keeping Roman occupied as much as she could, to get him through his time without Megan. Hopefully then they could both get their lives back on track.

Chapter Twelve

Ella hadn't wanted last night to end. After working all afternoon at her flat they'd headed over to Roman's house and before they knew it, it was already past 9pm. They'd spent time talking with Gianni, discussing a possible menu and the overall timing of the food. As soon as they had that all worked out they set to work on the line-up of the evening.

Like a pro, Roman had brought in a flip-chart from his office and Ella listened to all of Roman's advice about what they needed to do to make this night a success.

They scanned over each page of Dolores' book and made a list of potential artists. Ella recognised a few names that Dolores had mentioned during their conversations. 'Blossom Rose is a must.' Ella twizzled the book towards Roman and tapped the name. 'Blossom was with Dolores when she first got discovered. Fingers crossed she's in good health and will be able to make it. And there's Frank Divine, he was the one who pulled Dolores up on stage and got her recognised.'

Flynn jotted the names down on the flip-chart alongside their numbers.

'Who else?'

'Gracie Davies was always a regular at The Lakehouse, put her name on the list too.'

For the whole time Ella was working alongside Roman, she had a smile on her face that couldn't be contained and warmth radiated through her body. She was enjoying every second of planning this event.

After an hour they had a long list of potential names scrawled on the pad in front of them. 'There's way too many names there, all those people would fill a festival,' remarked Ella.

'You're right, but what we do is start at the top. I've tried to list them in some sort of order. We need to focus on the ones who performed with Dolores or had a connection to The Lakehouse in some way. We need to see the magic working between all these people. Some of these names may already have commitments, so we make the first call outlining the event, giving them all the details, when and where etc., and if they are available. Then we look back through the list. We have to decide how many songs they might sing, would they sing a duet with Dolores, what's the meaning behind the song, what's the relevance to the night? Everything has got to be right.'

Ella's head was whirling. She blew out a breath. 'It's like a military operation.'

'Exactly. I have contacts, which means I can get my hands on all the equipment we'll need, microphones… speakers. That won't be a problem.'

As Ella flicked through the book one last time, she saw a name she must have missed before. 'And whoever Charlie Love is, there is a big heart around his name, so my guess is he's a major player in this event. It looks like Dolores thinks very highly of him.'

'Maybe it's linked to his name: love… heart.'

'Oh yes! Well put him down. If nothing else, he's got a very cool name.'

They both looked at the flip-chart again. 'That's it, I think we've got our first list.' Roman stood back and placed the marker pen on the table.

'I can't thank you enough, I wouldn't have had a clue where to start.'

Roman tapped the flip-chart with his pen, then pointed at Ella. 'Start at the top and get ringing.'

Ella looked alarmed and immediately brought her hands up to her chest. 'M-me?' she stuttered. 'I can't go talking to any of these people. I just couldn't, I'd be too star struck. And why are you grinning at me?'

'Because you can and you will. I'm willing to help with all the technical stuff, but you're in full control of organising the guests.'

Ella watched as Roman walked over towards the dresser and picked up the landline. 'Here, it's still early. Let's see if we can get any firm yeses before your TV interview tomorrow, because that will really get the publicity wheel turning.'

'But Roman…'

Thinking back to last night, Ella found herself grinning as she made breakfast. She'd enjoyed spending time with Roman and she chuckled to herself as she remembered ordering him out of his very own living room whilst she rang the first number on the list.

'And you are grinning because…?' Callie walked into the kitchen and narrowed her eyes.

'Because I've had the best night, and preparations are already underway for the big event. We already have confirmed artists that will knock everyone's socks off…'

'We?' asked Callie, switching on the kettle.

'Roman is helping to organise the technical stuff. Honestly, I've learnt so much about event management in the last twenty-four hours! I absolutely loved it, even though I was extremely nervous when I was talking to the artists, but everyone was so kind. Today's plan is, after speaking with Dolores and Nancy, I'm going to upload a post on to the village community group page on Facebook, asking them to get involved with their own memories.'

'You've got it all in hand.' Callie looked impressed. 'Maybe there's a permanent job in this event planning but for all of Flynn Carter's business empire.'

'Wouldn't that be brilliant! Am I right in thinking that Flynn agreed this would be my job for the next couple of weeks, so I didn't have to waitress?'

'Yes, he wants you to concentrate on this entirely,' replied Callie, drinking her mug of tea quickly. 'I need to get across to the restaurant. I'll see you just after eleven for the filming.' She stood up and slipped her feet into her shoes. 'What are you wearing?'

'I'm not sure.' Ella hadn't thought that far ahead.

'Feel free to have a riffle through my wardrobe.'

'Will do, thank you.'

Ella tucked her legs underneath her on the settee and looked over the confirmed names for the event on the list she'd written down. She already felt a sense of achievement as there were some huge names on here, past and present, and she knew Flynn was going to be amazed. And she couldn't wait to tell Dolores.

As she put the list on the table, she thought back to how well she'd worked with Roman and was happy she was keeping her promise to keep him occupied whilst Megan was away.

Hearing her phone ping, Ella leant over and picked it up from the coffee table. Reading a message from Roman, she smiled. *Won't be sailing the boat this morning as I have the appointment to see how Megan is settling in. Good luck with the interview, and just for the record, Gracie has confirmed.*

What?!?!?! she typed back, her hands visibly shaking. *Am I allowed to mention it in the interview?*

YES! pinged back the reply in shouty capitals. *GO FOR IT!*

Brilliant! PS thinking of you today. Let me know how you get on.

This was amazing! Thinking ahead to her TV interview, Ella couldn't deny she was nervous, but she couldn't wait to share the line-up. All the old artists were coming together to support Dolores and The Lakehouse, and all of them were doing it out of the goodness of their hearts. All she had to do first was pick out her outfit and grab a quick shower. While her phone was in her hand, she quickly typed a message into the Heartcross community WhatsApp group:

Look out for the midday news, where I will be telling you all about 'A Trip Down Memory Lane with Dolores Henderson'! The event will take place at The Lakehouse on

Saturday the 1st, so keep that date free. More details to follow in an update on The Lakehouse Facebook page this afternoon.

Isla was the first to reply: *More details needed. Come on, spill!*

She and Flynn hadn't discussed dress code but Ella wanted it to resemble a glamorous Hollywood film premiere.

Dress code: Black tie and posh frocks! And anyone who has any old photographs of The Lakehouse or any old stories, do share your memories.

Putting her phone down, Ella went to look through Callie's clothes rail. She didn't want to look too formal during her interview or too casual. Glancing out of the window, she noticed the black sky in the distance and within seconds the rain began to pelt against the windowpane, sounding like bullets. Ella pulled out a long woollen coat that crossed over and tied around the waist, and she accessorised it with a beautiful floral blue scarf. There, it didn't matter what she actually wore underneath, this would be perfect, especially with the weather blowing a gale.

After a quick shower and a change of clothes Ella called in to see Dolores on her way out.

'Dolores, you can't eat cake for breakfast!' exclaimed Ella, noticing Dolores tucking into a huge sugary slice of lemon drizzle cake whilst watching the morning news.

Dolores gave Ella a wicked smile. 'At my age I can do whatever I want.'

'Your little black book is like gold dust; the line-up is already amazing and I'm on the news at midday being interviewed about the event. I'm a little nervous but secretly excited.'

'You have confirmed artists already?' Dolores placed down her fork and her eyes widened under her long false lashes.

'I do…' Ella flapped a hand in front of her face. 'And you'll never guess—'

Immediately Dolores held up her hands. 'Don't tell me!' she insisted.

'What do you mean, don't tell you! I'm bursting to tell you.'

'I want to hear it on the news, just like everyone else.'

'Dolores, you've just burst my bubble,' claimed Ella, itching to spill the beans.

But Dolores was adamant. 'I only have a couple of hours to wait.' She sat back in her chair and scooped up another huge forkful of the cake. 'Now go, before you tell me more.'

'Sometimes, Dolores Henderson, you act like a diva.'

'I know, and I should know better at my age.' She gave Ella a wink. 'But do pop back in on your way home. I'm just happy to have the opportunity to perform one last time, and I have you to thank for that.'

As Ella walked on to the High Street, she knew that Dolores really meant that from the bottom of her heart, and it made Ella extremely happy that she could make her last dream come true.

———————

Thirty minutes later, Ella arrived at The Lakehouse. Thankfully the rain had stopped for now but judging by the sky, it wouldn't be for long. She was greeted by Flynn who was amazed to learn that Ella had managed to secure some of the bookings in such a short amount of time.

'You really were the right woman for the job.' He beamed. 'Brilliant work, well done you!'

'I can't take all the credit, Roman helped to organise me,' Ella replied, stepping inside the restaurant and waving at Callie, who was behind the bar as Wilbur was sailing the boat today.

'But you made the phone calls and are making this happen. Nancy is already here. She's ready to roll when you are.'

Nancy was walking towards her holding a large fluffy microphone on a long pole, alongside a cameraman and a news reporter that Ella thought she recognised. 'We meet again so soon, and under very exciting circumstances.' Nancy looked towards Ella then gestured towards the reporter. 'This is Brett McCormick, he will be interviewing you today.'

'Very exciting circumstances,' repeated Ella, nodding a hello to Brett then following Nancy outside to the front of The Lakehouse. Nancy placed Ella with the restaurant directly behind them and the cameraman stepped back and positioned the lens on a tripod.

'We'd really like to be here on the night to film this iconic event and put it out across all the news channels,' said Nancy. 'Hopefully some of the footage can be used in a documentary all about Dolores' career.'

'Are you kidding me?' Ella was completely stunned; she couldn't believe what she was hearing.

Nancy slipped her a card. 'Here's my number, I want to work with you on making the event the best it can be.'

With a shaky hand Ella slipped the card into her pocket. She was actually speechless. Her head was in a whirl. Six months ago, she'd thought her life was over, but now she was standing in front of a news reporter waiting to be interviewed. Flynn and Callie had believed in her and now Ella believed in herself. So much had changed in her life, she was working hard, building a life for herself and she felt proud. Despite all the debts hanging over her, she wasn't going to let them drag her down, she'd moved on. Ella felt positive about her life, and you really didn't know what was around the corner.

'Right, we are good to go,' declared the cameraman.

'Fantastic,' replied Nancy. 'Let's get this done before that rain begins to fall again.'

The nerves were beginning to kick in for Ella now, and feeling a fluttery sensation in her stomach, she took a deep breath and hoped she didn't look as nervous as she felt. Glancing upwards, she noticed Flynn and Callie watching from up on the rooftop, smiling down on her. Ella flapped them away with her hand. 'Go away,' she mouthed at Callie, who gave her the thumbs up then moved back out of sight, so they weren't picked up on the camera.

'Are you ready?' asked Nancy. 'This is live. Don't swear! Try to relax and Brett will lead the way with his questions. Try not to look nervous and don't look directly into the camera.'

Ella nodded.

'And I believe you're ready to share some of the artists' names that have already confirmed?'

'I can.'

Nancy took a step back and lifted her arm in the air then lowered it. 'And... rolling!'

Brett looked directly into the camera whilst Ella was stood by his side.

'Today, we are standing outside The Lakehouse, the world-famous restaurant that was renowned in the past for its exclusive dining of the rich and famous.' Brett took a glance behind him and the camera swung over the restaurant.

'On Saturday the first of November, Dolores Henderson will be performing one last time, right here, alongside a star-studded line-up of artists, to celebrate her career. And to tell us all about it, and how you can get involved, is events co-ordinator Ella Johnson. Is it true that Dolores wakes you up at the crack of dawn, singing as the sun rises?'

Taken aback by her new job title, Ella beamed. The microphone was poised in front of her as she took a deep breath. 'It's very much true, and I can honestly say it's a lovely way to be woken up in the morning. Dolores is an absolute pleasure to have as my neighbour. And now, for one last time, she will be singing here in a very special event.' Once Ella started talking, she felt relaxed and didn't feel nervous at all.

'Are you able to tell us who Dolores' special guests will be on the night?'

'I can.' Ella knew that Dolores would be watching and she hoped that she'd done her proud.

'First she will be joined by Blossom Rose, who was Dolores' best friend and was there at the moment when Dolores was discovered. We will also be joined by Frank Divine, Richie Kirk and Gracie Davies who was a regular alongside Dolores here at The Lakehouse. This is "A Trip Down Memory Lane" that's not to be missed!'

'Thank you for joining me today, Ella.'

'Thank you!' she replied, looking at the camera for the first time.

'"A Trip Down Memory Lane with Dolores Henderson" at The Lakehouse. Tickets go on sale this Friday morning – I think you'll all agree, it's an evening not to be missed.' Brett looked directly into the camera. 'This is Brett McCormick reporting for BBC Scotland at The Lakehouse.'

There were a few seconds of silence, then Nancy shouted. 'It's a rap, they've cut back to the studio.'

Ella exhaled a breath she hadn't realised she'd been holding. The interview had actually gone quite well, and she'd enjoyed every second of it, and as soon as she got into her stride the nerves had evaporated. 'I loved that!'

Callie and Flynn must have been watching the TV in Flynn's office as they soon joined the group outside. 'Look at you, events co-ordinator,' quipped Callie. 'You were amazing – such a natural on screen.'

Quickly Ella turned towards Flynn. 'I didn't just give myself a promotion,' she said, trying to justify the job title. 'Brett just came out with it.' She must have looked stricken because Flynn soon jumped in to put her mind at rest.

'It's absolutely fine, that's exactly what you are, and a well-deserved job title at that – and maybe a pay increase for the next week or two.'

'I'll take that! Thank you,' Ella said, grinning.

After Nancy had finished talking to Brett, she said to Ella. 'You're a credit to this place! On the build-up to the evening we would love to interview yourself and Dolores. If you will have us?'

'Of course!' replied Ella, feeling her self-confidence building. Another interview! She was actually beginning to feel like a superstar herself.

As soon as Nancy and the crew left, Callie opened her arms wide and pulled her friend in for a hug. 'I told you Heartcross would be the making of you – you are shining!'

'And Callie is right, you're worth your weight in gold. This is great publicity for The Lakehouse and we have you and Dolores to thank for it.' Flynn looked down at his phone. 'Notifications are already coming in thick and fast to the Facebook page, and a lot of people are messaging to see if there is a pre-order route for tickets.'

'And listen to that,' remarked Callie. 'The restaurant phone hasn't stopped ringing since the interview aired.'

'Ella, you are magic,' said Flynn before disappearing back inside to take a call.

'The boat's about to leave.' Callie pointed to Wilbur who was about to untie the boat. 'Wilbur… wait,' Callie bellowed down the jetty, and he tipped his cap in acknowledgement. 'What are your plans for the rest of the day?' she asked, turning to Ella.

'I'm meeting Roman to organise what songs the guests are singing, then we can work out the playlist and timings.' Ella checked her watch. 'And I promised Dolores I'd pop back in and see her. I hope she's as happy as Flynn.'

'I'm sure she will be, now run! Wilbur is waiting for you.'

'Thanks, Callie,' Ella said as she turned to her friend.

'What for?'

'For giving me this opportunity. Somehow the past few months are already paling into insignificance.'

As Ella ran up the jetty and jumped on to the boat, she turned back and waved at Callie then sat down and looked out across the bay. She hoped they made it across the water before the rain started to fall again. For the next few days the weather was meant to be on the turn, with heavy rain predicted with storms. Ella was quite relieved she'd be working at home for most of that time, organising the event. Hearing her phone ping, she read a text from Roman. He seemed upbeat in his message, which Ella hoped meant it had gone as well as it could have with Megan this morning. He was meeting her at the flat in twenty minutes' time to discuss the songs each guest would be singing, as well as a conversation about what Dolores meant to them.

PS, I'll pick us up some lunch, came the second text before Ella had a chance to reply to the first.

After last night, Ella knew that she had a hundred and one conflicted feelings about Roman. She knew his life was still unsettled and she would never put any pressure on him, but she knew her feelings were growing deeper for him every day.

Oh, and Charlie Love has also confirmed, add him to the list.

Will do, Ella replied quickly. She had spent some time googling the name that was in Dolores' black book but couldn't find out anything about Charlie Love. Was he a singer, musician or manager? Ella had no idea.

Ella thanked Wilbur as the boat docked, then hurried along the coastal path and up through the village. She dodged the huge dollops of rain that were now falling from the sky and even though the wind was blustery, she felt like she was floating on cloud nine. She couldn't wait to see Dolores and hoped she'd done her proud.

Within five minutes, and now soaked to the core, Ella was knocking on Dolores' door and was greeted by her friend who had a huge beam on her face. 'You, my girl, have excelled yourself. This is going to be the best night of my career.' She helped to peel the sodden coat off Ella's back. 'The storms are coming; go and get warm by the fire whilst I make you a hot drink.'

Ella was thankful as she cupped her hands in front of the fire and was careful not to sit on McCartney who was stretched out on the rug, hogging the warmest spot in the flat right in front of the heat.

'So, you are happy?' shouted Ella above the whistle of the kettle.

'Happy? I feel like I've won the lottery… reunited with all my old friends – this is just going to be sensational.'

'The news team are coming to film on the night and there's a possibility they are going to produce a documentary all about your life.'

Dolores' eyes widened. 'All off the back of performing at The Lakehouse? Wow!' She handed Ella a hot mug of tea. 'That'll warm you up.'

'You are an icon, and you are going down in history! Oh, and we've had one more confirmation, Charlie Love. He was in your book, with a huge heart. Roman joked that's because his surname is Love, but we don't know if he is a singer or manager.' Ella looked up towards Dolores, whose face had suddenly paled. She staggered to a chair, then steadied herself as she sat down. 'Charlie is coming? Are you sure?' Both her hands were on her heart and tears began to roll down Dolores' cheeks.

'Dolores, what is it?' Ella had no clue if they were happy or sad tears. Feeling mortified that she'd made Dolores cry, she asked, 'Is it something I've done? Have I upset you?' Ella wasn't sure what to think. 'I didn't mean to…'

Dolores shook her head and reached across and cupped both of Ella's hands in hers. 'You haven't upset me, and these are happy tears. I just never, ever thought I would see Charlie again in this lifetime.' Dolores patted Ella's hand. 'You see…' Dolores took in a huge breath. 'Charlie was my one true love but we could never be together. We've written to each other for over sixty years.' Dolores didn't elaborate further. Lost in her memories, she sat back in her chair and dabbed her cheeks with a tissue.

'Thank you,' she said, and Ella knew Dolores meant it from the bottom of her heart.

Chapter Thirteen

'A couple of cheese and onion pasties and chocolate flapjacks to keep us going, courtesy of Rona,' Roman waltzed through the doorway and held up a carrier bag full of goodies before spilling them out on to the coffee table. 'There's enough Haribos to sink the *Titanic* and keep our sugar levels up. We have a busy few hours ahead of us.'

Ella noticed his mood was upbeat and she hoped it was because his meeting with Megan had gone well and not because he was trying to cover up a bad morning.

'How did your interview go? I didn't manage to catch it.'

'Never mind that, how was your meeting? That is a little more important than my five minutes of fame.' Ella gestured for Roman to sit down. 'You don't have to go into details; I just want to make sure you're both okay.'

'You're lovely. I can't remember the last time anyone asked me whether I was okay. On a positive note, Megan's still there and yes, we are both doing okay. Apparently, at first she was a little feisty, as she doesn't like rules and regulations, but her caseworker has said that is normal and she'll probably butt heads for a few more days until she realises she's not getting anywhere. She will have a shock being cut off from the outside world, but they confirmed that this morning she took part in a yoga class, which is great news. She's in the four-week programme, so I'm just hoping she has the will-power to see it through.'

'She wants this and she's there, so that's the first step. Take each day as it comes and remember, everyone is here for you both.'

'Thank you, I really do appreciate that.' Roman held her gaze for a moment before standing up and passing her a pasty in a white paper bag. 'Tell me, how has Dolores reacted to the line-up so far? I was thinking about it driving over here. Is she happy?'

Ella blew out a breath as she stood up and retrieved two plates from the kitchen cupboard. 'We've set the cat amongst the pigeons.'

'Why? What have we done?'

'Charlie Love... is the one that got away,' replied Ella.

'Dolores Henderson's one true love, but they couldn't be together.'

'Are you serious?'

'Absolutely serious. I'm not really sure of any of the details, but when I first arrived in Heartcross a letter was delivered here for Dolores by mistake. I gave it to her, but she literally hid it away from me. Anyway, it turns out that even though Dolores and Charlie couldn't be together, they've written to each other every six months for over sixty years.'

Roman blew out a breath. 'Sixty years! You're kidding me, right?'

'Dolores was actually tearful when I told her. She thought she would never see Charlie again, and now we are going to make that happen.'

'She's held a torch for Charlie for all this time?'

'And that's the reason why she never married anyone else. She never fell out of love. No one ever came close.'

'It sounds tragic, and now, by accident, after all this time, they are going to be in the same room?'

'Thanks to our phone call.'

'Is this a good thing?' Roman looked concerned. 'We don't want to throw Dolores into an emotional meltdown on the night. She needs to be on top form, especially if it's being filmed.'

'I asked Dolores if she wanted us to cancel Charlie's invite but she said no, she'd hoped one day they would get to see each other one last time. I'm actually feeling quite emotional about it all, but she wants to meet him in private before the event. Maybe in the afternoon, if we can arrange that?'

Roman jotted it down on his list. 'I'll see to that.'

Ella was pensive for a second. 'Can you imagine putting your life on hold and never falling in love again because you still loved that one person?'

'I can relate to that in a way,' admitted Roman, suddenly sounding sad.

'Oh, Roman, I didn't…'

'I know you didn't mean anything by it, but for years I threw myself into fatherhood, Megan always came first and…' He took a breath. 'I always felt guilty, that I wasn't good enough for anyone else. I blamed myself for Hattie's death. If only I hadn't encouraged her to go out that night, if only I'd slept in the same room that night, things would have been okay. But over time I've begun to see things in a different light.'

'Time is a good healer.' Ella gave a quick thought to Alex. With all the planning for the event at The Lakehouse, she hadn't given him much thought just lately.

'Right, let's get to work,' he said. 'I have the rest of the day and evening to work on this event as much as possible, and then it's back to sailing the boat tomorrow.'

Ella thought it was a good idea that Dolores would

introduce each act herself, then spend a couple of minutes reminiscing about the past – how they met, with a short amusing anecdote thrown in for good measure, followed by the artist's song, which they would sing together.

Twenty-four hours ago ringing an artist would have scared the life out of Ella but now, Roman and Flynn had boosted her confidence. They believed she was capable of organising this event and Ella was taking everything in her stride and proving them right.

She was scribbling on the pad in front of her, when she glanced up to see Roman smiling warmly at her. 'Why are you smiling at me?'

'Because you are really good at this, it's like you've found your calling. You have an amazing way with people, Ella. And you have great organisational skills.'

'Aww thanks, I'm learning from the best.' She smiled back warmly, tapping her pen on the table then pointing to Roman's phone, which had just started to ring.

'It's Callie,' he said, taking the call. 'Yes, she's right here with me.' He held his phone out towards Ella. 'It's Callie for you, your phone was constantly engaged so she tried mine.'

She took the phone from Roman. 'Hi, Boss, we're working like busy bees. Everything seems too good to be true, but it really is all slotting together with no hitches at all.' After speaking with Callie for a further five minutes, she hung up and gave Roman his phone back.

'Callie and Flynn are worried. For the next few days there's severe weather warnings and a storm looming over us. The bookings at The Lakehouse are virtually non-existent, so Gianni has suggested we round up the locals to get a few bums on seats so he can do a practice run of Dolores' menu for the big night. He's literally charging for the cost of the ingredients in exchange for feedback, and asked if we can post about it in the community groups. He knows it's short notice but hopefully we can entice a few of the villagers out into the dark dreary night.'

Taking a sip from her drink, Ella opened up her emails and spotted one from Flynn. She twizzled her screen towards Roman. 'Look at all these old photos and stories that the locals have sent in. It's amazing that everyone is getting on board. We need to go through all of these and put them into some sort of order.' Ella meant business and she was really enjoying getting her teeth stuck into this project... and spending time with Roman was an added bonus.

For hours Ella and Roman were on and off the phone, listening to the songs that the artists were going to sing on the night and organising everyone's memories into an order. All afternoon they laughed and joked and bounced off each other, and before they knew it Ella nudged Roman's elbow. 'Look!' She nodded towards the French doors of the balcony. 'It's pitch black outside and just gone 7pm!' exclaimed Ella, thinking the time had flown by. Her stomach growled with hunger and they both laughed. 'Do you fancy some food, or have you got plans?'

'The only plan I have is going home to an empty house and cooking for one. What do you suggest?' he asked, putting his pen down and raking his fringe out of his eyes.

'Shall I call Meredith and see if she will plate us a couple of pie and chips from the pub? I've still got a few things to do on this,' she looked towards her laptop, 'before I completely down tools.'

'That sounds like a perfect plan.'

Ella phoned across to Meredith, who was more than happy to plate up a couple of meals for the hard workers, and fifteen minutes later Ella hurried across to the pub leaving Roman to set the table. Callie was having tea at Julia's this evening and wouldn't be back until late, so that meant they could leave everything sprawled out over the table.

Five minutes later she was hurrying back up the stairwell clutching two hot plates. Roman had cleared a space and was sitting on the settee scrolling through his phone. 'I wonder what Megan is having for her tea?' he mused, as Ella placed the food on the table. 'Look at the size of that pie!'

Ella had to agree it was ginormous, but she was absolutely starving and was going to devour every bit of it. 'Tell me about Megan, what was she like as a little girl?'

Roman smiled and put down his knife and fork. 'From day one she was inquisitive, always looking around the room, smiling and gurgling. As soon as she learnt to speak, she wasn't afraid to ask questions, but the second she began to sing… her voice is beautiful. Megan always wanted to be in the entertainment industry, she auditioned for every school play, went to drama and singing classes. I was one proud dad. We've always had a brilliant relationship with just each other to rely on, but in the last eighteen months it became a struggle. It seemed like my little girl had just disappeared overnight. Her drinking escalated and has just become out of control. It saddens me to say it, but at the moment I just don't recognise her at all; my kind caring daughter has just vanished.'

'She'll be back, I just know it,' Ella reassured. 'Megan is in the best place.'

Five minutes later Ella leant back in her chair with her

hands clutching her stomach. 'I'm bursting, full to the brim, but that steak pie was to die for.'

With two empty plates in front of them, Ella looked at her laptop and shut down the lid. 'I declare we've done enough work today. Do you fancy watching a film or something? But saying that, I've only noticed one DVD around this place,' she scrunched up her face, 'and it's probably not your thing.'

'Try me.'

Ella chewed her lip for a second. *'Bridget Jones' Diary* it is, then.' She watched for Roman's reaction. 'Did you just roll your eyes?' She swiped his arm playfully.

'No, no… I promise I didn't roll my eyes; I can't think of a better film to watch.' He grinned, exaggerating an eye roll.

'You did so! Make yourself comfy, I'll get us some drinks.'

When Ella brought the drinks in, Roman had plumped up the cushions and made himself comfy on the settee, and had propped his feet up on the coffee table, causing Ella to burst out laughing. His multicoloured monster socks caught her eye. 'Very classy.'

'I love my socks.' He pretended to look hurt by her laughter. 'Socks say a lot about someone's personality.'

'You don't say,' she teased, sitting on the chair next to him and resting her feet next to his.

They both looked down at Ella's boring white trainer socks.

'Say no more,' he said with a glint in his eye.

Ella playfully hit him with the cushion. 'I am not boring.'

'You don't say,' he joked, repeating her very words. He tapped his foot against Ella's and sent a wave of shivers down her spine. Sitting next to Roman, they were only centimetres apart, and she folded her arms and fixed her eyes on the screen. Feeling comfortable in his company, they watched the film, sharing jokes and laughing, but after a while Ella realised that Roman had closed his eyes and fallen asleep.

She took the opportunity to study his face; he was more than handsome. She thought about how he'd uprooted himself, moved miles and sacrificed his own career to move Megan away from a situation to try and help her, which showed he had a huge heart. To be a single father and bring up his daughter by himself was commendable. Roman must be exhausted with everything that was going on in his life. Knowing she liked Roman, she watched him for a moment longer. The black cloud that had been hanging over Ella since Alex disappeared had begun to lift. She was feeling happy at home and at work, and all that was missing was that special something.

Even though Roman ticked all the boxes, Ella

questioned whether she was ready to trust again. She just knew she could never be hurt again. Switching down the volume on the TV, she dimmed the lights and gently covered him up with a throw.

She let him sleep as she carried on watching the film.

Chapter Fourteen

A storm was looming over Heartcross, but the majority of villagers were heading towards The Lakehouse to sample Gianni's taster menu for the big event. This was a dress rehearsal for Gianni as well as for the waiters, and all the members of staff selected to work on the night of the event had to sign a confidentiality agreement. No one was allowed to repeat any conversations that were overheard or ask for selfies, and the staff had to remain professional at all times.

Ella had joked that it was as crazy as signing the Official Secrets Act. Hamish had kindly offered to give Callie and Ella a lift to The Boathouse to catch the water taxi, as huge dollops of rain had already started to fall over Heartcross and the winds were wild. Weather warnings were broadcasting all over the news, but that hadn't dampened anyone's spirits, and everyone was looking forward to the night ahead.

On the way to the boat they picked up Felicity and Isla who were excited about Dolores' big event. In preparation they'd taken the day off work together and had travelled into the city, looking for the perfect dress for the 'Trip Down Memory Lane'.

'Look at this storm,' exclaimed Callie from the passenger seat as a fork of lightning lit up the sky in front of Hamish's car.

'Let's hope it calms down a little,' added Felicity, as Hamish parked right at the end of the jetty. Making a run for it, they shouted thank you to Hamish and sprinted towards the boat. The thunder rolled overhead like the fury of the Gods and tumbled towards them through the darkened clouds. The gangplank was down and all four on them ran straight on board and shielded undercover.

Roman gave Ella a huge beaming smile the second he spotted her. Last night he'd been out for the count and Ella had debated whether to leave him where he was. But just after 11pm she'd given him a little shake to wake him, and he'd been mortified he'd fallen asleep.

'Anything to get out of watching *Bridget Jones*,' she'd joked, and he'd agreed with a cheeky grin.

As Roman had packed up his stuff and headed to the front door, he'd hesitated and Ella had been sure he wanted to say something, or maybe even give her a goodnight kiss. Her heart gave a little skip, but the moment had passed, and he'd simply bid her a friendly goodnight. Ella knew once they'd crossed that line it would change everything, and although she was willing for that happen, there was a tiny part of her that was still uncertain.

'Do we get to sample the cocktails tonight?' joked Isla, looking towards Callie.

'Only if you're paying for them – do you want us to go bankrupt?' she teased.

Everyone was in good spirits despite the rain and Roman tipped his cap and started the engine. 'This isn't the best weather, so sit back and if you stay in the seats in the middle of the boat, it won't seem as rocky.' Straight away Ella noticed that Roman wasn't dressed in his usual uniform, but instead wore a more upmarket jacket accessorised with a pair of white gloves. It oozed 'designer', along with his aftershave. He really did look the part.

'New uniform?' Ella asked, admiring what she saw.

He nodded. 'My winter attire. Do you like it?'

'I do,' she replied, giving him a darting glance, followed by a silly grin before following Callie to the seats in the middle of the boat. Feeling a fast pulse, Ella knew they were flirting and she liked it.

'Look at this boat,' Felicity spun round.

The open-plan saloon and galley had a light and airy

feel with a split sliding canopy allowing each side to be opened separately. It was heated, the seats were plush red velvet around circular tables and fairy lights decorated the roof of the boat. The bar at the end came with waiter service, and the whole feel of the boat was magical.

'It feels like Christmas to me,' added Isla, taking her first glass of champagne from the waiter.

As they set off, the rain could be heard thrashing down on the roof of the boat but that didn't dampen anyone's spirits; they couldn't wait for their evening to start. Ella ducked with each thunderous boom, causing everyone to laugh. She knew it was silly but she couldn't help it.

Very soon The Lakehouse was in sight, and on the whole the crossing had been a little bumpy but nothing too scary. As Roman steered the boat in to calmer waters, Ella gasped; there were lights guiding the boat along the riverbank and the weeping willows sparkled in multiple colours.

'You've not seen anything yet.' Roman looked over his shoulder and Ella joined him at the helm. 'Look, what do you think?'

'I think it's the most romantic thing I've seen in a long, long time.' The restaurant looked like a magical wonderland. The lights were draped across the front of the restaurant, giving it very much a Christmas feel, and there were roaring fire pits burning under huge canopies. Despite the wind and the rain, the whole place looked magnificent.

'We are going for the full dress rehearsal tonight, aren't we? I'm surprised the rain doesn't put the fires out,' remarked Ella, thinking how dramatic yet beautiful it all looked.

'I think it's artificial flames just for effect, but on the night, there will be a red carpet trailing all the way up the jetty to the entrance,' added Callie. 'The left-hand side of the bay will be cordoned off for the paparazzi and the TV cameras, whilst the guests can line up on the right-hand side where they can say hello, shake hands with the stars etc. on the way into the restaurant.'

'It's all coming together!' Ella felt a tiny thrill of excitement. If it felt as spectacular as this on the night, it would definitely be a night to remember.

After cutting the engine, Roman pulled on his waterproofs before he ventured outside and secured the boat. Within seconds he was back on the boat and drenched. 'It's a short walk to the restaurant but it's brutal out there. Don't put your umbrellas up because they won't last two minutes in this wind. Here…' Roman handed out ponchos. 'You can dispose of them once inside.'

Everyone was grateful and even though it was only a

short walk across the jetty, they really were likely going to get soaked.

Just as they were about to make a run for it, Roman stopped Ella. 'I forgot to say, there was a man asking after you on the last crossing.'

'Really, for me? Did he give you his name or why he wanted me?'

Roman shook his head. 'Maybe it's something to do with the event? He's waiting inside for you.'

'Okay, thanks, see you later.' Ella looked at them all. 'Are we ready? Run!' She laughed, holding her hood as she ran for her life along the jetty. They all took off and Ella ducked her head under the veranda of The Lakehouse just as a tremendous clap of thunder rolled through the air. Once inside, they peeled off the wet ponchos and Wilbur disposed of them before handing them each a glass of champagne and showing them to their table.

'I could get used to this!' Felicity beamed. 'This is the life, champagne and fine dining.'

'Here's a copy of the set menu.' Ella handed them out from the middle of the table. Gianni had prepared an exquisite meal and every table was sampling the same delicious food so that Gianni could ensure that all the food was piping hot.

'This is food fit for a queen,' remarked Ella, running

her eyes over the dishes. 'Oh Wilbur, Roman mentioned someone was asking after me? Do you know who?'

'It's the gentleman just walking through the doors from the bathroom now.'

Ella stood up and glanced over.

'Jeez, who is that man? He's absolutely drop-dead gorgeous and such a snappy dresser too,' exclaimed Isla.

Ella was frozen to the spot, she felt sick to the stomach. She'd imagined this moment over and over in her head but had never expected it to actually happen. She was suddenly paralysed to the core.

'Are you okay, you look like you've seen a ghost.' Callie touched her arm. 'What is it?'

Ella's intake of breath could be heard all around the restaurant. She felt like her legs were going to buckle underneath her at any time. Her pulse was racing, her heart thumping and with wide eyes Ella turned towards Callie. 'It's Alex.'

Ella wasn't sure whose jaw had hit the floor the hardest – hers or Callie's.

'What the hell do you want me to do?' whispered Callie, under her breath as Ella let go of the chair and took a step in his direction. She could feel her whole body shaking.

Ella swivelled her head round and whispered. 'Act normal like you know nothing but call the police.'

Callie and the gang were amazing, they began talking

amongst themselves acting like nothing was going on and everything was normal, although it was far from it. Standing on the other side of the room, Alex wore the sickliest smile she'd ever seen. She couldn't quite believe the nerve of this man who had stolen everything from her. How had she ever fallen in love with him? She had no clue because right at this very minute he was making every inch of her body crawl.

'Hello, Ella; I bet you didn't expect to see me tonight?'

Ella had never expected to see him any night ever again.

'I think I've got some explaining to do. I've ordered you your favourite drink.' He bent forward to kiss her cheek but immediately Ella took a step back.

'Don't be mad, Ells. I can explain everything. Oh, and you look stunning, by the way – beautiful as ever.'

Ella used to love it when he called her Ells, but now it grated on her.

'Well that's good, because I'm all ears, and tequila was never my favourite drink, it was yours. I hate tequila.' She pushed the glass away from her. 'I hate it almost as much as I hate you. You've stolen a lot of money from me, Alex... if that really is your name?' Ella wasn't holding back.

Alex seemed to brush over it like it wasn't of any importance.

'Don't be daft, all your money is safe. My brother's business is on the up, thanks to you, Ells.'

Ella raised an eyebrow.

Was this really happening? Ella felt like she was stuck in the middle of some weird dream and any second she would wake up, but somehow, she didn't think she was going to be that lucky. She recognised his smell, the tiny scar above his eyebrow and the tattoo on his wrist. It was definitely him and this was real. She was in complete shock.

'We need to talk; you can't even begin to understand how sorry I am.'

'Sorry? I thought you were lying dead somewhere, hit by a car, a train. I had no clue what the hell had happened to you.' Ella could feel the anger rising inside and she wanted to lash out, and shake him, hit him with all of her might, and Ella had never been violent in her all of her life. The only reason she didn't was because she was trying to remain calm until the police arrived and could arrest him. Maybe then there might be a chance of getting some of her inheritance back, at least.

Even though her heart felt like it was going to pound through her chest at any given second, Ella had her wits about her. She was wiser now and she wasn't going to fall for his charms or that deep, intense look he gave her that used to turn her legs to jelly. She just prayed the police would hurry up.

Even though Ella hated tequila she was tempted to swig the whole glass back. 'So, what happened to you?' Ella couldn't wait to hear whatever story he'd concocted. 'You went to work and that was that.'

He tilted his head to one side. 'It's been terrible, Ells. I must have had some sort of breakdown. All I know is, I couldn't cope anymore. I felt like the world was closing in around me and I couldn't breathe. Work was off the scale, the pressure of more shifts at the hospital, I couldn't keep up with the schedule.'

Who the hell did he think he was kidding? Ella was shaking her head in disbelief, yet trying to keep every emotion under control. He wasn't even a doctor. Did he think she'd just sat back and never reported his disappearance to the police? What exactly was his game, because he was taking a huge risk turning up here.

'I felt numb, like my life was unmanageable,' he continued.

Ella wanted to stand up, shout 'Bravo, give this man an Oscar,' but instead she said, 'You poor thing. I can't believe this.' She saw Alex's mouth hitch into a tiny smile. Did he honestly think she was falling for this baloney?

'I had a breakdown, checked into a centre, had to get myself right.'

'I'm sorry to hear that, Alex. And did you not think to ring the woman you were living with and engaged to?'

'I was a broken man; I didn't want you seeing me that way. All I can do is beg for forgiveness. I love you, Ells, and I've missed you.'

'How did you find me?' Ella was curious how he'd ended up here.

'You're famous, all over the news for organising this prestigious event that's going on right here. Dolores Henderson is a huge star. I'm so proud of you! She's a friend of yours too? It's amazing. I always said you were destined for great things.'

'No, you didn't.'

Ella's bluntness didn't deter Alex's sob story in any way, shape or form.

'I want a part of this life with you. I want us back. We were in love, about to get married. We are two of a kind, Ella, destined to be with each other.'

Ella had a million and one questions whirling around in her head. Out of the corner of her eye she saw Callie using the landline behind the bar.

'Will you excuse me for a second, I really need to use the bathroom.' As Ella stood up a fork of lightning rocketed through the sky, lighting up the windowpanes. The thunder boomed almost instantly and the lights inside The Lakehouse began to flicker. The whole room gasped.

Flynn was quick to appear and address the room. 'Firstly, thank you all for coming and braving the weather just to help us out this evening. We really do appreciate it. The weather warnings are severe for the next hour, so if there are any problems with the electricity, can we ask you all to stay in your seats? Hopefully that will not be the case and the weather will calm down, but we will be bringing candles out to every table, so don't panic. Our waiters and waitresses will be filling up your glasses and your first course will be out very soon. In the meantime try and relax.'

As Ella began to walk away, Alex grabbed her wrist. 'What's happened was unfortunate, but I can provide proof from the centre I've been staying at. I was ill, Ella. I know this is all a shock but it's the truth. I still love you. We can make this work. I know we can.'

For a split second Ella actually wondered if he was telling her the truth. He seemed sincere, and if he could provide proof? But immediately her head batted those feelings away. She'd been in love with who she thought he was. He wasn't even a doctor, the police had said so, he didn't even work at the hospital. And surely, he could have been in touch to let her know he was okay, at least. Why was he back? Had he thought she'd landed on her feet again, mixing with the rich and famous, and wanted a part of it? Ella just had no clue who he really was. All she knew was that she no longer felt in love with this man; she was in fear of what he was capable of and she needed to take control.

'Let me just use the bathroom and we can talk.' Ella was thankful she sounded calm, as all she really wanted to do was get out of there and let the police investigate the situation.

Her whole body was beginning to shake as she walked towards the bathroom, and the second the door closed behind her she slumped against the wall and tried to control her breathing. Almost immediately the door was flung open and Ella brought her hands up to her chest and gasped.

'You frightened the life out of me.'

Isla was standing in front of her. 'They've sent me, as it may look odd if all of us pile in here. Are you okay? What's going on?'

Feeling shocked to the core, Ella's whole body was shaking, and she couldn't make herself stop. 'What's going on is, Dr Alex James is not dead; he's sitting in the restaurant claiming he's had some sort of mental breakdown, and he forgot who he was or where he was, and now he's seen me on the news it's jogged his memory of who I am, and he's still in love with me.' Ella barely took a breath.

'Are you kidding me? I suppose he's forgotten what he's done with all your money too? Oh, and the brand-new car he drove away in?'

'He said my money is safe.'

'And he's here to give it back to you?'

'I doubt that very much, but that's the only reason I'm not screaming blue murder.' Ella held out a trembling hand to Isla. 'Where are the police?'

'Dealing with lots of emergencies due to the storm, but they are on their way. You just have to keep calm. Nothing is going to happen to you whilst we are here. We'll sit tight until the police arrive,' reassured Isla.

'I feel sick to my stomach, I need to get out of here.'

Suddenly the lights in the bathroom flickered then blacked out altogether.

'It's the weather, the storm is brutal. The power is out,' said Isla, opening up the bathroom door to see Roman being blown through the back door of the restaurant by a huge gust of wind. He clutched the hood to his coat tightly and then pulled it down when he was safely inside. He shook himself, and raindrops dripped from the end of his nose.

'It's nasty out there.'

The storm sounded menacing with the wind howling and the rain lashing against the windows.

'Roman, can you take me home? I need to get out of here.' Even though Ella didn't relish the thought of stepping outside, she knew she had to get away from Alex.

'Is Gianni's cooking that bad?' Roman joked, but realised this was no joking matter when he saw the look on Ella's face and sensed something was immediately wrong.

'What's going on? Are you okay?' He looked directly at Ella, then touched her arm.

'Far from okay, I just need to get out of here. I'll explain when I'm on the boat. Is that okay?' Ella turned towards Isla. 'He's going to realise I'm not coming back in a minute, if he hasn't already, but there's going to be no way he can exit from the restaurant without the boat, so fingers crossed, the police will pick him up.'

'The police?' Roman's eyes widened.

'Just get her on that boat and away from here.' Isla gave her a quick hug. 'Now get yourself out the back entrance and message me when you are home and safe.'

Ella nodded and quickly took a coat off a hook in the staff corridor. 'I apologise in advance to whoever's coat this is,' she said, sliding her arms inside it and pulling the hood up.

'I just need to slip these invoices on to Flynn's desk for the taxi boat supplies, and I'll be with you in two minutes. You make your way to the boat,' Roman said and Ella nodded.

The second Ella stepped outside, the wind was pushing her harder and harder and attempting to lift her off her feet, but she held on firmly to her hood and fought against it with all of her might as she struggled to put one foot in front of the other and clung to the rail of the jetty. In the short walk to the boat, Ella worked every muscle in her legs as the rain stung her cheeks. The eerie sounds of the gusting winds were swirling around the cliffs. As she stepped on to the boat, the water was slapping against the sides. She stumbled towards the middle of the vessel, but then steadied herself as she got used to the boat's rocking. Soaked to the skin, she made her way to the captain's cubby-hole, a small private area at the back of the boat, in search of a towel, and began to dry her face. Roman would be on deck in a second and he'd get her home safe and sound in no time at all.

Thankfully, much to Ella's relief, she heard the engine fire up and the boat began to move.

She quickly shut the cubby-hole door behind her and made her way up the centre of the boat towards Roman. But as Ella stared at the figure at the helm, her heart hammered against her ribcage as she recognised the man's physique. 'Alex,' she muttered. 'What the hell are you doing?' Ella's voice was fraught, her knuckles were white as she gripped the seat hard.

Alex spun round and pulled down his hood. 'Let's take our own trip down memory lane, shall we Ella? We were so good together and we can be again.' The menacing look on his face shook Ella to the core.

'You are deluded. The only reason you're back is to try and screw more money out of me. Everything was a game to you.' With all of her strength Ella was mustering up for a fight. 'And what the hell do you think you are doing? The police are already on their way, so you won't be getting far.'

For a moment Alex's face seemed to soften. 'We just need to talk. You just need to listen to me.'

'And stealing a boat is going to make me listen to you?'

'I had no choice! I saw you running from me. That's not kind of you, Ella.'

Ella recognised his choice of words. When they had been together he was always telling her how kind he was, how he'd do anything for anyone. Now, he was trying to manipulate her into thinking she wasn't kind.

'Is lying about your identity being kind? Lying about your occupation? Pretending you work at the City Hospital when you don't? It beggars belief that you would walk out of that hospital entrance dressed up as a doctor, pretending you were something you weren't.' Ella was not holding back. 'And here was me, believing every word. You made me love you, you used the death of my parents to get close to me. You planned it all and stole my inheritance, and now you're back... for what? Because you think Dolores is going to give me money, or I'm suddenly going to be rich and famous? Who are you, Alex, and what are you? Because you are not a decent human being!'

Ella could see his knuckles turning white as he

gripped the steering wheel. 'You were an easy target.' He looked over his shoulder. 'I sat at that bistro for weeks, watching you. Think what we could do together now though.'

'What the hell are you talking about?'

'Flynn Carter, millionaire. Dolores Henderson must be worth a few bob, too. I want in.'

'In on what? You are delirious, sick in the head – these are my friends!'

This was a man she'd once shared her life with and what she thought was a future, and now she wished with all of her heart that she'd never clapped eyes on him.

Alex pushed the lever and the boat picked up speed, crashing furiously against the waves. Ella's life actually passed before her eyes. She felt dizzy, scared, but knew somehow that she had to get off this boat.

Ella looked towards the cold black water that was thrashing against the boat. She had no clue how far away from shore they were, but all she could think about was saving herself. She screamed as the boat jolted and hit the jagged rocks.

'Just take me back, Alex! Everyone will already be looking for me, they will have seen the boat sail away!'

But Alex wasn't listening, his face had darkened.

Something in the distance caught Ella's eye; lights bouncing towards them, another boat. Alex was driving the boat so hard, she was struggling to stay on her feet as water splashed over the sides. She took another look over her shoulder and couldn't gauge how far away the other boat was or whether it was actually heading in their direction, she just prayed it was.

Remembering the emergency stop button that Roman had shown her the first day she sailed across the river, she looked towards the dashboard. Her heart dropped as she realised this was a different boat but as her eyes frantically flicked up and down, she finally spotted a red round circular button.

'You didn't have to call the police, we could have worked this out, and because you've done that you've given me no choice.'

Ella looked into the distance. It was pitch black, but she could just about make out the coastline and realised Alex was heading directly towards the rocks. Ella edged her way forward and remembered Roman had told her not to press the emergency stop button if you were going at some speed, as it would throw you off the boat like a rag doll. Ella decided she'd rather take her chances with that than at the hands of Alex or being smashed against the rocks.

Preparing for the worst, Ella took her chance. She lunged forward and pressed the red button with all of her might.

They were both hurled forward with force. Alex lost his footing and rolled out on to the main deck. Ella's head smashed against the window, and she felt a sharp pain followed by a dull ache, then a trickle of blood running down her face. Alex was dazed and Ella attempted to stand up. He was shouting at her but all she could do was concentrate on locking the door to the glass cabin. Her fingers fumbled as she placed the fallen key in the door and turned it. Alex's face was now pressed up against the glass, his fist thumping against the door.

Trying to calm her beating heart, she saw the lights on the water moving closer and closer. Soon, they were at the side of her. Much to Ella's relief she saw the coastguard, the police and Roman. Thank God! All Ella could do was fall on to a seat and cry.

Within seconds the police swarmed the boat and arrested Alex. He stared at her through the glass as they took him away on the other boat. Ella's whole body shuddered, and she cursed the day he'd ever come into her life.

Taking a deep breath, she stepped straight into the arms of Roman, who held her tight. In shock, Ella sobbed and sobbed.

'It's okay, I've got you,' he murmured, kissing the top of her head softly.

Standing there, Ella felt mentally and physically battered and pulled away when she heard a voice.

'Please can you confirm your name?' There were three policemen standing at the side of her. Immediately one wrapped her up in a huge foil-like blanket. She could feel her whole body shaking uncontrollably.

'Ella… Ella Johnson.'

'Hi Ella, I'm Sergeant Moss, you're in shock and we are just going to take a minute to sit and get a warm drink inside you.'

Roman placed her hand in his and led her to the middle section of the boat. Another police officer handed Ella a drink whilst Sergeant Moss sat opposite her and twizzled the knob on the top of his radio. Roman never let go of her hand.

'I can confirm Ella Johnson is found and we are going to be heading back to the mainland in a couple of minutes. Please can you have an ambulance waiting on shore to take Ella to the hospital?'

'I don't need to go to hospital, I'm fine.' All Ella wanted to do was go home and sleep off this nightmare.

'You are going to hospital and I'm coming with you,' reassured Roman. 'No arguing.'

'I'm too cold to argue and my head hurts.' Ella lifted her hand to her head and felt the stickiness of the blood. 'My head really hurts.'

'You've got a nasty cut and will probably need stitches.'

Ella closed her eyes, feeling dizzy and a little nauseous.

'Try and keep your eyes open Ella, we need you to

stay as alert as possible.' With the boat rocking up and down on the water, Roman slipped his arm around Ella's shoulder. 'Rest on me but keep those eyes open.'

'I'll try.'

'You will try, because I'm not sure whether you've got the gist yet, Ella Johnson, but I kind of want you to stay around.'

'Sir.' Roman looked up at the sound of the police officer's voice. 'Do you know how to drive this boat?' asked Sargent Moss.

'I do.'

'Okay, can I ask you to take the helm? We will sit with Ella whilst you get us back to shore.'

As Roman walked into the driver's cabin, something caught Ella's eye on the floor. She bent down and picked up a mobile phone. She stared at the screensaver – a picture of herself and Alex wrapped up in each other's arms on their very first date. It seemed to her he was completely disturbed and had no clue what was real or not. And whilst she might have lost her inheritance, tonight she had very nearly also lost her life.

Chapter Fifteen

Ella woke up and for a second wondered where the hell she was, until she saw the wires protruding in every direction and saw that she was hooked up to a machine at the side of her bed, bleeping away.

Thankfully she'd stopped shivering and knew she was lucky to be alive. Ella remembered arriving at the hospital and after she'd undergone some tests the doctor confirmed she had mild hypothermia. She had a line of stitches across her forehead and a vague recollection that Callie had been by her side at some point, but her head hurt that much, she'd just drifted off to sleep.

Lying there in her own private room, Ella had no clue what time of day it was, but hearing a soft knock on the door, she looked up to see the nurse walking towards her with a hot mug of tea. 'How's your head this morning?

Would you like some painkillers?' she asked, looking at the chart. The nurse kindly helped Ella to sit up and plumped up her pillows.

'Yes, please, it's like a dull ache,' replied Ella, sipping her tea.

'You've had quite an adventure, haven't you?'

'One I could have done without,' Ella said as she closed her eyes for a brief moment.

'We need to keep you in for the time being. You've had a huge wallop and we just need to err on the side of caution.'

'What time is it?' asked Ella.

'Just gone 9am.'

The door opened and Ella looked over to see Roman walk into the room holding up a carrier bag and wearing his trademark smile. 'I was going to bring you flowers but apparently that's not allowed, so I've brought you fluffy PJs and socks... plain white trainer socks, even though I was tempted to bring monster socks and a bobble hat to keep the heat in. And I also brought these...' He pulled out a huge bar of chocolate, a flask of tea and pile of magazines.

Ella was impressed. 'You've thought of everything, thank you.'

'Callie sorted out the PJs. I'm here until 10.30am, then Callie is going to take over the second shift.'

'I have just the best friends,' Ella smiled and took the

carrier bag off Roman and immediately opened the chocolate and offered some to him. 'Thank God for the PJs.'

Pulling her blankets around her chest, the nurse checked Ella's pulse, temperature and noted them down on the chart at the end of her bed before leaving the room, while Roman sat down on the blue plastic chair at the side of her bed.

'That was quite a night. I don't even know how Gianni's food went down.'

Roman was looking at her with such admiration. 'You are amazing.' He smiled warmly at her. 'And I mean amazing, pressing the emergency button, locking yourself in the cabin.'

'I must have been bad in my past life,' she joked, while taking her painkillers from the small plastic cup the nurse had just handed to her. 'I don't feel amazing and I know I don't look amazing. I don't even want to go near a mirror.'

'War wounds, a few stitches. They will soon be gone.' There was silence for a second. 'Ella, this is all my fault. I left the key in the boat, which I know is a complete no-no, and if I hadn't, you wouldn't be lying here. I'm so sorry.' Roman looked troubled.

Ella reached across for his hand. 'Honestly, don't worry about that. I think it was a blessing in disguise, this way the police caught him, thankfully.' She took a sip of water from the glass on her bedside cabinet. 'You know, I'd never thought I'd ever set eyes on him again, and there he was, as bold as brass, sitting in The Lakehouse without a care in the world.' Ella took a breath. 'For a second I actually thought he was going to drive us into the rocks,' her voice faltered, and she felt the emotion well up inside. Roman leant across and laid his hand on top of hers. 'But he didn't, and you were so brave. Have the police been back in yet?'

Ella shook her head. 'I just want to know who the hell he really is and why did he come back a second time?'

'To chance his arm? Who knows how these people tick? It's beyond me. But he's arrested now and hopefully charged.'

'Let's hope so. How have I managed to get myself kidnapped at my age?'

Roman gave a little chuckle. 'It does sound funny, being kidnapped at your age.'

'It's just all so strange. The day he went missing, I was completed devastated, I thought he was dead and my life was over. And then the police discovered he'd lied about most things, maxed out my credit cards and conned me into handing over my inheritance. And now I actually wish he was dead, which is certainly not good-spirited of me.'

'In these circumstances I think I'd feel exactly the same.'

'I lived with this man for over a year and I don't even know his proper name. He was caring, loving and always made me feel like I was the only girl in the world. I felt lucky to have found him but now, looking back, it wasn't like that at all and I'm not feeling at all lucky now.'

'I honestly don't know what to say, except it's not your fault. These kind of people are professionals. I bet when he saw you on the TV organising an event for the world-famous Dolores Henderson, he got greedy, thinking there was another con opportunity. But you already saw him for what he is.'

'Thank God, they've arrested him.'

'They'll soon find out his real identity and at least you'll have some closure. It doesn't help losing your money, though.'

'But I have my life.'

'That's it, focus on the positives.'

'I came to Heartcross for a fresh start and it's all gone wrong again.' Ella let out a sigh.

'You aren't thinking of leaving, are you? Because if you are, you really do have brain damage!' teased Roman, giving her a warm smile. 'And look how far you have come in the past few weeks. Every event manager in Scotland would have wanted your gig, and it's going to be one of the glitziest nights in showbusiness.'

'No pressure!'

'And apart from that, I don't want you to leave. I've kind of got used to having you around. If you leave you will be missed.'

'But you will have a quieter life.' Ella tilted her head to one side and gave him a lopsided smile.

'Maybe I don't want a quieter life.' Roman didn't take his eyes off her for a second. 'Last night, when I saw the boat was leaving, I can't even describe the feeling in the pit of my stomach. I felt physically sick. All I kept thinking was, if anyone hurt you, I wouldn't be responsible for my actions.' Roman paused and took a deep breath. 'I want you in my life, Ella Johnson, and I know we've both been through the mill, but I'm hoping we can look after each other.'

Ella narrowed her eyes and smiled. 'Are you asking me out on a date, Roman Docherty?'

'I am indeed.'

Ella looked him right in the eye. 'Only on one condition.'

'Anything.'

'We don't go on a boat.'

Roman laughed. 'Deal.'

Hearing a knock on the door, they both looked up to see two of the police officers from last night standing in front of them. 'Can we come in?'

Ella nodded; she was hoping they'd discovered the

real identity of Alex James and they were going to lock him up and throw away the key.

'How are you feeling?' Sergeant Moss asked.

Ella swallowed back a wave of sadness that threatened to wash over her. When she spoke her voice slightly wobbled. 'I don't know why, but when people ask me how I am, I feel like bursting into tears.'

'It'll be the shock,' replied Sergeant Moss.

'But I'm doing okay, I have a scan booked in later and if I seem normal, hopefully I'll be allowed home.' She crossed her fingers in the air.

'Do you want me to leave?' asked Roman, respecting Ella's privacy.

She shook her head and took his hand.

'Have you found anything out?' asked Ella, looking towards the policemen.

'We have. Dr Alex James went by numerous names – we have a list as long as our arm – but his real name is Wayne Ridgeway.'

Ella raised an eyebrow. 'Not so glamorous as Dr Alex James.'

'Funnily enough, he was from a very rich family, one of five children, but it appears he was into petty crime and was a disappointment to his own parents, who left him nothing in their will, so he upped his criminal activity. This man has been reported by women all over the country and he aims big. He scours the newspapers and the TV news for accidents and deaths, and then suddenly appears in that area, and you know the rest.'

'And once you've handed over the money, he's gone.' Ella knew she had been well and truly taken for a ride.

'He always used a profession that would make him appealing to women – Doctor, Lawyer, Vet – giving the impression he had social status and financial security. He was a dangerous man and knew exactly what he was doing, he covered his tracks well.'

'Didn't he just.' Ella blew out a breath. She knew she'd been a fool, blinded by what she thought was love, but the only good thing to come out of this situation for her was that it was over. She felt a huge relief. Of course, she was sad she'd given her heart to the man, but now there would be no more love or head space wasted on him. He was gone and she was here. This was her time now.

'I suppose there's no chance of me getting my money back?' asked Ella, already thinking she knew the answer to that question.

'Never say never. We are looking into every scenario to try and make that happen. As soon as we know any more, we will let you know.'

As soon as the police left Roman asked her how she felt.

'Stupid. I cried for that man, thinking he was dead at

the time. I endured that gut-wrenching pain in the pit of my stomach. All that wasted energy.'

'But now you are back in control.'

'I feel relief it's over and I never have to look over my shoulder again. I hope he serves his time and Karma slaps him with a huge sentence.'

'Karma always comes back to bite you on the bum.'

It was approaching 10.30am and so far Ella's room had been like Chester station at rush hour. 'It's like the hokey-cokey in here – one in, one out, shake it all about,' teased Ella, but secretly she was pleased that everyone was coming to visit. 'There's no chance of me getting any rest,' she joked as Callie walked into the room.

'Don't be cheeky!' replied Callie, hovering at the end of the bed.

'Here, have this chair, I was waiting until you got here.' Roman stood and gestured to the chair. 'I've got to get to work. I'm on the late shift tonight, so please drop me a text after your scan and I'll be back in tomorrow.'

'Of course, and thanks for all this.' Ella nodded towards the chocolate and the magazines. 'Curtesy of Hamish.' He leant across the bed and kissed her softly on the cheek. 'And don't go getting into any more trouble whilst I'm gone.'

'I'll do my best.'

Ella knew that Callie's eyes were firmly fixed on her when Roman left the room. She perched on the end on the bed. 'What's going on between you two? I know that look.'

'What look?' Ella was trying to play it cool but then beamed.

'Are you…?'

'We are going on a date and that is all I'm saying.'

'Yay! I'm so chuffed for you. Honestly, you make the perfect couple and the way he looks at you! Roman was beside himself last night when he saw the boat sailing off.' Callie told Ellie how he'd hurtled back inside to see if Ella had stayed behind, and when they realised Alex had disappeared, it was all hands on deck. Roman had been blown around by the winds as he'd single-handedly tried to pull the speed boat from the back of the bay, but thankfully the police and the coastguard had turned up. 'Honestly, Roman was like a superhero, he jumped on to their boat and took over – he was going to save you, no matter what.'

Listening to Callie, Ella felt that magical flip in her stomach. This time it wasn't one of dread or fear, but the first flush of love. She knew she was falling for Roman more and more by the hour, if that was at all possible.

'And Flynn gave me this to show you. He passes on his best and said he'll pop in later with Julia, but look at this.' Callie delved into her bag and placed the magazine on Ella's lap. 'Turn to page sixteen.' Ella opened up the magazine and, as instructed, turned to page sixteen.

'Oh... my... God...' Ella strung out the words. Her eyes were quickly scanning over the article. 'I didn't even know there was such a thing. *Waiter of the month Ella Johnson is a huge asset to The Lakehouse restaurant situated on the outskirts of the River Heart. Her natural yet charismatic style and extensive knowledge of wines and food left our very own food critic Tiffany Downs sincerely impressed.'*

Ella beamed as she read over the article and studied the pictures of her going about her merry way in the restaurant. 'And where did they get those photos?'

'Tiffany spoke to Nancy – apparently they know each other from old – and Nancy had taken lots of photos on the day she came to film the TV news,' replied Callie.

'Waiter of the month? This was my first day at work!' Ella still couldn't believe it, Tiffany Down had praised her and The Lakehouse to the hilt. 'I feel like I should prepare a speech.'

'Not only is Gianni over the moon, but so is Flynn, who hasn't stopped polishing your halo. He's posted a copy of this article all over the restaurant's social media channels, and he's as proud as punch. You are smashing it, girl.'

'I'm actually speechless, I feel so emotional,' shared Ella, giving a satisfied smile. Apart from the fact she was currently lying in the hospital bed, Ella was full of positive thoughts. Since arriving in Heartcross she'd experienced the feeling of being able to conquer the world. She was surrounded by a community who had welcomed her with open arms and encouraged her to be the best she could possibly be, and she wasn't going to let any of them down, including herself.

'At this rate you will be saving The Lakehouse single-handedly. For your birthday I'm going to buy you a superhero cape.'

'Don't be daft,' replied Ella, waving off the compliment, 'it's all a team effort.'

'With you leading the way, and we are all right behind you.'

'And that's down to you – you gave me a job and a place to stay. Everyone should have a friend like you.' Ella meant every word; everyone should have a Callie in their life.

'Ditto,' replied Callie, leaning across the bed to give her best friend a huge heartfelt hug.

Chapter Sixteen

TWO WEEKS LATER

For the last forty-eight hours, even though Ella had been run off her feet, she'd had the best time. In seven hours' time all of her hard work, with the help of Roman, would be showcased to everyone who attended The Lakehouse, and she couldn't wait. Roman had spent the morning setting up all the sound equipment whilst Ella had organised the huge screen behind the stage which would project images from the past sent in by the villagers of Heartcross. The whole place looked beautiful, and reminded Ella of a magical winter wonderland. Dolores' favourite white flowers filled the corners of every room and the top of the grand piano was dotted with tea lights. Fairy lights were draped over the bay trees which looked beautiful at each end of the stage, and bottles and bottles of champagne were chilling in the huge fridges in the wine room at the back of the restaurant. All of the special guests supporting Dolores with her 'Trip Down Memory Lane' were arriving late afternoon. Flynn had put them all in the finest deluxe suites up at Starcross Manor and they were to be ushered across to The Lakehouse with the utmost high security.

'How are Dolores' nerves holding up?' asked Roman as he kicked off his shoes and draped his legs across the coffee table.

Ella jokingly pointed at Roman's feet. 'Make yourself at home, why don't you?'

'Well, we have been dating for a couple of weeks now,' he grinned, 'so, you know…'

Ella shook her head. 'Dolores has no nerves whatsoever. I called in just before we sailed across to The Lakehouse this morning, and she is absolutely itching for the night to begin. However, she is feeling more anxious about this afternoon. She'd spent ten minutes deliberating about what to wear for her meeting with Charlie.'

'I think I'd be nervous too. Fancy meeting your true love after all these years! I mean, what if Dolores is disappointed and thinks she wasted all those years hankering after someone she couldn't have, and now she wishes she hadn't?'

'Aren't you a true romantic? For your information, they have written to each other for years and kept in touch, but I've no idea why they were kept apart. Maybe we'll find out this afternoon. I'm absolutely intrigued. Changing the subject... How's Megan?'

'So far so good, another two weeks to go, and fingers crossed she's turned a corner. The hardest part about all this is, I can only support her from afar, there's no outside contact allowed, no technology, no social media. She has to focus on learning to love herself again.'

'And she will, I've got a good feeling about it all.'

Hearing the letterbox clang, Ella picked up the mail that had landed on the mat. 'Junk, junk. Even more junk and I've no idea what this one is.' The envelope was addressed to her but she didn't recognise the writing. She turned over the envelope in her hand and sat down next to Roman.

'What have you got there?' he asked.

Ella shrugged. 'I have no idea,' she replied, hooking her finger under the envelope and opening up the letter.

'Woah!' Ella's jaw dropped wide open. 'Is this for actual real or some sort of cruel joke?' She handed the cheque over to Roman.

'It's signed by Wayne Ridgeway.'

Ella couldn't believe her eyes as she stared at the letter. In her hand she held a cheque for seventy-five thousand pounds with what seemed like a sincere hand-written apology. Ella let out a long shuddering sigh. 'I really wasn't expecting this. I know it's not the full amount he conned from me and it's a year of my life I can't get back, but it's better than nothing. Why would he even give me some back?'

Roman was re-reading the letter. 'How do you feel about the last couple of sentences?'

Ella stared at the words on the page: *Just for the record, I never meant to hurt you and you will always have a place in my heart. I know it's not all the money but it's all I have and I am sorry. You were different from all the rest.*

She swallowed down a lump in her throat. 'Numb, indifferent. Call me cynical, but maybe he's after a shorter prison sentence.' She shrugged. 'If anything, the last year has taught me not to look backwards but just to keep going forwards, because that's when incredible things happen.' Ella snuggled into Roman's chest then looked upwards and placed a soft kiss to his lips. 'That may not be all my inheritance back, but it will pay off the debts and allow me to sail forward, hopefully not in a storm.'

Roman laughed. 'Ella Johnson, you are an amazing woman.'

'I know,' she said, nudging his elbow playfully. She looked down at the letter one last time then pushed it aside. 'Are we ready to take Dolores to meet Charlie?'

'I'll tell you something, my life isn't dull with you around.' He gently slapped her thigh with his hand and jumped up. 'You go and see Dolores, I'll fill Bette up with petrol and I'll meet you out the front in say... twenty minutes?'

'Perfect,' replied Ella.

———————————

Ella rapped on Dolores' front door, but there was no answer. She put her ear to the door and couldn't hear a sound. Knocking again, she pulled down the handle and walked inside.

'It's only me,' she shouted as she walked into the living room.

Ella stopped dead in her tracks and stared at Dolores who was standing in front of her. She didn't recognise her at all and had to look twice, she looked so beautiful. Dolores looked down to the floor then back up towards Ella, looking like a frightened rabbit in the headlights. Immediately Ella recognised her vulnerability, and understood that this was an important moment in her personal life. After all these years, and everything she had accomplished in her career, Dolores was still in love.

She was beautifully dressed, in a long flowing polka-dot dress with ruffles around the collar and wrists. Her flamboyant make-up had been toned down and her brunette hair hung straight down her back – there wasn't a long blonde curl in sight. Ella's mouth had dropped wide open as she looked between Dolores and the wig that was hanging over the arm of the chair. Ella gasped. 'Dolores, you look… stunning.' Ella stepped forward and kissed Dolores on the cheek. 'You look ten years younger.'

'I thought I'd ditch the bright-blue eye-shadow and the lashes. This is how I used to look: elegant, long flowing dresses, and I've hidden behind false eyelashes for years, when look…' Dolores fluttered her eyelashes. 'I covered myself up for years, hiding behind the façade that I'm an eccentric old lady, which was a good show, because I could usually get away with anything, but that was because I wasn't happy. Today I feel happy again.'

'Because you're meeting Charlie?'

'Yes, because I am meeting Charlie. I've loved Charlie with all my heart for all these years, and if it wasn't for you Ella, this would never be happening.'

Ella held out her hands. 'I'm so excited for you. What's the plan? Where are we meeting Charlie?'

'At The Boathouse, and then we are sailing across to The Lakehouse for lunch. I've booked our old favourite table, the one we always sat at, and Flynn has seen to it that we have our favourite cocktails waiting. I have to admit, in the whole of my career, singing in front of royalty, performing in front of thousands of people… I have never felt… so nervous – it's terrifying!'

'Don't be nervous, enjoy your time, and Roman and I are right behind you, all the way.'

Ella picked up Dolores' small suitcase. 'Come on, let's go and meet Charlie, and drop you both off at The Boathouse. This is where your *real* trip down memory lane begins.'

Dolores gently cupped her hands around Ella's face. 'You deserve every bit of happiness in your lifetime. My career was amazing, but I didn't get my happiness in my personal life until now. Just seeing Charlie for one last time is all I ever wished for, and now my heart is thumping so fast, it had better not bloody give way before I get there!' Dolores laughed.

'Don't say that!' Ella was close to tears, but seeing how happy Dolores was at this moment in time made her heart swell. 'Roman's waiting downstairs, are you ready?'

'I've been ready for years, but it's times like this I bloody wished I had dabbled in Botox.'

Ella laughed. 'Dolores, you should be bottled.'

'Please don't pickle me when my time is up.'

Walking out on to the High Street, Dolores looked like a movie star. Her dress floated behind her whilst her natural hair bounced lightly above her shoulders. She looked the picture of happiness. Hamish appeared in the shop doorway. 'I'm glad to see that wig has finally disappeared.' Dolores spun round and gave Hamish a huge beam. 'Thank you for being the best son.' She held his hands.

'Don't go going all gushy on me now.' He kissed his mother on her cheek. 'No go and get Charlie – it's been a long time coming.'

'Thank you, son.'

Ella fanned her face with her hands then stepped forward and hugged Roman, who was waiting by Bette. 'What's that for?'

'Just because I feel like I've found my prince and now Dolores is about to get hers.'

'You daft bugger,' he said, tilting her face towards his and kissing her on the lips before turning towards Dolores. 'Your carriage awaits.'

He swung open his arm and Dolores wrinkled her forehead. 'I think it's about time to treat yourself to a new car. Bette looks older than me,' she joked, accepting Roman's hand as he helped her into the front seat.

He laughed. 'Yes, it may be about time.'

Ella strapped herself in the back seat but shuffled to the edge and leant forward, with her elbows resting on their head rests. Roman set off up the road and headed towards the bumpy track along the side of the river.

Ella was feeling nervous for Dolores. She had no clue what had kept Dolores and Charlie apart for all these years, but at long last they were going to have their own trip down memory lane. 'What's the first thing you are going to say?' asked Ella, feeling the nervous tension in the air.

'I've no idea,' replied Dolores. 'I've rehearsed this moment over and over in my head but now my brain decides to go to mush.'

'Here we are.' Roman glanced over his shoulder at Ella and parked Bette at the side of The Boathouse.

'Do you want to get out of the car, or shall we stay inside until we see another car?' asked Roman, switching off the engine, but Ella interrupted before Dolores could answer.

'Here we go.'

Driving towards them was an electric-blue Bentley. 'Now that's posh – and we've arrived in Bette.' Ella was staring at the car out of the windscreen.

'Charlie wouldn't be bothered if I turned up on the back of a donkey,' replied Dolores, who looked over her shoulder and touched Ella's hand with hers.

'This is it. Good luck, Dolores.'

'Thank you, dear girl. I'm more nervous now than when I met the Queen.'

'You've got this.'

Roman and Ella held their breaths as Dolores got out of the car and shut the door behind her.

'It's like a love scene out of a movie.' Ella slid into the front seat next to Roman and placed her hand on his knee. He leant across and kissed her on her cheek.

'I have to say, I'm as nervous as hell and have everything crossed for a happy ending,' he said. 'It's all happening today, isn't it? How are you feeling about tonight?'

'I'm so excited to see it all come together, but I think I'm most excited about watching Dolores light up every face inside The Lakehouse when she sings.'

'It's going to be a magical night.'

In silence, they watched as Dolores walked forward but stopped halfway between Bette and the Bentley. Ella's heart was beating so fast, goodness knows how Dolores was holding up, meeting the love of her life after all these years. 'I wonder what he looks like?' asked Ella, her eyes fixed forward.

Roman put his hand up to his shoulder and took hold of Ella's hand. 'We are about to find out.' They watched in anticipation for the first glimpse of Charlie Love. The Bentley's car door was opened by the chauffeur and Ellie let out a sigh. 'He's not come, he's sent someone else, she must be his assistant.' Feeling the crushing disappointment, Ella was about to climb out of the car and rush to Dolores' side, but Roman stopped her.

'Look.'

Ella saw a tall, slim Indian woman dressed in an exquisitely cut blue trouser suit with red ballet shoes, walking towards Dolores, who was smiling. They began to walk faster towards each other and within seconds their arms were flung open and they fell into each other's embrace.

'What's going on?' asked Roman, looking at Ella, then back towards Dolores. They watched from afar as the two women hugged and kissed.

'My guess is, Charlie Love is not a man.' Wide-eyed, she looked towards Roman.

For a second, they watched the women embrace, before Dolores turned around and waved her hand in Ella's direction.

'That's our cue. Come on, let's go and meet Charlie.'

Hand in hand, Ella and Roman walked over towards them, and Ella noticed Dolores was physically shaking. 'Ella, Roman – let me introduce you to Charlie… Charlotte Love.'

Chapter Seventeen

Ella had to admit, discovering Charlie was Charlotte had totally knocked her socks off. She was never expecting that in a million years. Dolores was looking radiant and her whole face was lit up with happiness. The moment Ella had set eyes on Charlie, she was even more intrigued by their story.

'We are going to sail you across to The Lakehouse and get you settled, then Roman and I have a few last-minute preparations to take care of, ready for this evening.'

Ella noticed Charlie slip her hands into Dolores' as they ambled along the jetty towards the boat. Roman held out his hand and helped them step on board. 'If you would like to take a seat at the table over there.' Roman had laid a white crisp cloth over the table with an ice bucket in the middle with a bottle of champagne chilling. 'You ladies relax and enjoy yourselves.'

'I can't believe we are going back to The Lakehouse.' Charlie placed her hands on her heart. 'It really is a trip down memory lane.'

Roman and Ella hugged as the ladies made their way over to the table. Roman gently pulled away and held Ella's hands in his. 'All this, it's made me think, that life is too short.' He took a breath and looked lovingly at Ella. 'After what happened to me and to you, Ella, I never thought I'd find happiness again but...' He took Ella's hand. 'I have, and this,' he nodded towards Dolores and Charlie, 'makes me so happy seeing them here, finally together. My only assumption is, they couldn't be together because of the times they lived in back then?'

'I'm not sure, but I'm going to go and find out.' Ella stood on her tiptoes and kissed Roman softly on the lips. 'And just for the record, I'm the happiest I've ever been.' She hugged him again before turning to look at Dolores and Charlie, who were in deep conversation. For a second Ella watched them; they were so at ease with each other, it was like they'd never been apart. Ella knew that they'd written to each other for all those years, but they still had a whole lifetime to catch up on.

As the boat set off across the water, Dolores popped the cork on the champagne bottle and poured everyone a glass. 'I feel like I'm in the middle of the most romantic love story ever. Tell me everything, I want to know everything!' Ella said.

Dolores looked towards Charlie and squeezed her hand.

Charlie took a sip from the champagne flute and Ella could see her eyes were filling up, just thinking about it all. 'Back in our times things weren't quite like today, the love we shared would have been frowned upon, but even more so by my family. You see, my father had already arranged my marriage. It killed us that we couldn't be together.' Charlie looked adoringly towards Dolores. 'And my real name isn't Charlie Love. Every time Dolores said my name, she used to say "love" after it, so it just became a joke.'

Ella was taken back. 'What is your name?'

'My real name is Shehrnaz, but I always pretended I was a Charlotte, because I liked the name and I fitted in more with my friends. But then Dolores changed it to Charlie in case we were ever talking about each other and we ever slipped up. But these days you can call me anything.' Charlie smiled. 'I'm too long in the tooth to care.'

'You will always be Charlie to me. The Lakehouse was where it all began, we met here on a Thursday night when I was singing, and from then on this place was our safe haven.'

'I always had to sneak out of home, I wasn't allowed out and I was a little bit of a rebel.'

'A little bit?' joked Dolores.

Charlie continued. 'Back then, your parents' word was law, you respected them, we had to do what other people said and what was expected of us, even if it wasn't what we wanted...' Charlie's voice faltered. 'And it's not that I've ever wanted for anything in my life... except you.' Charlie was tearful. 'But I'm not thinking about that now.'

Ella could feel their pain.

Charlie continued. 'My mum Navela was led by my father, she worked hard sewing clothes all day, every day, and we helped her after school. The more she sewed, the more money we had. My father had numerous prospects in mind for me and, if I'm honest,' she looked towards Dolores, 'they chose well for me. I married a good, decent man and lived a very good lifestyle. But for all those years, I was hiding the truth of who I was, in here.' Charlie pressed a hand on to her heart.

'It must have been so difficult for you both,' said Ella.

'Prince George was a good friend of ours; we met him here at The Lakehouse. He was our ally, he knew we were in love and, to shield us from the press, he took us away on holiday on his boat,' reminisced Charlie.

'The best summer I've ever had.' Dolores was smiling and staring into Charlie's eyes.

'Until we arrived back, and it was all over the press that the prince was proposing to Dolores, and then she had to pretend to break his heart to keep our secret.'

'George was a gem and he played along. He was so good to us. We could never have had our time together if it wasn't for his help, but there was no way I could get out of my arranged marriage. I couldn't have disrespected my family.'

'And where is your husband now, Charlie?' Ella could see Charlie's eyes tearing up.

'He passed away ten years ago, and I know we could have seen each other sooner but…'

'You don't need to explain, you have your family, your children and I know you wouldn't have done anything to hurt any of them,' Dolores said, looking tenderly at Charlie.

'And now all my children have grown up and I have grandchildren too. But when you called,' she looked towards Ella, 'I just knew it was time. I told my children about Dolores that same day.'

Ella was in awe as she looked between them both. The combined age of the two women must be around one hundred and eighty years, and they both still looked in the prime of their life.

Dolores squeezed Charlie's hand. 'You were brave.'

'It was the hardest thing I've ever done, but they held me tight and told me they loved me. They encouraged me to come today and said I deserve all the happiness in the world.'

'Thankfully times have changed, and people are a lot more honest and open about who they are. Hamish has always known that Charlie was the love of my life. As soon as he asked questions about who his dad was, I couldn't lie. I wanted a baby but didn't want a man... George had contacts, and I adopted Hamish.'

Ella's eyes widened. 'I need more champagne!' This was a story of true love. Charlie and Dolores had started their lives together in secret but now could quite openly enjoy the time they had left together. This was the fairy-tale ending for both of them, and Ella knew that they were going to live every second to the max.

'I always had a deep sense of hope that we would be reunited one day, and here we are.' Charlie held up her glass. 'To us and life.'

They both watched as The Lakehouse came into view. Charlie and Dolores gasped at the same time. 'That view still gets me every time,' exclaimed Charlie. 'Just look at it.'

'All this, your story, has made me hold on stronger to what I've found.' Ella looked across towards Roman who must have sensed he was being watched and glanced over his shoulder.

'Here we go, ladies,' he said, cutting the engine of the boat. 'What have I missed?'

'Way too much, I'll fill you in on the ride home.' Ella slipped her hand around his waist. 'I know how lucky I am to have found you.'

Roman planted a soft kiss on the top of her head.

'I told you in those tea leaves you'd find true love, and I'm always right.'

'Please tell me you are not still pretending to read tea leaves?' Charlie let out a hearty laugh. 'This one used to pretend to read the leaves of the artists back-stage, and half the time she made it up.'

'Dolores, did you make up my reading?' exclaimed Ella with a huge smile on her face.

For a second Dolores looked shifty. 'I can neither confirm nor deny but look, I told you love happens when you least expect it, and I was right.'

Ella was shaking her head and laughing as they stepped off the boat. 'We'll see you inside and then we must head off. Roman will put your suitcase in your dressing room, but later you have to pretend you've just arrived and walk down the red carpet.'

'My last red carpet, and I would love it if you, Charlie, would walk by my side.'

'It will be an honour.'

Ella watched the interaction between them with her hands on her heart and blinked back the happy tears. They were just so beautiful to watch together.

Wilbur greeted them with a smile when they all

stepped inside The Lakehouse. He kissed Dolores on both cheeks and then stared at Charlie. 'Shehrnaz, it's been a long time.'

For a moment Charlie stared at Wilbur.

'You don't recognise me, do you?' he said.

It took Charlie a second. 'Don't tell me you were the boy that hid under the table to watch the acts? And I used to pass you crisps and Coke from the bar?'

'The very one! My parents owned this place and now my son, Flynn, does.' Wilbur held out his hand. 'And if I remember rightly, your favourite table was right in front of the piano, so you could watch the performances close up.'

Dolores turned towards Ella and Roman. 'You did this, if it wasn't for your idea, this wouldn't have happened. This is going to be the best night of my career and one of the best nights of my life.'

'It's been a pleasure to organise all this and to see you two reunited.' Ella kissed them both on the cheek, leaving Wilbur to show them to their table.

Hand in hand, Ella and Roman walked down the jetty. 'I've got a warm, fuzzy feeling inside,' she said. 'They looked so happy together! Could you imagine getting to their age and finding each other again?'

'We all get there in the end, I promise.' Roman stopped walking and slipped his hands around Ella's waist. 'And I'm glad we got there sooner rather than later. I completely adore you and I'm glad you turned up in Heartcross.'

'I'm glad I did too.' Ella snuggled in close, feeling safe and content in Roman's arms. Tilting her face upwards, Roman gazed into her eyes then kissed her so tenderly, it sent shivers down her spine.

A couple of hours later, when Ella walked back through the front door of the flat, Callie was tapping her watch. 'Where have you been? We need to get ready! Which dress are you going to wear?' Callie pointed to the two dresses hanging up from the back of the door in the living room.

Ella couldn't make up her mind. 'I'm not sure, I'll have a quick shower and then decide.' She looked over at Callie who was smiling down at her phone.

'And what's that smile for?' asked Ella, narrowing her eyes.

'I've got a date tonight; well, after he finishes work.' Callie bit down on her lip.

'What? Who? You've kept this very quiet.'

'Gianni!' replied Callie, waiting for Ella's reaction.

'Holy Moly! No way! Callie, that's brilliant.' Ella's face lit up with excitement. 'We can go on double dates.'

'The first being tonight.'

'It's going to be brilliant. Let's put on some music whilst we get ready,' suggested Ella. 'And this afternoon was magical, I've got so much to tell you about Dolores and Charlie, it's just made today extra special.'

'True love always prevails,' remarked Callie, opening the door to be greeted by a delivery man who was hiding behind an enormous bouquet of blooms and a long cardboard box.

'A delivery for Ella Johnson,' he announced chirpily, handing them over to Callie.

'It's for you,' called Callie.

Ella took the flowers and inhaled the scent. 'They are gorgeous.' She opened the white envelope and read the card inside: *Good luck for tonight, you are amazing, Roman xx.* She clutched the card to her chest. 'So thoughtful.'

She handed Callie the flowers and looked at the box in wonderment and eagerly began to open it up. Inside the contents were hidden beneath delicate blush-pink tissue paper. Her heart skipped a beat as she unfolded the tissue paper and lifted out the most stunning dress she'd ever laid eyes on.

'Wow! Look at that!' exclaimed Callie.

Ella's eyes were brimming with happy tears as she held it up against her body. The dress was made from a grey shimmery satin, gathered at the waist and floating to her ankles elegantly. The soft scoop neckline looked stunning, sewn with sparkles and sequins that glinted in the light.

Ella was speechless.

'It's absolutely perfect, Roman did well,' Callie said. 'Just stunning.'

Ella laid the dress back in the box and even though she wasn't wearing the dress yet, she already felt like a million dollars. Her heart was bursting with happiness.

Thirty minutes later, after applying her make-up, she curled her hair and pinned the top layer, allowing the curls to cascade loosely around her face before slipping on the dress. Ella stood in front of the long mirror and smiled at her own reflection, knowing in the last few months she'd come a long way and that it was all thanks to Callie, Roman and the community of Heartcross who had welcomed her with open arms. Her skin looked radiant and her eyes sparkled as she checked her appearance one last time and stepped out into the living room, where Callie was waiting for her.

'Oh my God, look at you.' Callie eyed her approvingly. 'That dress is beautiful. You look stunning.'

'Thank you, and you do too.' Ella air kissed Callie, then they both gave a little shimmy in their dresses.

'Are we ready to get this show on the road?' asked

Callie, picking up her bag. 'There's a limo picking us up and Roman is meeting us at the boat.'

Ella couldn't wait to see him and thank him for her dress. Hearing the doorbell ring, Ella looked out at the limo through the window. 'It's here.' She felt flutters of excitement as she lifted up her dress and carefully walked down the stairwell. At the bottom of the stairs she was greeted by a chauffeur wearing a uniform and a cap. He opened the car door before holding out his hand to help Ella step into the limo.

Travelling in style, it only took five minutes to reach the jetty, and the boat was already waiting for them as Ella stepped out of the limo and gasped. Seeing Roman, Ella felt her skin ripple with goose bumps. His suit was exquisitely cut, sharp and well fitted, his satin lapels were perfect alongside his bow tie and he was wearing the most gorgeous smile. Walking towards him, Ella began to feel nervous and as soon as she reached him, he held out his hands and took hers in his. 'You look stunning,' he whispered, kissing her on her cheek.

'Thank you and so do you.' Her heart was thumping so hard, she let out a long calming breath. 'I love my dress, you have impeccable taste.'

The paparazzi were gathered at the side of the boat and everyone posed for photographs before stepping on to it. Flynn had hired another captain to sail the boat so Roman could sit back and actually enjoy the crossing.

Ella held his hand the whole time whilst everyone chatted amongst themselves.

The tiny bay was packed with people as the boat approached The Lakehouse. Ella saw Nancy and the TV crew alongside numerous press, whilst the villagers and diners were all waiting patiently behind the cordoned-off area. A red carpet trailed up the jetty all the way to the entrance and as soon as the boat docked Ella could see Dolores and Charlie already speaking to the fans gathered outside.

Ella beckoned Dolores over when she spun round. Dolores and Charlie hurried towards the boat and were greeted by the cheers of the artists on board. Dolores was overwhelmed, dabbing her eyes with a tissue but also smiling widely. 'Blossom, Blossom – I can't believe it!' She hugged her old friend and held her hand before turning towards Frank and Ritchie. 'This is just surreal.'

Reunited with her old management and friends, they all enjoyed a glass of the good stuff on board before stepping off the boat and walking the red carpet all together. They were instantly hit by the continuous flashing of bulbs from all the cameras. 'So this is what it's like to be famous,' Ella whispered in Roman's ear.

Ella saw Felicity and Isla and the rest of the villagers cheering as everyone walked past. Hamish and Wilbur were standing at the entrance waiting to escort Dolores and Charlie inside. All the stars stopped to sign autographs and have their pictures taken.

'Ella!' Ella spun round to see Nancy beckoning her over to where she was already chatting to Dolores.

'Ella, how are you feeling? You made all this happen.' Ella knew the camera was rolling – the whole arrival was being televised for the late-night news – and placed her arm around Dolores' shoulder. 'It wasn't just me who made this happen, there's a long list of truly fabulous folk to thank, including this special lady.' She squeezed Dolores. 'And all the wonderful artists who are walking this way. Each one has a connection with Dolores and we have a special night ahead of us watching all those special moments tonight on stage. And can I just take this opportunity to thank Gianni, who has been slaving away all day over the most exquisite menu.'

The atmosphere was electric and Ella clung to Roman's hand. She wasn't expecting the paparazzi to take her picture but each and every one wanted to know how she'd managed to pull such a successful star-studded evening.

The star-studded line-up finally began to make their way inside The Lakehouse and were greeted by Flynn.

Ella smiled at Hamish, tucked under his arm was McCartney looking smart wearing a red velvet bow-tie. As soon as the artists were settled at their table, the rest of the guests began to file through the door. The whole community of Heartcross was out in full force and each and every one of them looked stunning, their dresses extravagant, their make-up perfect and all the men suited and booted. They were all out to support The Lakehouse and, of course, Dolores.

'I feel like I'm floating on air,' whispered Ella.

'And so you should be, you did all this.' Roman kissed her on her cheek and held her hand tightly.

'With a little help from some friends,' she replied.

Inside The Lakehouse, Ella was completely blown away. There were clusters of guests drinking from champagne flutes, sitting around their tables and an army of staff circulating with more glasses of fizz. The TV were set up along the back of the restaurant with a smaller camera positioned near the front. The whole room was bubbling with excitement. Roman had checked and double-checked the sound, which was all working correctly, and he placed a microphone on top of the piano. The whole room was decorated with fairy lights and white roses filled every spare space in the room. Ella was completely lost for words at the extravagance of it all. She weaved a way through the guests and accepted a drink from a passing waiter before she sat down at the table alongside Roman and Callie. Everything was running like clockwork. Dolores was in her element, working the room and chatting with everyone. Gianni appeared at the side of the table and Ella noticed him slip his arm around Callie's waist before disappearing back in the kitchen.

Within the next ten minutes a pianist came out to play whilst everyone enjoyed the delicious delights of the extravagant three-course meal that Gianni had prepared. Even Tiffany Down looked impressed as she shared a table with Nancy alongside some of the press photographers.

Once the food had been completely devoured, Flynn stepped onto the stage and Ella noticed how proud Julia looked from the table at the side of the stage. As he took the microphone, silence fell over the room. 'Welcome to each and every one of you for joining us tonight.'

Ella's heart was beating in double time, so goodness knew how Dolores was feeling, but she appeared to be taking it all in her stride.

'As we all know, The Lakehouse has been around for many years and originally was owned by my very own grandparents. Hundreds of famous names have passed through those doors, but one in particular we hold close to our hearts. Many years ago Frank Divine took to this very stage and spotted Dolores Henderson dancing in front of him with her friend Blossom Rose. After he invited her up on to the stage Dolores began to sing, and by the end of the night she had been signed by Richie Kirk, Frank's management, who are all sat here.' Flynn nodded towards their table. 'This is where Dolores Henderson began a career that spanned decades and tonight she will take to this stage one last time.' Flynn took a breath and searched the audience and spotted Ella. 'When I re-opened The Lakehouse, I was expecting it to follow in its past footsteps and become an instant success, but that wasn't to be, until this girl turned up in Heartcross. Please will you welcome to the stage Ella Johnson.'

Ella's heart was thumping, Roman gently shoved a surprised Ella on to the stage. 'Go and get up there.'

As Ella stood up from her seat there was rapturous applause. Walking on to the stage, she was brimming with emotion.

'It was Ella's idea to bring you "A Trip Down Memory Lane with Dolores Henderson". Not only has she organised this event for you all, she's brought together the world-famous artists that are going to perform for you this evening with Dolores. We have Frank, Ed, Gracie, and of course, Dolores herself.' The crowd was cheering, the air was charged, and everyone couldn't wait for the performances to begin.

'Ella's passion for this event and her social media activity have boosted The Lakehouse's bookings, and this place is getting well and truly back on track. So thank you, Ella.' Flynn looked towards her. 'I think it's only right that Ella introduces tonight's first performance.'

Flynn passed the microphone to Ella who moved it to her mouth.

She glanced around the room, every set of eyes were looking in her direction. She'd noticed that the acts and Dolores had moved from the main room and were now getting ready to perform in the backstage area.

'It is my absolute privilege to introduce to you all, "A Trip Down Memory Lane with Dolores Henderson"!'

The whole of the restaurant were up on their feet clapping as the lights dimmed and footage of The Lakehouse was projected on to the screen behind the stage. The band began to play and everyone watched the images of Dolores from the past. Frank walked on to the stage holding Dolores' hand and they sat down on a couple of stools in the middle of the stage and stared up at the screen, which was showing younger versions of themselves performing together that very first time at The Lakehouse. It had taken Ella over a week to find a copy of that special night and Dolores clearly couldn't believe her eyes. She gripped Frank's arm as the whole room watched the moment when she was discovered, her very first performance at The Lakehouse.

The whole night whizzed past in an absolute blur. Ella was in awe of Dolores, her energy and stage presence keeping everyone captivated the whole time. Each artist provided a story that had the audience in stitches regarding Dolores, and she sang duets with each and every one. The Lakehouse was alive, and back on the map. This night was going down in history, not only for Dolores and The Lakehouse but for Ella too. It was truly a sensational night and she never wanted it to end.

'I need to congratulate you, this night is amazing, you should think about this as a full-time job.' Charlie took a couple of glasses of champagne from the passing waiter and gave one to Ella. 'Cheers.'

'Cheers,' replied Ella, thinking about Charlie's words. She'd enjoyed every second of making this evening happen and she was going to chat to Flynn about further events. Ella was excited for her future at The Lakehouse and in Heartcross.

Dolores stood in the middle of the stage with the spotlight shining right on her. 'I have had the most fantastic career, and been blessed with the most fantastic son,' she blew a kiss across to Hamish, 'and the most fantastic friends. This night has meant the world to me,' she gave a look of admiration towards Charlie, 'and I can't thank Ella enough for organising tonight, and Roman for all the technical stuff. Now, I have one special performance left before everyone joins me back on stage.'

Ella looked towards Roman, she didn't know about any other special guests, what was going on?

'Please welcome Roman Docherty on to the stage!'

The room erupted in applause as Ella watched Roman take Dolores' hand before he sat down at the piano.

'What's all this?' asked Ella, looking at Charlie. 'I didn't even know Roman could play the piano.'

'Those two have been practising for the last week, this is going to be magical.' Charlie cupped her hand around Ella's and all eyes were on the stage.

'This is one of my favourite songs of all time, "Somewhere over the Rainbow".' Dolores nodded towards Roman.

Everyone's heads turned towards the piano, the glow from the candles revealing a magnitude of warmth and love in Roman's eyes, He turned his head slightly towards Ella and the smile he gave her melted her heart. As his fingers began to glide effortlessly over the keys, she closed her eyes. She felt breathless, as Roman played the notes, weaving a story – their story. As soon as Dolores began to sing, everyone gasped. She was still a superstar, and no one could take their eyes off her. Ella held up her arm towards Charlie. 'Goose bumps.'

Charlie mirrored her actions. 'Snap.'

There wasn't a dry eye in the place. Even Gianni was dabbing his eyes with a napkin as he joined Callie at their table.

No one uttered a word through the performance, the

whole room watching Dolores Henderson perform the last song all by herself, this magical moment capturing everyone's heart.

Just as Ella knew Roman had completely captured hers.

As soon as the song came to an end everyone was up on their feet. Roman joined Dolores centre stage and they both looked towards Ella and Charlie as they took a bow together before gesturing for them both to come up on the stage. They all hugged each other, before Dolores put the microphone to her mouth. 'Hamish, my son, as much as you don't like the limelight, please come up and join me for one very last song.'

Hamish didn't object and proudly took his mother's hand.

As the band took their places, Dolores announced, 'Please welcome back on stage all my special guests tonight for one last song. Next month it's Christmas…'

Everyone filed back on to the stage holding hands. As the band struck up the melody for 'Last Christmas', snow began to fall all over The Lakehouse. The whole audience were up on their feet embracing the artificial snow. This was a magical end to Dolores' last ever performance and she deserved nothing less than a standing ovation.

'I think we both have our happy ever afters,' Charlie whispered to Ella.

'I think we do.' Ella smiled. 'And when did you learn

to play the piano? That blew me away,' she whispered to Roman.

'I've been playing since I was five years old,' he replied as he slipped his arm around Ella's waist. As the song came to an end the scene in front of them was like a magical winter wonderland. As the applause rang out Dolores was emotional, tears streaming down her face. 'Thank you all for letting me sing one last time. Tonight it was me and you, and our "Trip Down Memory Lane". And if it's okay with you, I'm officially announcing my retirement!'

The applause never stopped as everyone still stood on stage, hanging on to this special moment.

'I hope we're like that when we get to that age,' Ella said, looking into Roman's eyes.

'I promise life will be plain sailing from now on… no pun intended.'

'Just the quiet life for us both now.'

'Thank God.' Roman took Ella in his arms and kissed her tenderly on the lips. Overcome with emotion, tears were welling up in her eyes – happy tears. 'Me, you and Megan.'

'I can't wait.' Ella knew she had fallen in love. Roman was her happy ever after and all of her previous heartache had led her to Heartcross for that very reason… Roman.

Ella looked out over the audience, she felt proud, her

eyes filling up with tears. She was happy, Dolores was happy and the whole restaurant was alive. Coming to Heartcross was the best thing she'd ever done.

'You know, when everyone says, once you arrive in Heartcross you never leave,' Ella said, looking straight at Callie, 'they're right. You did this, gave me a lifeline, and I can't tell you how much I love you.'

'That feeling is mutual. Does that mean you're staying?' Callie asked hopefully.

'Of course, I'm staying.' It had been a hell of a year, but Ella knew this was her future and it began right now.

Within seconds everyone was up on the dancefloor. The night had been a huge success and The Lakehouse was back on the map.

And as Roman held Ella's hand tightly and she looked around the room, she was overcome with emotion. This night was her perfect night. She'd found her reason for arriving in Heartcross and she was never going to let him go.

A Letter from Christie

Dear Readers,

Firstly, if you are reading this letter, thank you so much for choosing to read *The Lake House*.

I sincerely hope you enjoyed reading this story, if you did, I would be grateful if you'd write a review and share your thoughts on social media. Your recommendations can always help other readers to discover my books.

This is the fifth book in the Love Heart Lane series and my twelfth book to be published. The Love Heart Lane series has become a huge part of my life and I'm really not ready to let go of all the characters just yet. It's a collection of books I'm super proud of and the good news is there are still a few more books in the series to come!

So far this year has been a challenge, after filing for divorce and moving out of my family home I began a new adventure. In February, I moved into a ramshackle cottage that didn't have a working bathroom, with a rundown kitchen and not a decent space to write my books. I felt like I was glamping but with no glamour in my life! Then we were hit by a pandemic, the country went into lockdown and with no service constantly displaying on my phone, continuing power cuts to my old dilapidated shack and no Wi-Fi installed I was then thrown into home schooling on top of writing my books. However, despite living through these difficult times 2020 has taught me a lot in life, you fall out with people you never thought you would. Get betrayed by people you trusted with all your heart. And get used by people you would do anything for. But life also has a beautiful side to it. You will get loved by someone you never thought you would have. Form new friendships with people that will establish more meaningful and stronger relationships. And overcome things you thought you'd never get over. We all have chapters that end but I take pride in knowing that this year has moulded me into a strong independent woman in charge of my own destiny. I've developed as a writer, I'm dreaming big, working hard and staying focussed. The very best part of my book is still be written and I couldn't be happier.

This book, *The Lake House* was sparked from a floating

hotel back in my home town of Northwich in the 1980s. The iconic Floatel was built on the River Weaver and saw early success as the only hotel in the town centre. But due to the credit crunch it spelt the end for the unique structure off London Road and demolition took place in November 2009. I was always fascinated by the structure of the hotel and even back then I imagined a hideaway restaurant further up the river and the only way to dine there was travelling by boat – the idea for *The Lake House* was born many years ago!

Huge thanks to everyone that has accompanied on my writing journey so far. I truly value each and every one of you and it's an absolute joy to hear from my readers via Twitter, Facebook and Instagram.

Please do keep in touch and look out for *Primrose Park* – the next book in the Love Heart Lane series is coming very soon!

Warm wishes,

Christie xx

Acknowledgments

A book is a huge team effort and even though my name might be on the cover a lot of hard work goes on behind the scenes. As always thank you to the brilliantly supportive cast at One More Chapter HarperCollins UK, you have been instrumental in supporting and promoting my books and crafting this book into the best it could possibly be. Thank you to the wonderful Charlotte Ledger, who cheers me on and always believes in me when I don't – I'm so grateful to you for turning my stories into books – you are the best!

Emily Ruston, my brilliant editor, who brings out the best in me. She is just wonderful to work alongside and bounce ideas off. You have given me many a seed to grow a book from and I love working with you – long may it continue.

Special thanks to my gang, Emily, Jack, Roo and Mop – you are simply the best.

My writing partners in crime, Woody and Nellie, as much as you both drive me insane I would never be without you.

Thank you to my best friend, Anita Redfern, who keeps me sane, you have got me through some proper storms in the last three years – you rock.

High fives and a glass of gin to these lovely ladies, Bella Osborne, Glynis Peters, Deborah Carr and Terri Nixon for providing continuous laughs along the way.

Writing can be a solitary profession but when your book flies out into the big wide world it's a team effort and I have the most amazing squad of loyal readers who pre-order my books before they are even written. It's because of you I am lucky enough to do the job I love so much. Please do keep sending all your lovely messages, tweets and comments, they mean the world to me – I thank you from the bottom of my heart.

Much love goes out to all the terrific bloggers and reviewers for getting behind my books in such an overwhelming way. I am eternally grateful for your constant sharing of posts and your support for my writing is truly appreciated – thank you.

I have without a doubt enjoyed writing every second of this book and I hope you enjoy hanging out with Ella and Roman. Please do let me know!